MIRROR, MIRROR

"Jehane, what's this?" Silvertop asked.

Jehane leaned over his shoulder. Pale blue light washed out of the mirror; she saw a long hall paved in white. "It's the tower of Acrilat," she said, barely managing a whisper. "The god of Acrivain. It's mad. I don't think It wants you looking at It, Sil."

"I looked at It," said Silvertop, without taking his eyes off the mirror, "because It's looking at us. It's here. It's working in Liavek." He held out his free hand. "I need the peach."

Jehane never found out what he needed it for. The light from the mirror turned red, and then hot white. Silvertop yelped as the mirror exploded in a shower of glass and ivory, and the wizard's entire apparatus cracked and fluttered and flung itself about in the air. . . .

"Liavek is a place worth visiting. Get there before another volume comes out."

—VOYA

LIAVEK
WIZARD'S ROW

edited by
**Will Shetterly
and Emma Bull**

ACE BOOKS, NEW YORK

This book is an Ace original edition, and
has never been previously published.

LIAVEK:
WIZARD'S ROW

An Ace Book/published by arrangement with
the editors and their agent, Valerie Smith

PRINTING HISTORY
Ace edition/September 1987

LIAVEK

WIZARD'S ROW

edited by

**Will Shetterly
and Emma Bull**

ACE BOOKS, NEW YORK

This book is an Ace original edition, and
has never been previously published.

LIAVEK:
WIZARD'S ROW

An Ace Book / published by arrangement with
the editors and their agent, Valerie Smith

PRINTING HISTORY
Ace edition / September 1987

ISBN: 0-441-48190-6

Ace Books are published by The Berkley Publishing Group,
200 Madison Avenue, New York, New York 10016.
The name "Ace" and the "A" logo are
trademarks belonging to Charter
Communications, Inc.

For Gene, Pat, Steve,
Nancy, Jane, Kara,
Pamela, Megan, Barry,
Charles, Nate, Greg,
Charles, Mike, Brad,
Caroline, and Alan.

CONTENTS

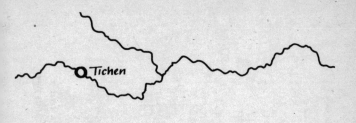

EMPIRE of TICHEN

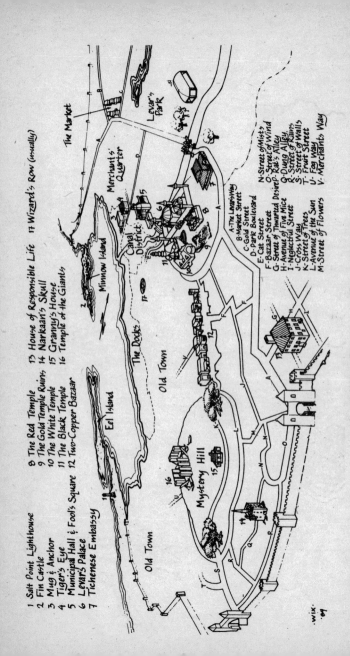

1 Salt Point Lighthouse
2 Fin Castle
3 Mug & Anchor
4 Tiger's Eye
5 Municipal Hall & Fool's Square
6 Levar's Palace
7 Tichenese Embassy

8 The Red Temple
9 The Gold Temple Ruins
10 The White Temple
11 The Black Temple
12 Two-Copper Bazaar

13 House of Responsible Life
14 Narkaan's Skull
15 Granny's House
16 Temple of the Giants

17 Wizard's Row (usually)

A - The Livar's Way
B - Market Street
C - Gold Street
D - Park Boulevard
E - Cat Street
F - Bazaar Street
G - Street of Thwarted Desire
H - Avenue of Five Mice
I - Neglectful Street
J - Cross Way
K - Street of Trees
L - Avenue of the Sun
M - Street of Flowers

N - Street of Mists
O - Street of Wind
P - Rat's Alley
Q - Dung Alley
R - Street of Rain
S - Street of Walls
T - Fog Way
U - Fruit Street
V - Merchants Way

The Market

Merchant's Quarter

Minnow Island

Canal District

The Docks

Old Town

Eel Island

Old Town

Mystery Hill

Levar's Park

An Act of Mercy

by Megan Lindholm and Steven Brust

KALOO RATTLED DOWN the stairs that led from her attic bedroom above the Mug and Anchor to the tavern's common room. The little silk fan she had pinned inside her robe rasped against her breast; her feet barely kissed each step in passing. This was her birthday; her luck time would begin this afternoon, and if she was going to invest her luck she hadn't a moment to waste. Those precious moments when one might take the luck created during one's birth time and place it in an object, to be called on at will for magic, came but once a year. She had waited long enough; by this evening she would be able to hold her luck in her hand. She rounded the corner at the base of the stairs and slammed her head into the shelf that held the extra lanterns. There was a warning rattle of crockery and Kaloo winced, expecting all of them to come tumbling down around her. But they didn't. "Lucky thing," she said to herself, rubbing her bruised forehead. She heard her own words and had to grin.

"You're getting taller, girl. Grow any more, and I'll have to re-carpenter the inn to fit you."

"I guess so," she replied cautiously. T'Nar, her foster father, sat at one of the scarred trestle tables before the low fire burning in the hearth. The usually noisy room was all but empty today. The sailor folk that made up their trade were all on the docks now, mending net, tarring seams, and generally preparing boats for another season of fishing. Kaloo was a little surprised to see T'Nar still here. A mug of beer was going flat on the table before him.

Silence hung a moment in the room. T'Nar picked up his mug in his wide scarred hands, turning it slowly while watching the beer inside. From the tar on his fingers and the rigger's knife in his belt and the smell of oakum in the room, she knew that he had been working on one of the boats. He didn't seem to fish as much as he once had, but every spring when the fleet was busy with repairs, his skills were in demand.

She hadn't seen much of him lately, but it wasn't the fault of

1

his long working hours. She suspected he had been avoiding her as much as she had him. Lately they couldn't say ten words to one another without it turning into a quarrel. Better not to speak at all. She shrugged and headed toward the kitchen, where L'Fertti, her tutor in matters of luck and magic, was usually to be found these days.

"Taller and older." T'Nar's voice stopped her again. "Going to be tall and slender."

"I guess so," she said guardedly. He was speaking so slowly and carefully, as if each word were heavy with meaning. Was he drunk, this early in the day? Or could he possibly be as melancholy as he sounded? She looked at him carefully, and found herself staring. When had his beard become so grizzled, the lines in his face so deep? Hard to recognize the man who had caught and tossed the child Kaloo, or been able to carry the ten-year-old girl kicking and squirming under one of his thick arms.

He sighed heavily. "Kaloo. You're getting to an age when you have to know things. About yourself. Things that may change the way others think of you, the way you think of yourself. Things maybe you should have known . . ."

"Yes?" She took two quick steps forward. She sensed secrets hovering in his words, things she suspected he knew and had never admitted. Such as who her parents had been, and why they had abandoned her in a ditch for him to find.

But her eagerness seemed to make him reconsider, for he fell silent, staring up at her. "Yes?" she repeated again.

He only gazed at her, his dark eyes pained. She had a sudden, uneasy feeling that he wasn't seeing her at all. He spoke unwillingly. "You look almost . . . well, but . . ." He shook his head suddenly, forbidding himself something. With a visible effort he smiled. When he spoke, his voice was falsely gay. "It's time you had some clothes that fit you. That's what I was thinking. That robe you're wearing is too short and too wide. Doesn't suit you. That's all."

He took a sip of his flat beer. Kaloo glared at him, then turned abruptly away. She was getting tired of the way he treated her. She wasn't a child anymore, as he and Daril seemed to think. She knew the robe didn't suit her. Angry words bubbled up in her, but she choked them down. She didn't have time to argue with T'Nar today. She had more important things to do. And if she succeeded, she'd soon change the semblance of this garment to something more flattering. Maybe some Zhir pants and a tunic, in pale blue.

She pushed through the swinging door that led to the kitchen. Voices spilled out to greet her. ". . . and then roll the vegetables in the freshly crushed herbs before adding them to the pot-boil, Daril, thus combining the essence of the flavors before cooking. That's all I'm suggesting."

L'Fertti was leaning against the wall of the pleasantly cluttered kitchen. The pot-boil in its blackened kettle was simmering over the kitchen fire, sending out tendrils of savory steam. Daril was busy chopping vegetables on the heavy wooden kitchen table. Her back was to them both as she spoke. "And I'm suggesting that I've been making this pot-boil since I was old enough to stir a kettle, and it's not going to change now. You know a bit about herbs and spices, I'll grant you, but this is my family's recipe, more than one hundred and fifty years old. No street wizard is going to change it now!"

"Street wizard!" L'Fertti bristled, but Kaloo interrupted.

"L'Fertti. About my lesson today. . ."

"Later, Kaloo. This afternoon, perhaps. Daril, how you can call me—"

"Later won't work, L'Fertti. It has to be now."

The asperity in Kaloo's voice drew both their attentions to her. The look of puzzlement faded suddenly from L'Fertti's face. He spoke in a warning voice. "On the contrary, Kaloo. I think we should skip any lesson for the day. I think you ought to consider taking a nap." He filched a wedge of spiny-heart tuber from Daril's cutting board and crunched into it as he gave Kaloo a warning stare.

"She does look a bit peaked," Daril observed, whacking the vegetables into chunks. "But she always does right before her blood-time. And cantankerous, just as she is now. Didn't you tell me you had an herbal drink for that kind of peevishness, L'Fertti?"

"As a matter of fact, I do. You take dandelion root and—"

Kaloo exploded. "I am sick and tired of the way everyone around here treats me! Daril, how can you speak of my blood-time before L'Fertti! And you, you're supposed to be tutoring me in mastering my luck, but you spend all your days in the kitchen arguing with Daril over recipes and simpering at the eggs-and-milk girl! I shall never invest my luck at the rate you teach me!"

Silence reigned for an instant in the kitchen. Then the two adults exchanged glances.

"Simpering?" L'Fertti asked in an acid voice. "I?"

Daril shot him a conspiratorial glance, then spoke soothingly.

"Well, my little Kookaloo, why don't you let L'Fertti teach you to mix his herbal cure today, then? It's a useful thing for any woman to know, whether she aspires to be a wizard or not. Might get rid of that nasty bloaty feeling that can make a woman feel like ripping into the first person to cross her. And—"

Kaloo ignored her, fixing her narrowed black eyes on the lounging wizard. Her voice was low and cold. "I want my lesson, L'Fertti. And not about herbal cures. You know what I'm talking about."

"Correction, apprentice. I know what I'm talking about. You obviously have no notion of what you are asking. I strongly suggest you spend the day quietly."

"No. I have other plans, and I intend to carry them out. With you or without you." Kaloo delivered the ultimatum quietly.

L'Fertti snorted. "I don't know what you think you can do without me, but go ahead. Go right ahead and try. Maybe it will teach you a lesson you do need, very much: humility. And respect for one's teacher. Go ahead. Prove to yourself just how little you know."

"I will." Kaloo turned, her whole body shaking with anger. She flung the swinging door open, and strode out through the common room, past T'Nar, who looked up suddenly.

"Kaloo. I've decided it's time."

"So have I," she answered bitterly, striding past him. From the corner of her eye, she saw him rise and come after her. Let him. He'd never keep up with her. She'd lose him in the alleys before she was three blocks from the inn. And serve him right. Serve them all right. They thought she was such a child, such a helpless infant. Wait until she returned this evening. Then they'd see. The Kookaloo nestling they'd raised was about to spread her wings. She could feel her luck inside her, rising like a summer squall. It swept her into the bright spring streets of Liavek.

The stump of Dashif's left leg still hurt a little where the wooden peg joined it, but not enough to wreck his mood. His master, the Regent, was keeping him busy, but not too busy, and today he was on his own.

As he left the palace he concentrated on his walk, practicing to get rid of the limp. His spies had heard no rumors of his new weakness, so his enemies probably didn't know of it, which was good. The railroad business was working its way to a nice conclusion, and his dreams of Erina, whom he had murdered so long ago, had become less haunting since he had heard—or imagined?—her voice forgiving him from the land of the dead.

The thoughts flitted through his mind as he found a footcab and commanded it to take him to the docks. He had time now to deal with his own business. A girl who had saved his life, though he had terrorized her. His spies had kept a watch on her until he was feeling himself again, for there was no urgency.

He took in the air near the canal. The scent of broiling fish made him mildly hungry, and the sky was a deep blue that almost made him hurt from the beauty of it. He decided he was going to enjoy this. Today he would find who she was, and why she'd been following him. It was strictly a personal matter and there was no hurry. And, for a change, no particular danger.

He checked the charges on his pistols and replaced them in his wide leather belt. The cab stopped outside the Mug and Anchor. Dashif paid the cabman with a full levar. He was feeling magnanimous.

Kaloo was out of breath and her hair stuck to the back of her neck. She jumped, caught the top of the rickety wooden fence, and hauled herself up to it. For an instant she had a view of the canal, the blue-brown water cluttered with traffic, and then she was over the fence, dropping into the untended jungle that L'Fertti referred to as his herb garden. She crunched through the standing dead stems of last year's growth to his back door. She hoped it wouldn't be warded.

It wasn't. It swung stiffly open to her push, revealing L'Fertti's tiny kitchen and cooking hearth. Flies buzzed over something grayish in a dish on the table. Probably old porridge. Very old. The table was dusty, the hearth completely cold. It was getting so the wizard spent more time hanging about the kitchen of the Mug and Anchor than he did making his cures and potions. Well, and why wouldn't he? He had Daril's cooking, Daril's company, and Kaloo to order about. And the sailors were beginning to buy magic salves for gurry-infected hands and arthritic aches from him. Kaloo expected that when Daril found out about his trade with her customers, she'd put an end to it. But, for now, L'Fertti was gone and his home would supply Kaloo with everything she needed for her investiture. It gave her a sense of justice.

She took out the fan and spread its colors on L'Fertti's dusty table. That would hold her luck, once she'd captured it. From her pocket she took the tattered guidebook. She tried to imagine how L'Fertti would look if he knew she had this. He wouldn't have been so high and mighty this morning.

She unrolled the spindled pamplet. YOU, TOO, CAN INVEST YOUR LUCK! proclaimed the ornate purple letters on the yellowing cover. A border of cabalistic signs and mysterious calligraphies framed the words. She had bought the pamphlet for three coppers from Dumps, Saffer's friend, who always had booklets like *Zhir Love Secrets,* and *Potions for Lovers,* and *Ten Ways to Summon Rikiki.*

Kaloo wiped her sweaty hands down the front of her robe. She opened the pamphlet to the table of contents. She decided to use the Basic Investiture for Beginners this time, and found that page. Next year she'd try one of the fancier settings, when she could afford the crystal bowls and expensive perfumes they required. But for this time . . . she ran her finger down the list of required equipment. Black candles L'Fertti always had, and the herbs were no problem. A lock of hair . . . she'd use some of her own. The same for the spoonful of maiden's blood. Just as well she hadn't spent her virginity yet. She had no idea where else in Liavek she'd find that ingredient. The rest seemed to be standard wizard's equipment. With a bit of rummaging in L'Fertti's cupboards, she'd find what she needed. Humming to herself, she got up to kindle a fire and put the kettle on. She had an hour or so before she could begin. Calmness came over her as her purpose grew strong. By tonight, power would be hers.

Dashif was perfectly aware of the silence that settled over the Mug and Anchor when he stepped through the door. He relished the effect. He looked around, hoping to spot Kaloo at once. It was a rather tidy little place, a bit dark, permeated with the sharp aroma of pot-boil and waterfront folk. A small fire burned in a great hearth at one end of the room. Seven patrons stopped their conversations, but avoided looking at Dashif or each other. One plump middle-aged woman, the host to judge by her apron and the mugs in her hand, stared at him boldly.

Dashif showed her his teeth and approached her. Before she could speak he said, "You must be Daril. I'm looking for Kaloo. Where is she?"

Dashif noticed, out of the corner of his eye, that one of the patrons gave a start. Daril noticed it, too, and spared him a glare, then met Dashif's eyes again, her jaws clamped tightly together. "Why do you want to know?" she countered after a moment.

"Don't question me. Fetch the girl at once."

Out of the corner of his eye, he saw the patron, a lanky gray-beard, stiffen. Daril said, "I don't know—" and stopped as Dashif removed a pistol. He took two steps over to the patron, cocked the weapon, and held it to the old man's head.

"Does this fellow matter to you, mistress?"

Daril paused, her eyes flickering between the two of them. Her eyes were very wide, her face pink, but she tried the bluff anyway. "Not especially. If you don't mind all these witnesses, you just go ahead and shoot him."

"Daril!" cried the old man. Then he turned to Dashif. "Sir, I beg of you . . ."

"Tell me where she is or shut up."

"She's left," he said quickly. Then, licking dry lips, he ventured, "But for a few coins—"

"L'Fertti!" cried Daril.

"Ah," said Dashif. "So that's who you are. All right, tell me where she is. If you don't, I'll kill you. Try any of your silly magic and I'll turn you into a three-legged stool and feed the fire with you."

L'Fertti turned pale. "I don't know," he said. "She ran out."

"Well, you're a wizard and she's your apprentice. Find her."

"I can't."

"Then you're dead."

L'Fertti clawed at his beard, then closed his eyes in sudden concentration.

"L'Fertti, no!" cried Daril.

Dashif looked at her again. "Another outburst from you, mistress, and I'll kill you, and I'll still find out what I want. I happen to know that Kaloo cares for you. Be wise for her sake then, if you haven't the wit to do so for yourself."

A long moment dragged before L'Fertti jerked upright in his chair. "That little minx! She's at my house, rifling through my supplies. What she thinks she's doing, I don't—" Then he sat back. "Oh, no."

Dashif studied him for a moment, then said, "This is her luck day?"

L'Fertti nodded. Daril gasped. "You!" she cried, and started moving toward the wizard. Dashif transferred his pistol to his left hand, but still held it at L'Fertti's head. With his right hand he slapped Daril. She gave a cry and staggered back.

L'Fertti stood up and said, "Sir—"

"Where do you live, L'Fertti?" asked Dashif in his best soft, sinister voice.

L'Fertti sat down again and buried his face in his hands.

• • •

Now that she was actually going to do it, the directions in the book seemed less than clear. She'd had to nick three of her fingers to get the spoonful of maiden's blood, and the closest thing to a silver vessel in L'Fertti's cupboard was a tarnished sugar bowl. She set the fan across the booklet to hold it open, and frowned at the crude illustration. It called for the lock of hair, but never mentioned where to put it or what to do with it. She shook her head irritably and set the lock aside. She wiped her damp palms down her robe. Time to start. No sense putting it off.

There had been a time when she hadn't even known her birthday and luck hours. L'Fertti had helped her to discover them, and to recognize the subtle signs of it. It was here, it was now. Time to invest her luck. No more waiting. Now.

She lit the black candle, glanced down at the pamphlet. She let three drops of hot wax fall into the vessel of blood. They congealed and floated. She glanced at the book again. Now the words. She whispered them, nonsense syllables that didn't resemble any language she had ever heard. She felt nothing. But according to the book, she was supposed to have a floating sensation by now. She chanted the syllables again, more firmly. Nothing. Nothing at all. And she felt nothing of the subtle tingling she had come to feel whenever L'Fertti guided her through one of the tiny magics he permitted her.

Panic scrabbled inside her. No. Be calm. Do one of his exercises. Breathe in, hold, breathe out. Try to be aware of your skin, of cloth touching it, of floor beneath you, of air against your face. Center yourself within your body. Relax.

And now she felt it, a floating, not of body but of mind. As if her thoughts were coming unhooked from her mind. The glob of black wax in the blood. It looked like a . . . like a . . . . Unsettled, she looked away from it. Her eyes snagged on the candle flame. She stared into it, entranced. Felt it pull at her. Birth luck raced through her like a riptide, tore her free from the moorings that held her to her everyday life, carried her away. The candle flame was like a brightly lit tunnel. She roared through it like a runaway coach, racing away from her life, back to other times, other places, other identities. She knew she should seize and master her luck, but not yet, not yet. It was so strong, and there was so much yet to see, if only she would let herself go, surrender to it. It whispered, it promised; it was taking her to the heart of all secrets, to the center of herself. It flowed around her, pushed her on like a wind drives a sail-car, from one brief image to the next. The coast of Minnow Island wreathed in silver mist. A candlelit table, a woman's slender hand resting atop a man's, the couple's faces lost in shadows. A man, built like T'Nar, but much younger, bending his back to the sweep of a dory's oars. A rumpled red cloak, flung wide atop the sweet earth in a meadow of tall sun-yellowed grasses. A man standing beside it. Kaloo felt her identity shrinking, her self receding as she came closer to him. She couldn't find room to care. She stood by the cloak and watched him. He was dragging a white shirt off his head. His arms were lifted, the shirt hiding his face but baring a tightly muscled belly, a line of hair that rose from his navel to widen over his chest. He drew lithely muscled arms from the shirt's loose sleeves. Something in the way he moved promised—no, threatened—great pleasure. He bent slightly, pulled the shirt free of his head, and let it fall to the grass. He straightened, shaking a head of dark curly hair. He lifted a smiling face to her. Dark, dark eyes, eyes she knew, eyes too close to hers—

He shook her and slowly the dazed look left her eyes. She stared into his, and for a moment he would have sworn he was holding Erina—the old Erina. But then her expression changed to confusion, and then to fear, and she started to scream.

"Shut up," said Dashif. "You don't have time for that. How long is your luck time?"

Kaloo shook her head. Dashif shook Kaloo. "How long?"

"I don't know."

Her eyes fell to his right hand, which held her instructions. He glanced at them, scowled, crumpled them up, and threw them across the room.

"No! I need those—"

"As much as you need evisceration," he agreed.

"But—"

"If you don't quiet down and listen to me, your luck time will be over and you will die. Do you understand?"

The hand of terror had drawn her expression, but Dashif took no pleasure in it. At last the girl nodded.

"Good," said Dashif. "Sit down over there. Get rid of these things." He kicked away the candles and the hair. "Now, you need an object to invest in—"

"I know that!" She sounded indignant. Dashif almost smiled.

"Good. Take it in your right hand. Yes, now . . . *Where did you get that?*"

Kaloo stared down at the fan she held, and began trembling again. "I just—I don't know. What's wrong?"

"Nothing. Never mind. I knew someone once who invested

her luck in something very similar." He shook his head to clear it. He didn't need this now. He had questions to ask this girl, and he couldn't ask them if she sickened and died due to a failed investiture. But now what? When he'd had magic, he had invested his own luck a score of times, but how to coach someone?

Well, he'd been at the births of two of his children. How different was this? It was a birth, of sorts. The midwife had said he had helped those times, so he could help now.

With more confidence than he felt, he said, "Relax. There's nothing to worry about. This has been done for thousands of years by millions of sorcerers before you. Let your body relax. Feel the fa—your luck object. Touch it, test its weight, study it, look at its details. Soon it will be more than it is, and so will you.

"Feel your power, your luck. It is there, but it is yet unreal, or unrealized. Now it will become real. It is easy to make a small change in the fan with your luck, isn't it? To heat it up or cool it down? Cool it a trifle. Do you feel it? Now you have the link to it, and the hard part is over." What a lie! "All that you need to do is let your luck flow, because the path is there. Can you imagine the path? A trail, a hallway, a road, a riverbed. A riverbed, with your luck as the river . . ."

As Kaloo relaxed, a peculiar clarity came over her vision. She saw all things with unshielded eyes. She felt more a spectator than an actor as she stared at the fan in her hand. Odd, she had never really seen it before. Oh, she had held it, opened it and gazed on the scenes painted there, but never like this. A river scene was painted on the fan. How had he known that? And as she looked at it, the river flowed with her birth luck. Flowed, and cooled the fan in her hand. Cooled it, just as he had said.

He was helping her. She suddenly knew it. She didn't know how, but she was sure it was his magic that suddenly filled her with confidence and strength. He was lending his experience to her, guiding her. She couldn't fail. All she had to do was listen to him and obey him. He'd help her finish the investiture. He knew what he was doing. The ominous power of Dashif's luck was near legendary in Liavek. A thing to fear—she nearly lost her grip on the flowing birth luck. Yes, a thing to fear, but also a thing to believe in. Later she would sort out why he was helping her. For now, she would accept it. With his help, she knew she could do this. She stared at the fan and, with a sudden intensity, willed her luck into it. Pushed it in, tamped it down, trapped it in the folds of the delicate paper. Almost kept it there.

"It won't stay." She looked up from the fan to tell him, to ask his help. He crouched before her, his eyes on a level with her own. Beneath those dark eyes, twin scars ran vertically down his cheeks, as if he had wept a thousand tears and their scalding passage had eroded his face. She felt caught in the maze of his face, in the lines of maliciousness and hard power that crossed and contradicted the lines of sorrow and regret. She leaned closer, her attention dragged into his face, studying how life had marked him. She wanted to reach out and touch him, smooth away the pains that had changed him so. Someone lifted a hand, reached out slowly. "My poor Dashif," she said with infinite pity. She touched his cheek, tried to smooth away the mask that covered the face of the man who had fathered . . . who had fathered . . .

The muscles of Dashif's face had hardened under her hand, setting it into a grimace of puzzlement, outrage, or something else. She knew him suddenly for what he was, and jerked back her hand from that contact. A rising thunder behind him suddenly crescendoed as the door split and T'Nar avalanched through it.

T'Nar roared at Dashif, rage depriving him of speech. He glared from Kaloo to Dashif, and his face contorted with hate, his skin turning a patchy red and white. "You struck Daril, and now with my Kaloo—!" The stocky old seaman choked on his accusations and abandoned any attempt at speech. He flung himself forward, his thick-fingered hands darting for Dashif's throat.

Sitting, deep in concentration, with my back to an unguarded door, thought Dashif. I deserve whatever happens to me. But even as he was cursing himself he was moving, and the old sailor—what was he babbling about?—was left grasping air.

Dashif shot out a foot, low to the ground, and caught the sailor's ankle. The sailor fell. Dashif kicked him in the head. The sailor tried to stand. Dashif kicked him again. The sailor moaned once, then was still.

Kaloo whimpered, "No."

Dashif drew a pistol.

Kaloo said, "No."

Dashif cocked both barrels.

Kaloo cried, "No. Please!"

Dashif pointed the pistol at the sailor's head.

Kaloo screamed, "Father! Don't!"

He stopped and turned to her. He felt himself trembling. "What are you saying, girl?"

Her eyes had become huge, and a knuckle had found its way to her mouth. She said nothing. He looked into her face, and this time, when he saw Erina, he knew he was seeing Truth.

The scars on his face burned as from salt on a wound. He carefully released the locks of his pistol, lest he set them off with his trembling. He replaced the pistol in his belt, and his movement was slow and dreamlike. He knelt beside the girl.

"Can such things be?" he said, and his voice felt hoarse and strained.

"Please don't hurt him," she said.

He glanced down at the unconscious sailor. "I won't. I promise." He returned his eyes to the girl... his daughter. Could it really be? She stared back at him, and it was Erina, who had said, "I forgive you."

Then he shook himself. "We have little time, child. We must finish."

She looked at T'Nar, fallen to the floor. Struck down by the man who had fathered her. He had fallen out of her reach, and she suddenly felt she would never be able to reach him again. Would never be able to touch him as his Kookaloo, as his fostered nestling. She was something else now. She was Count Dashif's daughter, child of the most ruthless and feared man in Liavek. Daughter of nobility and intrigue, heir to power and wealth. Power and wealth, such as she had imagined her invested luck would bring her. She looked again at T'Nar.

"You must finish your investiture. Your time is slipping away," Dashif insisted. He knelt before her, his eyes devouring her face. He repelled her. She desired nothing that he was a party to.

She forced herself to look at him. "I can't. I don't want to."

"You must. Or you will die."

She locked eyes with him. Every ounce of Daril's upbringing and ethics recoiled from this man. But something deeper in her, something that seemed always to have lurked in the shadows of her soul, recognized a kinship. He would never have wondered at his daughter's need for privacy, for times of solitude. He would have expected his child to invest her luck. He would have recognized the unchildlike drives that motivated her, and he would have channeled them.

He put his hands on her, and she refused to flinch. Daril's child would have cowered. But her very defiance marked her as Dashif's as she said, "I won't."

His grip on her wrist tightened. His other hand held the back of her neck. He forced the hand that held the fan up before her eyes. "You will," he said. "Because you cannot help it. Look. Look at the fan. Your luck flows there. You know it. You see it. It flows there because you want it to. You want your luck to flow there, because you want the strength you can tap there. You want the power you can trap there. If for no other reason, so you can say no to me, and perhaps mean it. So you can say to me, 'I forbid you to kill that man!' instead of, 'No, please, don't hurt him, please.'" He put a pleading whine into the last words, mocking her helplessness.

Anger and hatred surged through her, fury that anyone should be able to speak to her so, to treat her so. And with the anger, riding it, she suddenly saw the greater part of her luck. It was tied to her frustration, to the deep-seated anger she had always suppressed. They had kept it from her, all these years. She could not doubt that they had all known, Daril and T'Nar and Dashif himself. They had kept it from her, the knowledge of her birth, even of her luck time. Kept from her that which was hers.

But no more. Even as the overpowering surge of anger passed through her, she saw it rush into the fan. The river surged and boiled with a wave of fury and luck. It would overflow its banks, it would sweep away the delicate flowers and graceful trees that banked it. Her luck would rush away downstream and leave her here, weak and dying. She did not know how to contain it.

And then she knew: as he did. With icy calm and contempt. With cold, iron control and a face that was a mask. She sealed it off, sliced it off cleanly. All the baggage of her journey from childhood, the fears and pains, wild hopes and crashed joys. Emotions that had seared or soared within her. Hatred and anger and love and joy. And luck. All boxed and bound into a fan. Contained where only she could tap it. Invested.

Dashif was no longer touching her. She did not know when he had taken his hands away, nor how long she had been staring at the fan. It didn't matter. He was rocked back on his heels, studying her, looking at her face. It didn't matter. What he was looking for was no longer there. She snapped the fan shut and held it closed in her hand. Her soul hummed within it.

"You did it," he said softly.

"Yes." No emotion to her answer. She felt . . . weariness. That was all. No elation, no joy such as she had imagined. She wondered if it was this way for everyone who invested his luck. She found she rather liked holding her emotions tightly shut in her hand. Like her father. She met Dashif's eyes without smiling. Behind him, T'Nar's eyes were open and Dashif's death was in them. His knife was in his hand, the old blade gleaming. She looked into Dashif's face, at his dark eyes, at the jawline they shared, at his curling locks that had come to her as unruly waves in her hair. As the old seaman stood up behind him, she did not betray anything. For she felt nothing at all.

Dashif felt the movement behind him and lunged to the side. The swipe meant to part his head from his neck breezed past his cheek. He thought he had made it in time, but then, as he stood, he felt the side of his head aching.

He backed up immediately. The old sailor had a short, ugly knife in his hands and hate in his eyes. There was blood on the knife, but no time for that now. There came a flash of pain from his missing foot, but there was no time for that, either, as the knife flashed down.

He lunged, rolled, and came to his feet again. The sailor came closer. *It was all the stuffing in my empty boot. My kicks aren't as disabling as they used to be.* He backed away again, looking for his chance. The sailor crouched low, eyes intent as he moved forward. Dashif risked a glance around the room. A chair was almost right behind him. If he could get his hands on it, he could disable the sailor with it.

The sailor lunged again and Dashif jumped backward. He felt the chair behind him. On impulse, he sat in it. When the sailor's knife came down, Dashif presented his left leg as a sacrifice. The knife bit into the wood. The sailor looked startled. Dashif twisted his leg and the knife went flying. It clattered to the floor near Kaloo. She didn't move.

Before the sailor could strike again, Dashif was up and there was a pistol in his hand. He kicked the sailor in the groin, then hit him in the head with the pistol. The sailor went down. Dashif cocked the pistol.

"You promised not to kill him."

The voice penetrated, as from another world. He looked up. Kaloo. Yes. The side of his head ached. The girl shrugged. Her eyes were like ice. Dashif pointed the pistol at the sailor.

"You promised," she repeated. She wasn't pleading, she was stating a fact.

An object on the floor between them caught Dashif's eye. It took a moment before he realized it was his ear. He swallowed the bile that rose in his throat and realized that soon he'd grow dizzy, then faint, and he'd be at the mercy of the sailor.

"Promised," he said. "Yes. I suppose I did." He uncocked and replaced the pistol. He pushed back his cloak, removed his own knife, and carefully sliced off one of his puffed, ruffled, pure-white sleeves. He tied it around his head. How much blood had he lost? Would he pass out? How long would it take? Another minute? Five? Ten? What would she do?

She must have seen the sailor coming up behind him, yet she hadn't warned him.

"You are, indeed, my daughter."

"Yes."

"It is sad."

She seemed to understand what he meant. She said, "Yes."

"You lived, just now, because you became cold. You won't live again until you feel the warmth." She didn't understand, but didn't seem to care, either, and that was worse. Dashif said, "I love you, my daughter," because he suddenly knew that he did, and it hurt far more than his severed ear. He said, "I will find you again, or you can find me. You don't have to fear me. Ever."

It was the second time she had seen him bleed. Yes, and the second time she had seen him defeated. This time . . . all that blood, sliding down the side of his head, soaking and spreading across the shoulder of his white shirt. He might . . . she snorted, a harsh sound, dismissing the thought. Let him take care of himself. Hadn't he let her take care of herself, all these years?

She looked around the room, feeling a strange detachment from its disarray, even from the man who groaned on the floor. It felt like the time T'Nar had had to cut the big hook out of her palm, and she had wanted to faint, but couldn't. Somewhere, she knew she was badly hurt, but she couldn't find the pain. T'Nar's hand twitched against the floor. He'd recover. She'd seen enough tavern fights to know that, and she also knew from what she'd seen that Dashif's kicking leg was a false one. T'Nar's heavy canvas trousers would have absorbed most of the impact.

Too much had happened, too fast. She felt she could not get a grip on all of it. She had invested her luck, found her birth father, and taken control of her life in one short afternoon. Now she badly needed to find a quiet spot to think it all through.

T'Nar groaned again. She looked at him, feeling nothing so much as annoyance. He was a messy detail to be tidied up before she could have any time for herself. More than that? she asked herself. She groped after warm childhood memories that had gone still and lifeless. No. Just an irritating old man, one more loose thread to tie up.

She went to him, slipped an arm behind his shoulders, and heaved him up to a sitting position. His eyes opened, squinted at her. "He's gone," he noticed. Then, "My poor little Kaloo," he said thickly.

His pity disgusted her. He should keep it for himself. "You have to get up," she told him. "We have to get you back to the Mug and Anchor."

"Yes. Yes, you're right." He heaved himself to his feet, leaning on her. Kaloo staggered sideways under his weight, nearly slipped on something on the floor. She glanced down, expecting the rubbery wilted peel of a potato.

An ear. Dashif's.

She stared down at it, fascinated. She couldn't lift her eyes from it. She almost wanted to laugh at so ridiculous a thing. She felt T'Nar give her a gentle shake. "Come, girl. Don't be so downcast. I never meant for you to find it out this way. I always thought I'd find a time, a place . . . But it doesn't matter, now does it? The only way it can make a difference is if we let it. Right? And we won't. You'll always be my own little Kookaloo. Now let's go home."

She scarcely heard him. He leaned against her, propelling her toward the door. She stepped over the ear and went. She didn't think she'd ever come back here. She'd made too many mistakes here, and she suddenly could count them all. Trusting L'Fertti, that old phoney. Letting Dashif learn not only her luck time, but the item that housed her invested luck. Staying for T'Nar to wake up. The time for mistakes was over. She'd need a proper teacher, and she knew that now. And a place of her own, a place to be alone and to think. She found herself evaluating her possessions. Did she have anything she could sell for a month's rent?

What was the old man babbling? ". . . better once we're home. And we needn't tell Daril, need we? I mean, the two of us used to keep secrets all the time, didn't we? And this one would just hurt her, wouldn't do anyone any good at all. We'll say Dashif thought you were someone else, someone he knew . . ."

Kaloo let him mutter on, let the words flow past her. As well, she thought, to say that you thought I was someone else. Someone you knew . . .

He found his way to the door, the world still crisp and sharp. The scars on his face hurt. His left foot itched. His head throbbed, and blocked out all sound. He discovered that he was on the street, and that he had somehow found a footcab. He saw himself paying the cabman, and almost heard himself as he asked for the Levar's Palace. He forced himself to concentrate on what the cabman was saying over the roaring in his head.

". . . too much, my lord."

He forced a reply from a thickened tongue. "I may be unconscious when we arrive. See that I am carried into the east door, where they will treat me. Leave your name, and I will give you a purse of gold when I am well."

The cabman's eyes grew wide, and he nodded.

The jolting of the ride hurt even more for a while, but then he became numb. The back of the cabman's head swirled, and became Erina's face, and she was saying good-bye. Then it swirled, only a little, and it was Kaloo who stared out at him, somber and cold. Dashif knew the path she had set out on. But he also knew that, at last, he had paid his debt to Erina.

He was smiling when unconsciousness finally overcame him.

Green Is the Color

by John M. Ford

ARIANAI HAD GONE two blocks down the narrow, empty lane before she realized she'd missed Wizard's Row. Or it had missed her; sometimes the street vanished on a moment's notice. It was never individual wizards' houses that came and went, always the whole Row. She wondered just who decided the issue.

It was a gray, gloomy spring afternoon, matching her mood. She half hoped for rain, though she wasn't dressed for it, in white cotton shirt and pants and a thin flannel cape. Rain would at least be something definite—she could point to it and say, "Look, it's raining, no wonder we're all unraveled."

No, she thought. She didn't need cheap excuses. She needed Wizard's Row, and that meant she needed someone to give her directions.

There wasn't anyone on the little street, and all the houses seemed to be shut tight. Some of the doors were boarded up. But a little way ahead there was a glow of light, a shopfront, two high narrow windows and a high narrow door.

There was a rattle like bones overhead. Arianai looked up. Hanging from a wooden bracket, apparently as the shop sign, was a puppet on a string. It danced in the slight breeze—didn't just swing, but actually danced, throwing out its elbows and knees. The only sound on the street was a whisper of air. There was something eerie about the marionette, dancing to no music.

Arianai went inside. It was surprisingly spacious within. The narrow storefront was only a third of the shop's actual width.

There were shelves filled with stuffed animals of cloth and fur, dozens of dolls, some with porcelain heads and arms, little ships with linen sails. More marionettes hung on the walls, and kites of paper and silk. A table displayed boards for shah and tafel and other games, dice, decks of cards; on another, two armies of toy soldiers faced each other in precise ranks, brightly painted in the liveries of Liavek and Ka Zhir four centuries ago. There were smells of sandalwood and hide glue, and a faint taste of raw wood in the air.

A long counter crossed the back of the shop. Behind it sat a pale-skinned man with long, slender limbs and very black hair. He was working at a piece of wood with a small rasp. Other tools and bits of carving were laid out on the counter within his reach. Behind him were more shelves, more toys; on the topmost shelf was a wooden train, a model of the one being built along the coast from Hrothvek to Saltigos. It had shiny brass fittings and red-spoked wheels.

"Good afternoon," the man said, without looking up. "Browsing is free. The prices are outrageous." His voice was pleasant without being friendly.

Arianai said. "Excuse me, master . . . I am looking for Wizard's Row. I seem to have gotten lost."

"You, or it?" said the dark-haired man.

"I'm not certain," Arianai said, and laughed, more from the release of tension than the joke.

"Well," the man said, "the Row is either ninety paces to the right of my door, or else it is not. Happy to have been of assistance, mistress." He held up the piece of whittled wood, blew dust from a hole. He picked up a length of braided white cord and ran it experimentally through the hole.

"That's a shiribi puzzle, isn't it?" Arianai said.

"It is."

"I'd always wondered where those came from. You see the White priests with them, but . . ."

"But you cannot imagine White priests making anything with their hands?"

"I'm sorry, I didn't mean to insult your faith."

The man laughed. "If I had a faith, that wouldn't be it." He put down the wood and cord, picked up another stick and a file, went back to work. He had long-fingered, spidery hands, quick and very smooth.

Arianai turned toward the door. An arrangement of soft toys drew her eye; in the center was a fuzzy camel as high as her knee, with a ragdoll rider perched on the hump. The rider, dressed in the robes of the desert nomads, had one arm upraised, with a yarn whip coiled down it—an ordinary pose, but there was something about the way the person was bent forward, and the camel's neck was bent back, that let Arianai hear the rider muttering and grumbling, and the camel—most obstinate beast that ever the gods devised—well, snickering. The toy was a perfect little sketch of a stubborn camel and its hapless owner, in cloth and stitches and yarn.

Perhaps, Arianai thought, there was luck in her wrong turn after all. "Who makes these toys?" she said.

"I do," said the black-haired man, "when I am not interrupted." Arianai was not certain if it was meant as a joke.

She said, "I am looking for something for a child."

"That is very usual in a toyshop." The man stopped his filing, but still did not look up. "Even if the child is oneself, many years late."

"This is a child who cannot sleep," Arianai said.

"Perhaps a music box," the toymaker said, examining the bit of puzzle in his fingers. "I have one that plays 'Eel Island Shoals' with a sound of waves as background, very restful. Or the flannel cat on the third shelf, beside the carousel . . . inside it are a cam and a spring; when wound up, it makes a sound like a beating heart. Some people find it quite soothing." The toymaker's voice had warmed. "Then again, all your child may need is something to hold. A woolen monkey, or a satin dolphin. A friendly caution —if the child has lost a pet, or greatly desires some particular animal, choose something different. Toys should not come with bad memories or unfulfilled promises attached."

"Why have I never heard of you before?" Arianai said.

The man looked up. His face was fine-boned, somewhat sharp, with hazel eyes of a remarkable clarity. "Why should you have?" The warmth was gone again.

"I am Arianai Sheyzu."

"Yes?"

"The children's physician. My house is just around the corner."

"Oh. Forgive me for telling you your trade, Mistress Healer. Please browse at your pleasure." He went back to his work.

"The child—her name is Theleme—is afraid to sleep." The toymaker said nothing, but Arianai went on, the words just spilling out. "She fights sleep for as long as she can, sometimes for days, until she falls into an exhausted sleep. And then she screams. Chamomile and valerian are no use at all, and she has become too frail for stronger drugs."

"I understand now why you were seeking Wizard's Row, Mistress Healer. I do hope that you find it."

Arianai bit her lip. "I'm sorry, master . . ."

"Quard."

"I didn't mean to burden you with my troubles."

"I never accept such burdens," Quard said. "To the right, ninety paces."

"Thank you." She turned to go.

"Take the flannel cat with you," Quard said in a quiet voice. "It's wound through the seam on its left flank."

Hesitantly, Arianai picked up the stuffed animal. As she moved it, she felt the springs inside loosen and the wooden heart pulse. Something in the mechanism purred softly.

"No charge for the loan," Quard said.

She looked at him. He was looking back, his eyes bright in his pale face like the eyes of a porcelain doll. Arianai tucked the cat under her arm, gave the man a hard stare back, and went out of the shop. Above her head, the sign-puppet kicked up its heels on a fresh wind from the sea.

Sen Wuchien was strolling through the Levar's Park when he heard the sentry call midnight. He paused for a moment, shivered, and felt an irrational impulse to touch the vessel of his luck. Instead he simply leaned slightly on his walking stick and thought on his vessel, drawing power into his bones to stop the chill. Foolish to have gone walking on such a chilly night, he thought, but the air was clean and pleasant, if damp. He would make tea when he got home, Red Orchid blend, and share it with his cat Shin; then all would be well.

His magic warmed him. With his empty hand he stroked the air, as if Shin's head were there, and tightened his abdomen, pulling power up to his eyes. Around Sen, the landscape brightened, sharpened. The images of catsight reminded him of an ink-and-water drawing; it occurred to Sen that he had neglected his brushes of late. That was not good. New rituals kept the magic responsive, the power fluid.

He stretched his vision, watched an owl gobbling a mouse, a badger waddling off toward its hole, a pair of lovers in deep consideration. He thought, amused, that he would do a pillow-book painting, the sort young people did, indeed the sort he had done as a young man in Tichen. And the text . . .

> *Backs shape heaven's arches*
> *Dark hair braids with fingers*
> *As the tea grows cold.*

Sen realized that he was tracing the calligraphy in the air. It was idle, no light trailed from his fingertips; he had moved, but not invoked. He was old now but not yet so careless. He wiped the power from his eyes, let the magic flush of warmth drain away, and walked on.

He heard a musical whistle, turned his head. There was a figure sitting on a boulder, a long white pipe to its lips. Sen Wuchien wondered that he had not seen this one before—he was not indeed so careless. There was power involved here. Sen looked closer.

The person wore a sashed full robe in the classical Tichenese style, all pure white with the sheen of silk, and white slippers. The face was smooth and finely featured, a young woman's or a beautiful boy's, Sen could not tell, with black hair in a long braid across one shoulder. The piper played a few notes, bowed slightly. Sen Wuchien bowed in return.

Sen said, "I had supposed to meet you in Tichen."

The piper gestured meaninglessly with the white flute, which Sen could see was made of a long bone. The bone of what? he wondered. It was too long to be a man's, or even a horse's. Sen said, "Pardon me. I spoke falsely without intent. I meant to say..." But he could no longer recall what he had meant to say.

The person in white stretched out a slim hand, pointing the bone flute at Sen, and spoke in Tichenese. "Come, if you are coming."

Sen smiled at the thought of having some option in the matter, and put his hand on the flute. It was very cold. Sen controlled his trembling without the use of his power, and looked into the face of the white piper.

"Oh," Sen said, "it is *you*—"

He looked at his hand. It glowed with a cool green light. He tried to let go of the bone flute, but could not. He reached for his power, but his mind was cold and would not move that far. Through the green haze that now wrapped his whole body, Sen looked again at the piper's face, understanding now why he had been offered a choice, and that in fact the offer had been real.

But as the cold caressed his heart, Sen Wuchien thought that he had already made the choice, thirty years ago.

The Levar's Park was large and not heavily patrolled; it was about an hour and a half before the two Guards came by on their rounds. They saw the glow long before they could see what it came from.

The next day was still gray, and drizzly as well. The puppet over the toyshop door seemed to clutch at himself and shiver in the wind, and there was a sad drip-drip from his nose and his toes.

Lamps were lit inside the shop; Quard sat near a lamp with a large glass lens that threw light on the doll's face he was painting. As he stroked cobalt blue on the eyebrows, he said, "Did you find Wizard's Row?"

"Yes," Arianai said, "and a strange thing happened there."

"Most who seek Wizard's Row are disappointed if one does not."

"The Magician at Seventeen and Doctor Twist both recommended you."

"As what?"

"As one who knows something about dreams."

Quard put down his work, wiped his brush with solvent. "In addition to an entire street named The Dreamers', the apothecary at Canalgate calls his boat *Dreams*. Maydee Gai at the House of Blue Leaves retails them fairly and to most tastes; Cimis Malirakhin is most to mine. Liavek has many splendid theaters, though I do not attend them. I'm a toymaker."

Suddenly a chipmunk appeared from beneath the counter, nodding and chittering, a blue nut in its paws. "Yes?" Quard said to the animal, then, "I quite agree. She has made a mistake." *Squeak, squeak?* "Yes, Doctor Twist will probably refund her money, but Trav? Never. It would offend his moral principles."

Finally Arianai realized that the chipmunk was a puppet on Quard's hand. "You do that very well," she said, "but I'm not so easily insulted."

"No insult intended," Quard said, now sounding tired. "I only wished to get a point across. Sometimes puppets are better at that than people." He pulled off the glove-puppet and put it on the counter, where it looked rather unpleasantly like a dead real chipmunk.

Arianai said, "You haven't even seen the child."

"I assume that you have confidence in your own abilities as a healer. And you have already named the most noted sorcerer in Liavek, as well as the craziest. What is there for me to look at?"

"It was the wizards who named you."

"So you said. Perhaps I've upset them somehow. They are subtle and quick to anger, you know."

"Surely you must care what happens to a child."

"Because I'm a toymaker? Bad proof, mistress."

"I think you did prove it to me. When you first spoke, about choosing toys."

"As a children's healer, you must know a certain amount about lice and worms. Do you love them?"

She stared at him. He had picked up the doll-mask, and turned the lamp lens to examine it.

"She slept last night, master. With your cat in her arms, she slept for almost the whole night."

"Then you have no further need for me. You may keep the cat."

After a moment Arianai said, "The girl is dying."

"So are we all, Healer—with all due respect to your profession."

For several minutes there was no sound in the shop. Then Quard said, "Did Trav tell you I'd be difficult?"

"Who?"

"The Magician."

"He did not tell me you would be hateful."

"Trav is like that. Bring Theleme tomorrow at five hours past noon."

It took her a moment to realize what he had said. "There's a long night between now and then."

"True. Five tomorrow."

She felt puzzled and relieved—too much of both to be really angry. "Tomorrow, Master Quard. Thank you."

The wizard Gorodain sat in his attic room, contemplating a tabletop. The wood was covered with a disk of glass, etched with a six-pointed star and inscriptions in the language that had centuries ago evolved into the S'Rian tongue. From each of the points of the star, a line led to the center of the disk; above the intersection was a small, darting green flame that burned without fuel or ash. One of the points was empty. Small objects rested on the others: a small bronze mask on a chain, a leather shoelace coiled in a complex knot, an arrowhead, a wooden doll, a silver dagger with a wickedly curved blade and an emerald in the hilt.

The previous night all the points had been filled, a little paper scroll on the sixth.

Gorodain examined the objects on the glass as a man might look over a crucial position in a game of shah—which, after a fashion, this was. The creation of the board, the collection of the pieces, had occupied most of thirty years. This was no time to rush the endgame.

He picked up the mask. It had horns, and finely crafted eyes that were chips of carnelian in onyx. He put it down again on its point, looked out the garret window at the moon rising through torn clouds. It was nearly eleven o'clock. Time to start.

Gorodain concentrated on the vessel of his luck, reached out with an imaginary hand, closed fingers of power on the bronze mask. He began to push it along the cut-glass line, toward the flame in the center.

He met resistance. He concentrated again, pushed harder. The mask wobbled but did not move. Gorodain felt his strength draining away. He ceased to push.

He raised his right hand, brushed his smallest finger against the boss of the ring he wore. A small blade, no bigger than a fingernail trimming, flicked out. He drew back his left sleeve, spoke some words, and nicked the skin of his arm. A drop of blood fell into the green flame.

The flame guttered, flattened, pooled on the glass. A darkness appeared, and Gorodain looked into it. He saw a man with pale skin, lying on a narrow bed, one arm thrown out straight, the hand clutching the bedpost.

So, Gorodain thought, the key was not yet fully in the lock, the door was closed to him tonight. It was possible still for him to send another nightmare, perhaps force the issue. But that would cost more of his already depleted magic, and the ritual of feeding the flame was exorbitantly costly. There would be time. He had waited thirty years; he could wait another day. He made a gesture and the flame went out.

It had rained all day, and by five in the afternoon showed no sign of stopping. Arianai and Theleme met no one on the street except a pair of cloaked and disgruntled City Guards, who looked after them as if bewildered that anyone would take a child out on a day like this.

They sloshed and bustled down the side street—it didn't seem to have a name posted anywhere—to the sign of the dancing puppet, which now stood nearly still, just shivering in the wet.

There was no one in the front of the shop, though lamps were lit. "Master Quard?" Arianai said. There was no answer. A small light came from a door behind the long counter.

Arianai took the damp cape from Theleme's shoulders. The girl was five, or perhaps six, but her face was ancient, hollowed under cheekbones and dull, unfocused eyes. "Wait right here, Theleme," Arianai said. "I'll be back in just a moment. Don't go anywhere, now."

Theleme nodded. Arianai went behind the counter. "Master Quard?" she said into the dimness beyond the doorway.

"No farther," Quard's voice came back softly. "How did the night go?"

"The cat did help," Arianai said. "She slept for a few hours—but then she began to scream again."

"All right. Go back to her. I'll be out."

Arianai did so. She saw that Theleme was slowly looking around the walls of the shop, at the toys. Perhaps, Arianai thought, they had made an opening; perhaps the key was in the lock.

Quard came out. He wore a long robe of blue and yellow, with a matching skullcap. Without a word, he went to the windows and lowered the blinds. The lamps were already lit. Then he bowed low to Theleme, and settled down to sit cross-legged on the floor before her, his clothes billowing around him. The effect was at once clownish and impressive.

"You would be Mistress Theleme," Quard said in a respectful tone.

Theleme nodded.

"I am Quard Toymaker, Quard of Dancing Wood, and your friend the healer Arianai has brought you to me, through the storm and the cold and the wet, because I need your help in a thing."

"Yes, master?"

"Sit down, mistress." Quard spread his arms above his lap. Theleme looked at Arianai, who nodded. Theleme sat down, cradled on Quard's knee.

"Now, mistress," he said, "do you know of the Farlands? The Countries of Always-Cold?"

"Anni has told me stories."

Quard shot a curious glance at Arianai, then said, "There is a princess in the Farlands—just about your age."

"What does she look like?"

"I have never seen her," Quard said, "but they tell me she has yellow hair like yours, and violet eyes like Mistress Anni's, and the pale skin of all Farlanders."

"Like yours?"

"There you have it. Now, mistress, the princess is to have a birthday soon. Lean close to me." He whispered in Theleme's ear, and she nodded gravely.

Quard said, "Now you understand how important this matter is?" Theleme nodded again. Any Liavekan, even the youngest, understood the seriousness of revealing a true birthday.

"Now, mistress, comes my problem. The princess must have a gift for her birthday. But there are so many things in my shop, and I know them all so well, that I cannot choose one for her. Do you think you can help me?"

Theleme put a finger to her mouth. She turned again to Arianai, who smiled and nodded.

Quard helped Theleme stand up again, and she began to wander around the shop, looking wonderingly at the toys. She put out a hand hesitantly, drew it back.

"Please touch," Quard said. "You will not break them."

Theleme searched among the toys for a third of an hour. Arianai caught herself fidgeting; Quard just sat, smiling crookedly, his hands crossed in his lap.

Arianai noticed that the backs of Quard's hands were entirely smooth, without a single hair. His face was just as bare below his eyebrows, without the shadow of a beard. Was Quard a woman? she wondered. The flowing robe made it difficult to tell. Not her business, she supposed. If this succeeded, she did not care if Quard was a troll.

Theleme had picked up a toy and was bringing it to Quard. It was the soft camel-and-rider Arianai had seen on her first visit. Quard held out his hands and received the doll. "Why, this is it, Mistress Theleme; that is just the present for the princess. I never would have guessed it." Quard stood up in a fluid motion, holding the stuffed toy in both hands. "Perfect, perfect. I must arrange at once to send this to the Farlands."

Theleme looked up at him, still as a sculpture, watching with dead eyes as the toy camel left her.

Quard turned away, then spun full circle, his robe floating out. "Wait," he said, and sat down again. "Come closer, mistress."

Theleme did so. Quard said, "My eyes are not what they once were, you know. Will you look closely at this toy, *very* close, and tell me if anything is wrong with it? A princess's gift must be perfect, you know."

Theleme took hold of the toy, began to minutely examine it. As she did, Quard reached slowly to the back of her neck, began to rub it. Theleme leaned over the soft camel. Quard stroked downward. Theleme's head tipped forward and was pillowed on the camel's hump.

Surprised and a little alarmed, Arianai said, "What did you—?"

"Let nature take its course," Quard said softly, and then pressed a finger to his lips. He leaned close to Theleme and said, "They will ask me why, you know. Not the princess—she will be delighted, I am sure—but all the lords and ladies at court, they will want to know, 'Why that toy? Why a camel?' Surely you know how lords and ladies are, when they see something that is special to you. They always want to know why."

Eyes still shut, Theleme said, "Yes, Master Quard."

"Tell me what the princess should say to them."

Theleme said, in a startlingly clear voice, "The green man is there. He has to go away."

"Is the green man bad? Is that why he has to go?"

"He wants to hurt the princess. He wants her to die."

"Do you see the green man, Theleme? Is he here?"

"Yes.. Yes!" The child struggled. Arianai bent forward. Quard hugged Theleme and said, "Look away from the man, Theleme. Look away. Do you see something coming there? Do you see a camel, and a rider? I think they're coming. Do you see them?"

"Yes . . . I see them."

"And does the rider have a whip? Can you see the whip in the rider's hand?"

"Yes."

"Look, Theleme! The rider's reaching down for you. Catch the rider's hand as the camel comes by. Quick, now! Catch it!" He gripped Theleme's hand in his own.

"I have it!"

"I'll pull you up now!" He tugged gently at Theleme's hand. "Hold tight, hold tight! We have to ride fast!" He slipped his hand around Theleme's waist.

"I'm holding, master!"

"Now, we must ride for the green man. You have to be brave now, Theleme, for we must drive him out. Do you see the whip in the rider's hand?"

"Yes, I see it. I'll try to be brave."

"Very well. Here we come. And here comes the whip." Quard gestured to Arianai. She raised her hands and clapped them as hard as she could. Theleme twitched, but held tight to the stuffed camel.

"Here it comes again!" *Crack!*

"Is he running, Theleme? Can you see the green man run?"

"Yes! He's running! He's running away..." Theleme's voice faded, and she relaxed in Quard's arms. He rocked her gently.

"I think she will be better now," he said finally. "Here—can you take her?"

Arianai did, and Quard stood up, the stuffed toy under his arm. He put it in Arianai's arms beside Theleme, who cuddled it without waking. Then he walked to the door. "I'll go up to the corner and get you a footcab. There must be an enterprising few of them out in the slop." He opened the door, letting cool air in from the dark outside. "Well. It's stopped raining."

"Quard, I—"

"I doubt she'll remember the story about the princess as any different from the rest of the dream. If she does, tell her that I made another camel, just for her."

"Quard."

"Let me get the cab. You don't want to carry her home, do you?"

"I wouldn't mind. If you carried the camel."

"'I'll carry the child if you carry the camel.'" Quard's voice was suddenly flat. "That must be the punch line to a joke, but I don't remember it."

"Come and have tea. I'd like to talk to you."

"What, and wake Theleme with our pillow conversation?" sounding more sad than funny.

"Do you have other appointments?"

"There's your cab," Quard said, in a tone that made Arianai hug the child tight. He went running out the door, and was gone for minutes, and minutes, the door wide open. Then a footcab did appear. Arianai went to meet it, found the driver had already been paid. But Quard was nowhere in sight. Arianai closed the shop door and rode home. She put Theleme to bed, the camel still in the child's grasp, and then sat in her office making notes on the case and rereading medical books that had been dull the first time. Finally, at almost midnight, she went to bed, and her sleep was very sweet.

Shiel ola Siska blew through the narrow bronze pipe, sending a narrow jet of flame from the spirit burner onto the tinned wires in her left hand, brazing them to a circular copper plate as broad as three fingers. She tongued the blowpipe, spraying fire around the copper, producing a pleasing rainbow finish on the hammered metal. She slid her fingers to the other end of a wire, bent it around, then fused it to the plate. Another wire was curved and twisted over and under the first before being brazed in place; then the next, and the next.

The end product was a copper brooch bearing a coil of wires, tangled, complex, yet pleasing in form. The purpose of the item, the ritual, was antimagic: When luck was driven through the brooch, spells cast at the wearer would be ensnared in the coil, their energy twisted and untuned and dissipated. Certain spells, at any rate. "The most crucial of magics," ola Siska's instructor had taught her, "is the illusion that wizards are infallible, but their customers can foul up any enchantment."

And as with any magical device, it was temporary; it would lose its luck on ola Siska's birthday, or with her death. No wizard could truly create. A true adept could bind luck into a thing and make it truly magical—but only once, for the bound magic was gone from the wizard forever. The brooch was just a brief diversion of luck, as a spinning top that could stand impossibly on its point until it slowed and toppled.

Ola Siska stroked her finger across the wires. They played a faint series of notes, not quite music. She snuffed the spirit burner, took the brooch to a table covered in white linen. A high window let the light of the three-quarter moon shine upon it. She took up a pair of forceps, and with them lifted a small silver casting of a spread-eagled, naked man. She started to lower it into the nest of wires.

There was a slight rumbling beneath the floor. The copper brooch bounced into the air, rolled across the linen, and fell to the floor, where it kept rolling. Shiel muttered darkly and turned to catch it as it wheeled away—had she been thinking of spinning tops? Was that why the thing was acting so—

The brooch bumped against metal with a little tinny clink and fell over. The thing it had struck shifted; it was a boot, of lapped bronze plates.

Ola Siska looked up, slowly. Above the boot was a bronze greave, a knee-cover, then, resting on the knee, a jointed bronze gauntlet. The hand pushed down, and the knee levered up, and the figure of a man in full metal armor stood up, a bronze man shaded green with verdigris. His breastplate was heavily engraved with intricate designs, and his helmet bore winglike flanges at the temples. Its crown nearly brushed Shiel ola Siska's ceiling beams.

His faceplate was a mirror-finished sheet of metal, without features, without holes for sight or speech or air.

Her throat felt tight. So it had not been time and chill night air that had taken Sen Wuchien after all, she thought. She should have known.

She should have been *told!*

The bronze man walked toward her, holding out its hands. Ola Siska saw that its forearms were spiked down their length, like a crab's arms. She was quite certain that the jagged metal points had not been there a moment ago.

She flexed her hands. If she had not been at work, there would have been a ring on every finger, half a dozen bracelets on each of her wrists, each one the ritual of a spell. But she still wore amulets, around her neck and ankles, in her hair. And most important, she had the vessel of her luck safely on her person.

She caught her full skirts in her hands, swept them upward like a butterfly's wings, then released the cloth and touched a square pendant of interlaced steel and glass rods.

As the skirts fell, a circle of something like stained glass, though impossibly thin for glass, appeared before her. Grainy color radiated from the center of the disk, and thin black veins.

The bronze man collided with the colored disk. There were showers of sparks where his armor touched it. Ola Siska reached to the top of her head, pulled out two long golden pins. She raised her hands and breathed deep, feeling the power rise from her vessel to the pins.

A bronze gauntlet punched through the disk in a spray of colored fragments. Cracks shot through the glass, and in a moment it collapsed to the floor, and evaporated.

Ola Siska stiffened, but did not break the incantation. She threw the two pins. They flew true as arrows through the air, and pierced the bronze man's hands, nailing them to his breastplate. Ola Siska raised her right fist, slammed it into her left palm, and the pins shone with unbearable blue light, hissing as they welded themselves into place.

The bronze man struggled to pull his hands free, as Shiel ola Siska groped through her boxes of jewelry for the proper ritual device. There was a grating noise, then a rhythmic clinking, like a music box but deeper and flatter. Ola Siska seized a bracelet and turned.

The bronze man's arms had fallen off at the shoulders, and dangled from his chest by the nails through their gauntlets. From the sides of his breastplate, another pair of arms, thin and rod-like, was folding out, oiled cables gliding in grooves along their length.

Ola Siska dropped the bracelet—no use now to sever the thing's legs—and turned, and ran, out the door and into the night. She could hear the clanking of the bronze man behind her, and could not help but waste a moment in looking back: There were now spikes and hooks and blades down all its limbs, and steam hissed from its joints.

She ran up the street, trying to keep a grip on her thoughts and her skirts, unable to order her luck with the brazen thing behind her. She seemed to feel a dull red heat from it, but that was only in her mind, surely in her mind—

She paused, leaned against a doorframe, turned to face the thing. It was twenty paces behind her, taking slow long strides. There was no steam, no furnace glow, and even its steps were not overly loud; it had a sort of quiet dignity as it came for her. She held up a hand in a warding gesture, saw that her fingernails shone brilliantly green.

Into the pit with dignity, she thought, and hiked up her skirts and ran. She heard the clank of metal behind her, dared not waste the time to turn but knew it was gaining. Could it tire? *Metal fatigue,* she thought, with—irony? Ha, ha, ha.

Suddenly she thought of a place to run, a thing to run for. She had cast the spell away uncast, and now—

She stretched luck down to her right foot, felt the anklet there rattle and loosen. There was no time to stop, take the thing off, do this properly; it had to be timed just right—

Ola Siska kicked off the loop of silver. It sailed out before her, spinning, expanding from a bracelet to a belt to a loop broader than her shoulders; it struck the pavement; she leaped into it—

And landed on her hands and knees, gasping, half the city away, where Park Boulevard met the Street of the Dreamers. The shop called the Tiger's Eye was dark, its awnings folded. There was only the slight glitter of streetlamps on the items behind its windows.

Shiel tried to stand. She couldn't, not yet; the spell had drawn most of her strength. She was terribly cold. And her nails and knuckles were greenly luminous.

She pushed herself upright and went to the door of the shop, groped at her belt for a gold-and-silver key that hung there. She rubbed the pendant, pulling hard at the last of her luck.

Her hand spasmed and the key fell on its cord. Of course the shop would be sealed against magical entry. She pounded on the door, still short the breath to shout.

Behind her was a sound like a key in an unoiled lock. She looked into the dark shop, and in the glass saw the bronze man reflected, tall and shining and severe, his arms stretched out to her.

Ola Siska leaned against the door. With just a moment to recover herself, she could break the glass, reach through . . . no, that was too obvious, the inner bolt would require a key. There was no sign of a stirring within, no lights, just a twinkling like stars on crystal and silver and brass. Only an inch of wood and glass between her and that whole constellation of life.

Something blurred her view: It was her face, shining green in the glass. Was that truly the way it was, then? Was she really so tired of running?

She turned, leaning back against the door, hands on knees that glowed greenly through her skirts. She looked up at the bronze man, who stood above her with his metal hands outstretched. His face was green as well . . . no, it was just her reflection.

"Come," said the bronze man, his voice rasping and twanging like a saw cutting wires, "if you are coming."

"I could have run farther still," she said, breathless but with dignity. "I could." She held out her hand, but remained sitting, so that he would have to kneel to her, like a courtier and not a conqueror.

Which he obligingly did.

The sun came out the next morning, in more ways than one; Theleme woke wanting breakfast, and almost smiling. Arianai gave her some buttered toast and juice, knowing the child would be hungry but that her stomach would be in no shape for a heavy meal, and then they tossed on light cloaks and went for a walk along the canal.

As they crossed the lower bridge, they ran into a cluster of people on the street, around the Tiger's Eye, and a line of Guards keeping them away from something. Arianai recognized the officer in charge, a tall, hawk-faced woman with straight black hair, and walked up to her.

"Hello, Jem."

Jemuel, captain of the Levar's Guard, turned. "Hi, Anni." More softly she said, "Keep the little one away. It's not nice, what's over there."

"Can I help?"

"Not any longer, Anni. It's another green one."

"What? A Green priest?"

"Another glowing one—you haven't heard? The half-copper rags have been full of it."

"I've been busy, and you know I don't read the rags."

Jemuel said, "We've got two wizards dead in three nights. Not a scratch on either of them—but the bodies are glowing green as fireflies."

"Just a moment, Jem." Arianai led Theleme over to a baker's cart, bought her a sweet biscuit for distraction, then went back to Jemuel. "Glowing? Magic?"

"What it seems. Funny, though, you should even have to ask —Thomorin Wiln said that phosphorus could make a body glow so, but he tested, and there wasn't any, nor any other poison he could find. Phosphorus, imagine that. More ways to die than you'd think, eh, Anni?"

"Who were they?"

"Um? Oh. Two nights back was that old Titch who lived up on the canal, Wuchien; found him in the park. And this morning when Snake opens up, she finds Shiel ola Siska glowing on her doorstep."

"Snake," Arianai said distantly, thinking of Snake's skill with the camel driver's whip she always carried, thinking too of a rag-stuffed toy.

"—so there it sits," Jemuel was saying, "one not far from his house, the other a long way the wrong side of the canal; a man, a woman; a Titch and a Liavekan—no pattern to it except that they both did magic, no motive, no sense. And an ola Siska dead, so the nobility are demanding that Somebody Do Something." She sighed. "Guess who."

"Captain?" It was a young Tichenese, Snake's assistant Thyan. "There's kaf."

"Enough for one more?" Jemuel said, indicating Arianai.

"Of course. Hello, Healer."

"Well . . . will Theleme be any trouble in there?"

"I'll take care of her, mistress," Thyan said. "Part of the job. Do come in."

Jemuel and Arianai sat in wicker chairs, by a tiny brass table with the porcelain kaf service; Snake, wearing an embroidered abjahin with the long whip coiled incongruously at her waist, leaned against a cabinet, stroking her cup, looking as if she wanted to pace. Arianai recalled that the shopkeeper had quietly put out word that she was to marry shortly. Death on the doorstep must have been quite an intrusion.

"You did know ola Siska?" Jemuel said.

"Of course I knew her. Everyone involved with jewelry did. But I never carried much of her work. Mostly she sold through Janning Lightsmith, sometimes the Crystal Gull."

"Too expensive for your trade?"

"Thanks, Jem."

"Well?" Jemuel said, not apologetic.

Snake gestured with her fingertips. "Not to my taste. Shiel had a particular fondness for . . . well, strange images. Skulls. Human figures twisted up. And sharp edges: she showed me a necklace once that . . ." Snake ran a hand around her throat.

Arianai said, "There's a market for that?"

Snake said, in a more relaxed voice, "There's a market for everything. I'm no prude; I'll sell you a poison ring, or a pendant with a hidden dagger. But Shiel ola Siska's work seemed to . . . celebrate death, and pain." She looked around the shop, at the multitude of trinkets and oddments that crowded the place. "Let me show you something," she said suddenly, went behind the counter and brought out a velvet-covered tray. She raised a spherical pendant on a fine gold chain. "This is one of hers. I bought it for the craftsmanship, before I quite saw what the thing was."

The pendant was an openwork ball of gold and silver pieces; the gold bars were straight, the silver ones coiled.

"It's a shiribi puzzle, isn't it?" Arianai said. "What's that in the center?" She put her finger to the pendant.

"Careful!" Snake cried, and Arianai stopped her hand, just as she saw that the object within the shiribi puzzle was a silver figure of a man, curled into a fetal position with one arm outstretched.

Then Snake's hand shook, and the metal sphere bumped against Arianai's fingertip; and the ball collapsed on its silver springs, into a tight knot of white and yellow metal from which a pale hand emerged in a gesture of pure desperation.

"Kosker and Pharn!" Jemuel said.

"It'll certainly be salable now," Snake said, "dead artists and all that. But I've wondered ever since I first looked closely at the thing, would I want to do business with anyone who'd buy it?"

"You think it had anything to do with ola Siska being at your door last night?"

"I've told you already, Jem, I don't know why she was there."

"And you didn't hear her knock."

"If she knocked, I didn't hear it." She put the pendant down. "There *was* a privacy spell on the bedroom last night."

"Thank you for saving me the question," Jemuel said. "Anni? Something wrong?"

Arianai realized she was still staring at the shiribi puzzle. "No, nothing."

From several corners of the shop, clocks began to strike nine.

Jemuel said, "Pharn's teeth, it's three hours past my bedtime. If anything occurs to you—either of you—as a clue, you'll let me know, right?"

"Of course."

"Sure, Jem."

"Thanks for the kaf. I'll sleep better for it." She waved and went out of the shop, jingling the porcelain bells above the door.

Arianaï said, "Snake, you sell some toys, don't you?"

"Sure. Want something for the little girl you've been—"

"No, I . . . have you ever bought from Quard?"

"Quard? Yes, some marionettes. He makes the best string-puppets I've ever seen. He'd have a reputation and a half, if his shop weren't harder to find than Wizard's Row in a dust storm."

"Hard to find . . ."

Snake put her hand on Arianaï's shoulder. "Are you sure there's nothing wrong, Anni?" They locked eyes for a long moment, and then Snake said gently, "Oh. Yeah. Me, too . . . guess you've heard." She smiled, a little sadly. "It does make it harder to look at death, doesn't it?"

Arianaï nodded and went out. In front of the shop, Thyan was demonstrating cat's cradles for Theleme, who watched in amazement as the knots appeared and vanished. Arianaï said, "Time to go, Theleme. Thank you, Thyan," and handed the young woman a copper.

"I shouldn't take this," Thyan said. "It's part of serving the customers . . ."

"I didn't buy anything."

"Oh. I guess it's all right, then." Thyan grinned. From within the shop came the sound of a single clock striking nine, and Snake's voice calling, "Thyan!"

"Oops," Thyan said, "see you later," and ducked inside.

Theleme held up her fingers, tangled in brown string. "See, Anni? You pull, and snap she closes!" She tugged at the figure.

"Yes, dear, I see," Arianaï said, and licked her dry lips. "Let's go home, now, and you can nap."

"Well," Quard said as Arianaï entered the shop, "you are by far the most regular customer I have ever had." He had some of the miniature soldiers arrayed on the counter, with books piled up to represent hills and a blue scarf for a river.

"Tell me about shiribi puzzles," she said, trying not to look at the little metal men.

Quard shrugged. "They involve rods and strings. The object

of the puzzle is to take it apart, and then to reassemble it." He went to one of the shelves behind the counter, took down one of the puzzles; it was the size of a small melon, of dark oiled wood and white cord, with a blue glass ball caged inside. "Some, like this one, have a thing inside them, which is supposed to be 'freed,' but the problem is the same."

"Where do they come from?"

Quard looked up. "Toymakers, when they're not being interrupted."

"I mean—"

"I know what you mean. I was being hateful again. I don't know who invented them, but they're old, several thousand years at least. And most of them come from the far West, beyond Ombaya." He turned the puzzle over in his fingers. "The White priests have decided they mean something important, and wear them as symbols of whatever-it-is."

"You make them for the Whites?"

"I haven't yet. But then they haven't asked me."

"Have you made them to order?" she asked carefully.

Quard blinked his clear light eyes. "I was once asked to make one as a cage for an animal—a chipmunk, say, or a large mouse. I'd seen them before; the puzzle has to be made of something the pet can't gnaw, of course, but it can easily be fed through the openings, and when it runs for exercise the cage rolls around on the floor, which also cleans it . . . however, this customer wanted a bit more. The puzzle was to be designed so that a mistake in opening it would crush the animal to death."

In her mind Arianai heard the snap of metal. "Did you build it?"

"Is it any of your business if I did?"

She said slowly, "Do you know Shiel ola Siska?"

"The jeweler-mage. I know she's dead."

"It only happened this morning."

"They print the half-copper rags so fast these days, isn't it a wonder?" He put the puzzle back on the shelf. "Time I was going back to work. Theleme is well?"

"Yes. Theleme is well."

"I don't suppose I'll be seeing you anytime soon, then. Do come back if you need a toy."

"I'm still interested in shiribi puzzles."

"Well." Quard took down the puzzle again, spun it between his palms. "There really isn't much more to be said about them. Do you know the match take-away game, where a player can always force a win if he knows the right moves? Well, there's a general solution to these, a set of moves that will unravel any shiribi. Once you know it, they're no fun any longer."

"Any of them?"

"Quite simple and obvious, once it's occurred to you." He brought the puzzle down on the countertop and smashed it to pieces.

"Quard—"

"You *did* ask me for an answer, Healer. There it is. Good day."

Gorodain looked over his glass gameboard. The bronze mask was gone now; the flame had been almost greedy to receive it. The key was in the lock, and turned.

There had been a great deal of news-rag speculation on Shiel ola Siska's apparent attempt to break into the Tiger's Eye in her last moments. Gorodain was not displeased. It would confuse and distract the temporal authorities in looking for an answer, which they would not find. He had acquired the small mask from Snake's shop some years ago, through a series of intermediaries, all of them now comfortably dead; even if Snake should recall the item's sale, there was no way of tracing it to him. And the thing itself no longer existed.

It was just like ola Siska, Gorodain mused, to try to dispose of the thing by selling it, casting it to the winds of luck, so to speak; it was Shiel's habit of playing with sharp things that had brought her into the circle to begin with.

Just as it would be the pretty young healer's boldness that would bring them together, that would open the bottomless spring of death and let it flow. There were, in round figures, three hundred thousand living human beings in Liavek. Three hundred thousand deaths! The thought alone was wine to the senses.

Gorodain reached his magic to the carved glass and touched the knotted shoelace.

Teyer ais Elenaith lived in the entire top floor of a squarely dull old building in the Merchant's Quarter, fronting on the Levar's Way. The ground floor was occupied by a firm of admiralty lawyers, and the level between was packed with the lawyers' files and records, so that no one but the occasional tired clerk or nautically inclined mouse ever heard the thump of a foot from above.

The loft was one large room, closets and a tiny bathchamber

along one wall, heavy trusses and skylights overhead. Folding screens could fence off sleeping or dressing areas as needed. On the walls, dancing shoes and performance props, canes and bells and caps, hung from pegs. There were several full-length mirrors and a balance rail, and in a corner were a stack of music boxes and a large metronome.

A few sweet-scented candles were burning, but most of the light came from the moon through the skylights. All the folding screens had been set up on the studio floor in rectilinear boxes and corridors. Moonlight, direct and from the wall mirrors, added panels of silver light and black shadow to the maze.

Teyer ais Elenaith leaned against the wall, arms folded, one foot on the floor and one on the wainscot, examining the puzzle she had set up. She wore a loose shirt over trousers, all crimson silk of Tichen, with a broad leather belt, something she had once fancied on a sailor's hard body, riding low on her hips. Her dancing slippers were red kid, laced around her strong slender ankles. A nine-strand braid of gold wire wrapped twice around her long throat; a compromise, but one had to keep one's luck vessel within three steps—ordinary steps, not dancer's leaps—*and* make certain it didn't go flying during a particularly active movement. Probably the reason there weren't more dancer-magicians; of course, it also required a bit more working room than most rituals. She looked up at the ceiling beams; ais Elenaith was not a tall woman, barely five feet, and still the trusses were inconveniently low at times. Better, she supposed, than having columns interrupting the open floor.

She went to the corner and set the metronome ticking, its brass pendulum catching moonlight on each beat. She took a few loose-jointed steps, rolled her shoulders. One, she thought to the rhythm. Two. One, two, *three*.

She leaped into the shadow-maze, landing on the ball of a foot barely a span from one of the screens. She arched her back, stroked her hands down the screen without touching it, spun on her toe and sidestepped, froze again, leaped again.

Ais Elenaith worked the maze with her whole body, threading through it start-stop-turn-leap, moving ever faster, coming ever closer to the screens without touching them, the smell of sweat mingling with the candles, the only music the tick of the metronome, the steady chord of her breathing, the bang of her feet on the floor, all in harmony.

She came through the maze, stepped, stretched, then repeated it, faster. She came through and repeated, and now there was music in the loft, instruments called up through the luck around her neck, cittern and hammered harp and horn. Once again and there were bells and drums; once again and there was a chorus, and sparks showered from her hands and feet as she moved.

Once again, and she saw him, standing by the metronome, in front of the mirror, which did not reflect him.

He wore trousers tight enough to show every muscle—*every one*—of black silk that glistened in the moonlight, and around his broad bare chest was a leather harness with small gold bells, as the temple dancers of eastern Tichen wore. One gold earring, one bracelet, one anklet. He was barefoot, and his hair was tied back like a sailor's.

So, ais Elenaith thought, was this why so many went willingly? But she was more than a heart and a will. He would have to dance for her life. She spun, clapped her hands, stepped again into the maze, hearing the temple bells chiming behind her.

Step, turn, pause. Her music was now a bright passage for horn, counterpoint to the golden bells. One, two, leap, four. She waited for him to falter, to touch the maze. He did not. Perhaps he would not; it was not necessary. Arch, step, pivot, *kick*—

Her foot snapped out, and a panel swung on its hinges, slamming closed against another with a crack and a streak of red fire. She danced on, two, three, *kick*, and another screen closed up.

She circled the maze of screens, kicking higher than her chin, shutting the panels like a puzzle box, luck in her throat like the lump of arousal. Sweat spattered from her as she moved, the droplets crackling with waste luck. The candle flames were drawn toward the center of the room.

The spell drew close. Ais Elenaith cartwheeled heels-overhead three times and drove both feet into a painted wood panel. The screens all collapsed, one on another with a crescendo of slams. All the candles blew out.

Teyer ais Elenaith wavered on her feet. There were no more sounds of footsteps or bells or music, nothing but the metronome's tick, tick—

It stopped beating.

Ais Elenaith turned. The man held his finger on the pendulum. Then he held out his hand, palm up; he did not have to speak. She knew an invitation to the dance.

She bowed. She pulled the metal braid from around her neck; it only chafed, and she was out of magic for this night. It was a strain on the strength, so much more than dancing. She pulled the lacings of her kid slippers, kicked them off. Teyer ais Elenaith took the offered hand, and saw pale green light shimmer and bounce from the mirrors in the loft.

She began to dance. There was no hesitancy in it; she had always called hesitancy the death of the dance. And it was not hard at all, even without her luck. The stiffness that she had tried to ignore these last years was gone truly. She moved with her partner like two hands at the same task, and she danced for joy —what other way is there?

They spun to the door, and kicked it open, and moved lightly down the stairway to the moonlit street. The partner held out his hands, and she leaped into them, was lifted into the clear night sky. Something fell away from ais Elenaith, the last concealment of the veil dance she had done so long; it crumpled beneath her feet but did not hinder her step, the green light of its bones through its flesh only a backlight to her firework movements, as she danced away from Liavek with the partner she had always known would come.

The House of Responsible Life was a boxy building at Liavek's northeast corner, between the Street of Thwarted Desire and Neglectful Street. Though not far from a city gate, it was not in a heavily traveled part of Liavek. So the occupants of the House, the religion whose color was green, did see the crowd around them.

The Green order did not do anything at first. It was not their way to do anything: They were a faith of sworn suicides, concerned only with fulfilling all their earthly obligations and responsibilities before making an artistic exit from life. This was not too clearly understood by most Liavekans, and crowds had stared at the House before. The Order simply took no notice; there was work to do in the House and its gardens.

They noticed the first stone through the window.

Suddenly there were more stones, and angry shouts. Glass was breaking, and people were running, and wood splintered. A hole was battered in the garden fence, and bodies crowded through, trampling vines and crushing fruit, doing more damage by accident than design. Someone tossed in a little pig, which ran about rooting and squealing.

At the front of the House, a novice came out of the main double doors and hurried to close the window shutters; a shower of stones drove her to cover. Voices were loud and without meaning. Someone lit a torch. The crowd, some fifty people, moved forward.

The front doors opened again, and a man in green robes came out. He was not tall, with long hair and large brown eyes in a soft face. He walked down the three green steps, and went straight toward the mob, to the man holding the torch. Missiles shot past him; he ignored them.

The Green priest put both hands on the burning roll of papers and jerked it out of the holder's grip. He threw it down and stamped on it.

The crowd faltered, fell back a step. They muttered in a low rumble that was not quite speech. The Green priest stood still. The crowd started to surge forward again.

There was a gunshot, and then a voice: *"All right, that's enough!"* To one side, pressing in on the crowd, was a line of City Guards in gray. Most had swords out; a few carried flintlock shotguns, clumsy but able to splatter men like thrown tomatoes. The shot and the voice had come from a Guard captain with black hair and a fierce expression. Her double-barreled pistol was still leveled, and people were backing away from her as from a plague carrier.

The crowd was breaking up, people colliding with one another, drifting away from the House, falling down, getting up and running.

It was over almost as quickly as it had started, the street emptying out as the line of Guards pressed forward. The Green priest had not moved. The captain walked up to him.

"Hello, Verdialos," Jemuel said. "Nice morning."

"I can recall better," the priest said, "and worse." He turned to survey the damage to the House, then walked quickly to the bush where the novice was still huddling. "Are you hurt, my dear? No, that's good. Go inside now, and tell Cook I said to give you two honeycakes and some strong tea." He turned back to Jemuel. "The gardens?"

"I've got some people back there." She took her pistol off cock and put it away. "Dialo, I realize you're sworn to kill yourself, but weren't you trying rather hard at it just then?"

"Oh," Verdialos said, and his eyes went very round and white. "I didn't . . . well, it was their stoning the girl. It made me angry."

"Angry. You? If I put that in the report, no one will believe it."

"Would you then also put down that my order takes complete responsibility for the green deaths, so that won't be believed either?"

"We're doing what we can, Dialo. Do you want guards full time?"

"I'll put it to the Serenities, but I don't think so. It might only encourage another mob. We were fortunate today."

Jemuel nodded. "I wanted to tell you that I've been put on special duty to deal with this green mess. No offense."

"None taken. If we learn anything, of course we'll let you know."

"Thanks, Dialo."

"Thank you, Jem. Good death to you."

"I'll just say good day, thanks."

Jemuel took a footcab back to the Guard offices in the Levar's Palace; the runner grudgingly took a city credit slip for the fare, but insisted on a cash tip.

Jemuel made out the reports on the night's dirty work and the incident at the House of Responsible Life. The riot—she had to call it that—was really bad news; the Regent would want to know if Liavek were being pushed to the edge by the deaths, and the truth, that in a city of three hundred thousand you could get fifty people together to throw rocks on any excuse at all, would not reassure him a bit.

Only three deaths, she thought. More people than that died every night in the Old City, of starvation or other sharp edges. But these were all wizards, and even people who knew better— like other magicians—tended to think of wizards as immortal. And it was certainly a creepy way to go. Sen Wuchien's body was four days cold in the morgue, with nobody to claim it, and still glowing. Somebody wanted to keep him on the slab, to see how long he did glow. There was a typically morgue-ish joke about saving money on lamp wicks.

Her pen was starting to wobble. So this was special duty: she was supposed to end her shift with the end of the night watch, and here it was morning with a vengeance. She shoved her chair back from her littered desk, put her feet up, and closed her eyes. Immediately there was a knock at the door.

Lieutenant Jassil put his red-haired head in. "Captain? Some-one here to see you. It's Thyan, from Snake's place."

"Sure, Rusty."

The Tichenese girl came in. Jemuel gave her forehead a pat in greeting. "What news, mistress?"

Thyan held out a small shiny thing. "Snake thought you'd want to see this."

Jemuel looked at the object. *"Fhogkhefe,"* she said.

Thyan giggled and blushed slightly. "That's a good one, Captain."

Jemuel said, "You speak Bhandaf?"

"I work in Snake's shop, Captain. I can swear in sixteen languages."

"Come visit this office on a holiday night, you'll learn sixteen more," Jemuel said. "Come on, let's go talk to Snake."

Quard was reading when Arianai came in. He put the book down, said, "I'm sorry about yesterday. I was upset."

"Would you like to tell me what you were upset about?"

"No."

She nodded. "I guess the apology will have to do, then. Would you mind talking about Theleme?"

"She's not ill again?"

"No. She's fine. I wanted to ask—you seemed to slip into her dream so readily."

"You wondered if I knew something about green men?" Quard said, an edge in his voice. "Green men who kill?"

"That's not it at all," Arianai said. It was at least halfway the truth. "I was wondering . . . if we could work out where the nightmare came from, so she could be protected from having it again."

Quard nodded. "All right. What's the girl's family like?"

"She doesn't have one. She was left as an infant at the House of Responsible Life—"

"The suicides' order?"

"Yes, of course," Arianai said, startled. "I don't know why. Perhaps the person who left her misunderstood the name of the order, thinking it meant 'those who take responsibility for the living,' or somesuch."

"That is what the name does mean," Quard said, "in Sylarine . . . Old S'Rian."

"There's such a thing as *Old* S'Rian?"

"Everything has a past," Quard said softly. "What did the Green priests do with the child?"

"They thought about taking her in as a novice of the order. But it was decided that if she were raised entirely within the House, she could never come to an unbiased decision about her own death . . . isn't that odd, that a religion of suicides should be so particular about who actually dies?"

"Every faith excludes someone from paradise."

She laughed in the hope it was a joke. "Do you know, I cannot remember ever having heard of a member of the House actually taking his own life?"

Quard said, "They may not, until they have severed every link of responsibility to the rest of the world. The order isn't about death, really, but breaking links."

"There's a difference?"

"Yes, there is. That is another reason they would be unwilling to adopt a child, you know. Someone would have to take responsibility for her, and be bound again to life. To willingly take on such a bond would be practically apostasy."

Arianai paused. It was so hard to read anything from Quard's tone of voice. "Are you a member of the House?" she said.

"I once considered it. But we were discussing the child."

"Yes. . . . They gave her to the Levar's Orphanage. She lived there for five years. Until she began to sleep badly. Could the Green order have been the source of the 'bad green man' in her dreams?"

"It seems so obvious. But it was five years between the time the Greens had her and this . . . disturbance? You're certain of that?"

"Yes, certain."

"And she was only in the House of Responsible Life for a short time."

"A few days, I was told."

"Then . . . no. Surely that can't be it. Not with the dream so strong."

"*Does* it mean something?"

"No," he said, too quickly.

"You don't think—"

"Do you intend to adopt Theleme?"

"What? Well, I'd thought about it . . . or find her a foster family—"

"I think the best thing you can do to protect her from nightmares is to do just that. The Levar's Orphanage is, I'm sure, a fine place, but it surely can't be better than loving parents."

"I think you're right."

"Thank you. Now, please, I need to get some work done."

"All right, Quard." She held his hand; he looked at hers as if he were not certain what it was for.

When Arianai got home, Jemuel was sitting on the doorstep, in her officer's uniform.

"You're up early," Arianai said.

"I'm up late. I sleep when there's a chance these days."

Arianai said, "I've found a cure for—" and shut her mouth.

"So I hear. What does your gentleman friend do nights, Anni? Beggin' your right to privacy."

"Jem, do you know how long it's been since I've had a . . . gentleman friend?" She tried to laugh, but it came out forced and high.

"Your little patient told Thyan. Thyan's not very good about secrets."

"Third-hand gossip, Jem? Are you really so short of clues for your two dead wizards?"

"Yes. And it's three. The Hrothvek dancer, Teyer ais Elenaith, was found last night, in the middle of the Levar's Way." Jemuel reached into the pouch at her belt, put a small cool object into Arianai's hand. "Seen one of these yet?"

The item was a glass skull, not much bigger than the end of Arianai's thumb, filled with green liquid. The crown of the skull seemed to be threaded in place. "What is it?"

"Poison. Fast and neat. I'm told it doesn't even taste too bad."

Arianai sat down on the step next to Jemuel, with rather a bump. "Where are they coming from?"

"At last a question I can answer. Remember Old Wheeze the glassblower? His son, Little Wheeze, came up with the first ones. He claims it was his girlfriend's idea. Now there are five glassblowers turning them out so fast that there's a shortage of green poison. They're dyeing white poison . . . Pharn's fangs, I didn't mean that pun."

"But what's the idea?"

"Random green death, according to Little Wheeze's girlfriend. If you never know when you're going to suddenly glow green and drop dead, well, why not carry your own?"

Arianai looked at the skull. "And are they actually using these?"

"Not yet. I'm not going to worry until they stop shocking the grownups. When that happens, the kids'll need a new shock. And then we might be in trouble."

"Are you going to do anything about it?"

Jemuel produced another of the skulls, tossed it in the air and caught it. "Legal age to buy poison in Liavek is fourteen. So far, that's been strictly observed. There's no legal minimum to *carry* poison, because who would have passed such a dumb law? And if you use the thing, you can't be charged with much, except maybe littering, or blocking a public sidewalk, which come to think of it we're guilty of now. Move along, please, mistress."

They stood up. "We *did*," Jemuel added, "put the lid on a fellow who wanted to do them in rock candy and lime."

Arianai shook her head. "Would you like to come in for tea and a biscuit?"

"I'd rather come in for tea and a clue. . . . Anni, I do need help. Is there any chance that this friend of yours knows anything?"

"I don't think there is."

"Are you not thinking there is, or can you provide him with an alibi?"

"Jem, there's a line. Don't cross it."

"All right," Jemuel said, sounding nearly sorry. "I'll see you around, Anni. Say, what's your luck time?"

"Three hours. Why?"

"You might want to study magic. I think there's going to be a shortage." Jemuel went off down the street, juggling a pair of glass skulls and whistling "Positively Cheap Street."

Prestal Cade thought that her life had a rather marvelous symmetry to it: she had become a magician on her fifteenth birthday, successfully forcing her magic into a wooden doll in one long and nervous night. Then for forty more years she had practiced the mysterious and confusing art, leaving her birthplace in Ka Zhir for some time at sea, a few years in the Farlands, a few more in Tichen, before finally arriving in Liavek to stay as a quiet practitioner of the luck-craft.

She worked through dolls, composing her spells in carving and painting, dressing and detailing them; as a result, her magic was mostly involved directly with people—cosmetic spells, protection from hazards (while at sea, she had crafted a doll of cork, whose spell preserved absolutely from drowning), and the occasional bodily complaints, though always with the assistance of a healer.

And of course there had been the special doll, her part of the spell that they had all cast together, that was now coming back to them all and dressing them in green.

Well, she thought, that completed the symmetry. For after fifteen years without magic, and forty with, she had had fifteen again without. Fifteen years ago there had been a man who was jealous of her luck, her dolls, her craft. Durus had loved her, she still did believe that; she was convinced that it was because he loved her that he found the vessel of her luck and broke it, set her magic free so that all her spells failed at once.

Prestal Cade had been walking home from the greengrocer's when it happened. She felt her heart squeezed, she fell and was sick into the gutter as fruits and cabbages rolled away from her. *So this is it,* she thought, *the knock at the door and me without my magic to answer it.* But the Liavekans on the street, used to the vagaries of luck, knew better than she what was happening; someone, she never knew his name, gathered up her groceries and led her home.

There she found Durus on the floor, a knife in one hand and a small cedarwood doll without its head in the other. Had he only waited a few more months, the break in his heart would have healed, and the patch she had put on could have failed without harming him; but Durus was always impetuous.

He had not, of course, destroyed her vessel on her ill-luck day; on any given birthday since that night, Prestal Cade could have stuffed her luck into some new vessel, been a practicing magician again. But she had not. She was, she thought (when she thought about it at all) becoming old, and would inevitably start using magic to confuse that inalterable fact. She had seen all the places she had meant to see, except the Dreamsend Hills (and who ever got *there?*). She would only begin to repeat herself, another this, another that, another Durus.

Still, there was the one small thing, each night.

Prestal Cade stood in the largest room in her not-large house, as she did every night just before midnight. The only furnishings were a chair just big enough for her, and a table just large enough for a teacup and a cake plate. The rest of the room was filled with dolls, more than three hundred of them, tiny dolls made from a single piece of wood and some as high as her waist, with jointed limbs and eyes that moved; dolls clothed as kings and jesters, sailors and fops, heroes out of legend and beggars from the Two-Copper Bazaar. Some of them had been spell dolls, a luck-twisting purpose in their every feature, but most of them came after that. If not for those she had sold or given away, there would be twice as many of them in the room.

For most of those in Liavek who knew Prestal Cade, she was the Doll Lady, had never been the Doll Witch. It was, she thought (and this she thought rather often) a satisfactory name to depart with.

She looked among the dolls on their shelves, took one down. It was a little lady as tall as Prestal Cade's forearm, with a porcelain head and arms and a cloth-stuffed body, under a long, full gown of blue velvet. It had been the style of court ball dresses two centuries ago, preserved in children's stories. Prestal Cade adjusted the hem of the gown, saw that the tiny fur slippers were securely in place. She stood the doll on the floor, and waited for midnight to strike.

A wizard who could invest, but did not, had one trick left: on the minutes of each day corresponding to the moment of birth, the power flashed by. Only a little luck, the most immediate of all the instant magics, but sufficient, perhaps, to hold the line between power and the void.

The hour came by. Prestal Cade felt her luck rise. She reached out with it.

The blue velvet doll straightened up, began walking in stately fashion toward the door. When she reached it, she raised a porcelain hand, and the door swung open. The doll curtsied to the figure beyond the door; Prestal Cade bowed.

The doll did not rise. The moment was gone. Prestal Cade looked up, smiling. The room was already suffused with green light.

"Verdialos, you're crying."

"Oh. Am I?" His eyes went wide, which stopped his tears. He was sitting in the dining hall of the House of Responsible Life, over a cup of cold breakfast tea and a half-eaten slice of melon. "I'm sorry, Serenity." The title did not mean a great deal; the hierarchy of the Green Order was loose at best. It just was necessary to have something to call the people with more authority than others.

"Don't be sorry. Do you mind telling me what the matter is?"

"I was just told that Prestal Cade had died. Did you know her?"

"I don't believe so."

"She was a dollmaker."

"A wizard?"

Verdialos smiled slightly. "She had been. But her vessel was destroyed."

"*Oh*."

"Well, no, not like that, not *quite* like that, Serenity. Her luck was just freed, not lost. She could have reinvested, but she didn't."

"Do you know why?"

"Not so well that I would be comfortable saying so." He

picked up his piece of melon. "I was there the night her luck was freed, you see. It was fifteen years ago, and I was just barely a novice of the Order, and I saw this woman fall down. . . ." He examined the melon rind. "She had a bag of groceries."

"Groceries."

"I picked them up for her. I remember thinking, as soon as I'd sorted out what had happened, that I should convert this woman to the faith, that I should at least preach the truth to her. . ."

"But you didn't?"

"No, I didn't. There was so much going on at the time, you see."

"And now the woman is dead, and it's too late to preach to her. You shouldn't cry over what can't be mended, Dialo."

"I'm not," Verdialos said plainly. "I'm sad because I've lost something, and I can't decide whether it's a reason to live, or to die." He shook his head. "One would think after fifteen years as a priest I'd be beyond such ambiguities."

"I've been a priest rather longer than you," the Serenity said. "If it weren't for ambiguity, what need would we have for faith?"

Verdialos nodded. "Thank you, Gorodain."

"That's what I'm here for," the Serenity said, and started up the stairs to his attic room. "That's what we are all here for."

Arianai went looking for Wizard's Row, and was rather surprised to find it present.

Present, but scarcely all there: in place of the usual outlandishly styled houses, there were plain stones, shuttered windows, and silence, except for a raw wind blowing dust and trash up the street.

Number 17 was on this day a modest stone dwelling with lead-paned windows that admitted no view. A small enameled sign by the doorway arch carried the street number. The knocker on the heavy oak door was of black iron, and as Arianai reached for it, it rattled of itself and the door swung open.

Arianai entered a narrow corridor with a worn red carpet, hazy light filtering through small windows high up. The passage led to a room with one small lamp on a table: it was otherwise so dark that the objects on the walls, the walls themselves, were uncertain.

In a large leather chair next to the lamp sat The Magician. He wore a long red gown with brocade trim, black leather slippers. His face was difficult to see in the glare of the lamp, but his hands were as youthful as always. His small silver-blue cat was in his lap, the fat black one curled up at his feet.

"Arianai," he said, and that was all.

"Magician."

When he did not answer, she said, "Your hospitality is usually better than this."

"Times are usually better than this."

"What's the matter with the times? It doesn't seem to me to be a bad time at all. Unless of course you're a wizard."

"You are acquiring a bitter humor, Arianai. I wonder from where." His voice was that of a very young man, but it was shot through with ancient weariness, so terrible that she had to pause before answering him.

"You sent me to Quard."

"I referred Theleme's case to him. There is a difference."

"I'm tired of hearing about all these subtle differences! Is Quard involved with the dead wizards?"

The Magician was silent.

"You want a fee?" She threw a handful of silver on the floor. The sleeping cat jumped up and ran away into the darkness. She took a step forward. "I think you're scared. You're afraid you're going to die, too."

"Young lady," The Magician said firmly, "I *know* that I am going to die. It taunts me every year with its presence. I ceased to be *afraid* of it before your several-great-grandparents were conceived." He stroked his cat. "That is why these . . . colleagues of mine are dead: because they had no fear."

More quietly, Arianai said, "Is Quard a murderer?"

"No."

She licked her lips. "But is he the wizard-killer?"

"There is no way to answer that question in a way you will understand."

"Then tell me enough to understand! Please, Magician . . . Quard said your name was Trav."

"I've thought about changing it." He sighed. "What you are seeing now are the last in a long series of actions. Call them moves in a game. The object of the game is power . . . a power as much greater than our magic as the sun exceeds this lamp."

"Are you playing the game?"

"At present, only observing it."

"So who are the players?"

"Originally—thirty years ago—there were seven. Their leader's name was Imbre. He was an extremely powerful wizard, with a luck time of almost two full days. There was, in fact, a

time when he might have become The Magician of Liavek in my
place. But he had an obsessive streak in his nature that led him
into . . . experiments. And not long after the start of the one that
interests you, he died."

"Did you kill him?"

"Thank you for your confidence. His closest associate in the
seven killed him, fairly or not, I've no idea."

"And took over."

"There was nothing for him to take over."

"But you said the power—"

"It is not that kind of power. Not something that any of
Imbre's group—or all of them together—could use or control to
their own ends. All they could do was release it on the world."

"And if they did?"

The Magician said nothing.

"*And if they did?*"

"Do you pray to a god, Healer?"

"I . . . pray. Healers do that quite a bit."

"And what happens when you pray to whatever god it is?
Does some actual being use its power to touch you back? Or does
your own wish, your own prayer, give shape to some abstract
power?"

"What difference does it make?"

The Magician made a gesture over the cat in his lap. It began
to rise, levitating almost in front of The Magician's face. The cat
seemed to enjoy it, curling and stretching in midair. "I reach into
myself and do this," he said, "but I am not a god."

"How do you know?"

The cat sank back into The Magician's lap, presented its belly
for scratching, and was rewarded. The Magician said, "Because I
look back and regret my wasted efforts. Only mortals look back."

"Is Quard mortal?"

"If you cut him, he will bleed. But Quard is also a gateway to
the power that Imbre's seven reached for."

"He has the power?"

"No one *has* the power!" The Magician's voice softened. "Because Quard has a mind and a will, he may not simply be walked
over. Think of his will as being a lock on the gate. Imbre's successor has spent thirty years assembling the key to that lock."

"And the glowing dead—they're the first light coming
through the keyhole?"

"Spoken like a wizard."

"But if you know all this—if you've been 'observing the

game'—why in all the gods' names haven't you *done something?*"

"Because I believe that the play will fail, and by interfering I would do no good and might cause many more deaths."

"All right! Tell me what *I* can do."

"You have already done it," The Magician said tiredly. "You put the key into the lock."

Arianai stared. "I . . . what did I . . . do you mean Theleme?"

"Imbre fathered Quard to gain access to power. Imbre's successor fathered Theleme to gain access to Quard."

Arianai's throat clamped shut. The Magician just sat in his darkness, stroking his cat.

Finally she said, "Theleme . . . ? The . . . green man is her father?"

"Planted in her dreams for Quard to find."

"But you sent me to Quard!"

"I sent you *back* to Quard. His sensitivity to dreams is real. Theleme would have died without him, and the unlocking process would still have begun. Now do you start to understand just how complex this game is?"

"Tell me the rest of it! *Please.*"

"The rest of it is Quard's story. He will have to tell you."

"You could tell me more, but you won't."

The Magician sighed again. "I could tell you to leave Liavek, to have nothing more to do with Quard, but you won't. That is one mistake that I have made, and am bitterly sorry for: I forgot what it meant to be lonely, and not be proud of the fact."

"At least tell me the name of the green man."

"If I tell you, you will go to him. If I do not tell you, you will discover it anyway."

"Then you might as well tell me."

"No. I will not. So that I may pretend that my hands are clean. Good day to you, Healer Sheyzu."

The lamp went out. After a moment of darkness, Arianai found herself standing on Healer's Street, at the intersection with Wizard's Row; but the intersection, and the Row, were gone.

"I've been to see Trav," was the first thing Arianai said to Quard.

He did not look up from the piece of wood he was whittling. "On first-name terms with him now? That's good. Did you get your money's worth?"

"He told me you were involved with . . . some sort of power."

"I thought Liavekans always called it luck."

"Don't be hateful to me, Quard."

"I'd be glad to do it in your absence."

Arianai breathed hard. "Forgive me for wearing sandals," she said. "If I'd known the self-pity ran so deep around here, I'd have brought my boots."

Quard put down the rasp. "That's not a bad line."

"The Magician said I was learning."

"How long is your luck time?"

"What?"

"I didn't ask your blessed birthday, just the span of luck. How long was your mother in labor?"

"A little more than three hours."

"Not long for a Liavekan," Quard said.

"My family are healers, not magicians," she said. "We don't believe in prolonging pain."

Quard said, "Then you know that it *is* done."

"Of course. A student magician has access to power only for the duration of his mother's labor. I've heard of it being stretched out for forty, fifty hours." She shook her head in disgust. Then she thought of what The Magician had said about Imbre—two days' luck—and shivered.

"Is labor pain really as terrible as all that?" Quard said, with a sort of distracted curiosity.

"It is."

"Then to extend it for . . . say, twelve days . . . that would be a very bad thing, wouldn't it."

She stared. "*Twelve days?*"

"It would have been twelve weeks, if they could have done it. Twelve months, if only they could have. Imagine that: an unending luck time. But it does leave the question of one's ill-luck time, at the opposite pole of the year. I think they might have been satisfied with six months and a day . . . just to see what happened on that day when luck and counter-luck overlapped. An irresistible force and an immovable . . ." He gave a nasty, barking laugh.

"But your mother—twelve days? That's impossible!"

"No. Not impossible. With drugs and magic and clever surgeries, not impossible for the pain to last that long. But impossible to survive, yes." His voice rose. "My father and his little clutch of wizards stretched my mother's pain until there was no more flesh to cover it. And then, as she was dying and I was being born, just when any *human being* would have thought the

obscenity could not be increased, they cast a spell. It took all
seven of them, because the luck of a birthing woman is overwhelming—how else do you think the thing happens? These
seven people, with enough power between them to have done
anything, *anything* their souls desired, they, they—" He gestured
wildly. "—they *stopped* my birth instant, my mother's death instant, and we *hung* there, me struggling to be *born,* she struggling to *die,* for an *hour* from midnight—"

He fell forward on the counter, sobbing without tears. He
reached up and clawed at his hair, pulling the wig away, display-
ing a skull utterly smooth but for a few strands of false hair stuck
in spirit gum. He tugged at an eyebrow, and it came away as
well.

"Quard—" She reached around his shoulders.

"Three of them—" He shuddered, pulled away from her arm.
"Three of them were *women.*"

"Quard. You have a will of your own."

He straightened up. "A small one. . . . I destroyed my vessel of
luck, years ago. It was almost harder than the investment had
been. I did it at the wrong time, though. The luck is only loose,
not gone."

"As long as you use your will, your mind, no one can use
you. The Magician told me that."

"You don't understand. I was created for a purpose."

"I don't doubt your power. But the power belongs to you. No
one else can use it, if you don't let them."

"No. No. That was the experiment, but not the experiment's
purpose. Do you remember when we talked about the Green
faith? And I mentioned what its name meant, in the old language?"

"Yes."

"When that language was spoken, the Order was different
from the one you know. Now they spend their time plotting their
own deaths—and rarely succeed. But not so long ago, they contrived the deaths of others, and they did achieve them. Do you
see?" He leaned toward her, and his clear light eyes shone fever-
ishly. "Death as an art form. The death of the whole world as
their masterwork." He stood up, turned away from her, braced
his hands against the wall as if to keep it from collapsing upon
him. He took a deep breath. "My father didn't want a powerful
magician, you see. He wanted to create a god. To have Death as
his own obedient son."

Arianai went around the counter, put her hands on his knotted shoulders. "But he failed," she said gently.

"*No!*" He twisted away from her, pulling the shelf from the wall. A shiribi puzzle and a stack of alphabet blocks crashed to the floor. "No, he *didn't!* The death is in my soul, just waiting to come out in the world. Don't you see? Don't you know who the rest of my father's gang were? Sen Wuchien. Shiel ola Siska. Teyer ais Elenaith. Prestal Cade. All of them dead, and still they control me. I've killed them, in my midnight dreams, and I'm still the slave of their wish." Quard stared at the shelves of toys, and began to sweep them aside. Puppets were tangled and broken, music boxes spilled their tinkling clockwork, porcelain dolls shattered.

"Stop it, Quard," Arianai said firmly. "Do you think I haven't seen an unhappy child throw a tantrum before? I said, *stop it*."

Quard's shoulders slumped. He looked up. There were tears and dust on his face, and he smiled, a joyless doll's smile. "Tantrum? It's midnight, Mistress Healer. Allow me to show you a tantrum such as gods throw."

He stretched his hand toward a pile of ceramic bits that had been a doll's head. There was a flicker of green, and a small tornado swept the pieces into his palm. He closed his fingers around them, and squeezed; green light leaked from his fingers, and the bones showed through the skin. The hand relaxed. He flipped something to Arianai, and she caught it.

The object was a perfectly formed porcelain skull just smaller than an egg.

She threw it down. "Come home with me," she said quietly. "I'll change your dreams."

"What, in *bed?*" he said incredulously. "Wrestle and gasp and pledge the world, and then wake up counting the days till the world ends?"

She was too angry to turn away. "I'm not frightened, Quard."

"Then you're stark mad." He circled around her. "I can't stay here any longer," he said. "If I can't get away from my destiny, at least I'll be the death of someplace less than Liavek." He went into the back of the shop, paused in the doorway. "The toys are innocent," he said in a hollow voice. "Give them to children who will love them."

The door closed, the latch clicked. Arianai knocked at it, called to Quard, for half an hour. Then she went home.

Theleme was sleeping fitfully, tossing and turning. Quard's stuffed toys were beside the bed, apparently knocked aside by Theleme in her sleep. Arianai wound the spring in the flannel cat, listened to the soft beat-beat of its wooden heart, put it carefully against Theleme's chest. Theleme curled her arms and legs around the cat. Her breathing quieted.

Arianai picked up the camel and rider, carried them from the bedroom into her office. Some of the stitches on the rider's hood had broken, and it was askew; Arianai straightened it, put the toy on her desk. She poured a cup of nearly-cold tea, sat down behind the desk, and looked for a long time at the stuffed beast and its harried driver. As ever, the cloth tableau made her want to laugh out loud.

But she didn't. She put her head down on her arms and cried herself to sleep.

When Obas came to Liavek from Ombaya, he brought with him six shafts of ebony from the tree behind his house. The tree was old, and strong, and lucky; it had been planted on the grave of Obas's thrice-great-grandfather Udeweyo, a mighty wizard of earth and air, and the black tree's roots and branches kept his luck alive. Obas's mother had gone out into the yard where the tree stood to give birth to him, done the labor that gave Obas his birth luck on the ground that fed the tree, in the shade of its leaves.

Obas shaped his luck in the making of arrows, and when he left home his mother gave him the blackwood shafts, sealed in a pouch of moleskin, saying, "These are for no ordinary magic, not for wealth and not for power, not for the people of the lands you visit, for their own trees in their own earth will be strong enough for that. Someday, my son, you will need the luck of the house you were born in; these will touch you to Udeweyo's luck."

That had been fifty years ago; and in that span Obas had been hungry and poor, and he had been afraid, and he had needed luck that had not come to him; but he had not touched the ebony shafts.

Tonight the moleskin pouch was open and empty, and Obas was crafting the last of the six black arrows.

Their points were silver, and their flights were from a red flamingo, taken without harming the bird. The smooth black wood was carved with words and symbols, the carvings then rubbed with a mixture of herbs and Obas's blood. Each arrow had a name, and the names were Seeker, Binder, Blaster, Blinder, Flyer, and Slayer. Each arrow had a purpose—and the purpose would come for Obas at midnight, but Obas would meet it armed with ancient luck.

Just before midnight he put the arrows in a quiver and

strapped it to his back. Around his left wrist he tied a band of oxhide. He put on a short cloak of skin, and went out into the Levar's Park in the city's northwest, the place where Sen had died. He did not have to go to the park; he did not have to go to his opponent at all. He knew that he could be found. But he wished to meet the enemy in the open, under the sky, earth under him. Sky and earth might strengthen the gift of Udeweyo's luck; Obas did not know. But if he was to die, let it be in the room he was born in: the room of the world.

The park was quiet, and bright with the light of the nearly full moon. Obas smelled damp grass and cedarwood, heard a fly buzz past his ear; he turned, but the fly—if fly it had been—was gone. He was alone.

No, he thought, feeling luck stir in the soles of his feet, not alone.

Obas drew out the first arrow, the one named Seeker. The vessel of his luck, a broad silver arrowhead on a cord around his neck, was cool against his chest. His heart was slow and his breathing was even. He twirled the shaft in his fingers, filling it with his luck. Little lightnings flashed from the silver head down the shaft, making the carved chants glow, sparking from the red feathers.

With a snap of his wrist, Obas cast Seeker. It flew from his fingertips, trailing behind it a ribbon of silver light. The ribbon arched, bent, dove. Then Seeker began to whirl, spinning a ring, a braid, a column of light. The arrow struck the ground, its magic spent, and fell apart in black ashes.

Within Seeker's windings stood a tall warrior with a shield and a spear. He wore a striped skin, and his own dark skin was painted with figures of white and red and yellow.

In Ombaya the warrior's name was Barah. He was the First Hunter, the one who had learned to use wisdom to overcome prey stronger than himself. Obas felt suddenly old, and weary, and small. At the same time, he had hope: he did not fight an *inisha*, the wind or the earth, but the Hunter, who though a god had been a man. Barah could fail. A hunter might abandon the kill, if the prey proved too strong.

Obas raised the arrow Binder, spun it. It flashed and flew, striking the earth between Barah's feet. The shaft swelled, and sprouted branches, growing into a tree with its trunk at Barah's back. The branches reached for Barah's arms, the roots coiling to trap his legs. Barah struggled, but the tree drew luck from earth, and held him.

Obas drew the next arrow, Blinder, gave it magic, and cast it. It whistled like a diving shrike and flew toward Barah's eyes. The Hunter tried to raise his shield, but the branches pulled his arm aside. Blinder reached his face, and opened into a hood of blackness that tightened over Barah's head, covering his eyes, his ears, his nostrils, his mouth, so that Barah's face was a smooth ebony sculpture, all senseless.

Obas raised Blaster, whispering his luck into it. The silver arrowhead grew warm against his chest. The luck was there, the luck was strong. Hunter and prey had changed their skins. Obas cast the arrow, and it flew for Barah's chest.

Blaster erupted in fire that flowed down Barah's body, along his pinioned limbs, melting the skin from his bones. Dark flesh fell away, and the bones beneath showed green.

The fire spread to the binding tree, haloing it in the night. Bark began to slough from the branches, dripping thickly, like black mud.

Where the molten bark struck the Hunter's bare green bones, it clung, shining red over black over green, clothing the bones, muscling and fleshing them.

Barah stretched out his new limbs, still held in the tree's branches and roots, and tightened his new muscles. The tree groaned. Barah bent his back, and brought the tree up by its roots.

Earth fell away from the dead tree's roots, and tangled in them. Obas could see white bones: the skeleton, he knew, of Udeweyo, the breaking of his luck.

The First Hunter shook off the tree as a man throws off a cloak. Its trunk and Udeweyo's bones crunched together into black and white splinters. Barah struck his spear on his shield and took a step toward Obas.

Feeling his heart pound, his lungs strain, Obas raised Flyer. He cast the arrow, and as its flights brushed his fingers he grasped the feathers. Flyer lifted Obas, carried him into the sky.

He was afraid, he was fleeing. Could it be cowardice? The prey was too strong.

Far below, Obas saw Barah drop his shield to the ground, stand upon it. The wind rose, rippling the grass. Barah's shield rose on the wind, carrying him aloft. Barah raised his spear and flew after Obas. Together they soared above the housetops of Liavek, curving over the shining pan of the sea, riding the wind toward distant Ombaya.

Barah rose above Obas, stood on air, a dark shape against the moon. His spearpoint flashed in the moonlight. He threw the spear.

Obas raised his left wrist. The band of hide around it began to grow, until it was a shield. Obas raised it as the spear flew toward him.

Barah's spear struck Obas's shield, and pierced it.

And stopped, the spearhead barely two fingers' breadth from Obas's heart.

Obas let the shield and spear fall away. They caught fire, a green shooting star toward the roofs of the city. Obas grasped his last arrow, the one named Slayer. He pulled at his magic until his heart burned, and then he cast the spell. Slayer shot burning at Barah's heart, and the First Hunter's shield was between his feet and the wind.

Barah reached out and plucked Slayer from the air. As he held the arrow, it seemed that neither he nor Obas were flying, but simply standing, two men face to face in the darkness. Obas looked into Barah's eyes. The hunter was mighty. The prey was not.

"Come," said the voice of Barah, louder than the wind, "if you are coming."

The moonlight took on a green cast; Obas looked at his open hand, empty of arrows, and saw that the green light came from him.

Barah cast Slayer back at its maker.

Obas's vessel of power melted, and the liquid silver trickled down his skin. If he cried out, it was lost on the wind. He lost his grip on the arrow Flyer, and he fell. Below him, the towers of Liavek thrust up like the bones of Udeweyo, and embraced him.

It was nearly noon when Arianai awoke. She dressed at once and went out to buy a *Cat Street Crier;* the front page had the news of Obas the Arrowsmith, found dead in the Levar's Park with the ground dented beneath him, though the earth there was not soft and there was no mark on Obas's body. Excepting of course the green glow of his bones.

Arianai crumpled the paper, shook her head. She carried the sleeping Theleme next door, leaving her in the care of that healer's nurse, and went to the toyshop.

The sign-puppet showed no more motion than a hanged man. Arianai tried the door, found it unlocked. Quard was not in the front of the shop; quietly, Arianai went around the counter and into the back.

It was a mess even by young-bachelor standards, shelves and tables and most of the floor haphazardly covered with paint jars and glue pots and tools, partially finished toys and drawings for others, odd books and dirty dishes, with dust and wood shavings filling all the gaps.

Quard was asleep. The bed was small and hard, but so finely carpentered it must have been his own work. He was sprawled on his stomach, head turned to one side. His wig was off, and the smooth complete hairlessness of his head and neck and face made him look like an unfinished doll.

She put two fingers to his temple. His pulse hammered. His eyelids twitched as he dreamed.

"Who killed Imbre?" she said into his ear. "We can stop him if only we have his name."

"No," Quard muttered. "Can't go there."

"Imbre. Who was Imbre's friend? Who killed him?"

"Die, all die."

"We have to drive out the green man. Who is he?"

"Gorodain," Quard said. "Friend, priest, kill. Gorodain."

She kissed him and went out, went north, to the Street of Thwarted Desire, and the House of Responsible Life.

She asked to see Gorodain. The clerks sent her to a small office, barely big enough to pace comfortably. Its walls were painted a pale green. Arianai thought that she was becoming quite physically sick of green.

After a few minutes an unprepossessing man came in. "Are you Gorodain?"

"My name is Verdialos," he said, in a lame little voice. "I am . . . oh, say that I deal with requests."

"I'm not here to die."

"But you are looking for someone who is?"

"I want to talk to the priest called Gorodain. Tell him it's about five dead wizards."

"I will tell him that. But he won't see you on that matter."

"Then tell him it's about Imbre."

"All right," Verdialos said equably. "Dead wizards and Imbre. Please wait here. Sit if you like."

"Your chairs aren't very comfortable."

"Most of our visitors have other things on their minds." Verdialos went out.

He was not long in returning. "Serenity Gorodain regrets that the press of duties keeps him busy for the next several days. If you would care to make an appointment, or leave your name . . ."

He sounded vaguely uneasy.

"Arianai Sheyzu, eighty-five Healer's Street." Then she recalled what The Magician had said, about her discovering the green man's name. The Magician was one of the murkiest of an opaque lot, but what was in the fog was always truth.

Verdialos had started writing the address. He looked up. "Are you well, Mistress Sheyzu?"

"Yes," she said. "I've got no intention of dying anytime soon."

"A good death to you nonetheless," Verdialos said.

Shortly after the Healer Sheyzu had gone, Gorodain came into Verdialos's office. "Did she leave her name and address?" the Serenity asked.

Verdialos gave him the paper. "Forgive me for asking, Serenity . . . but my schedule is rather light this week, and if I could assist you . . ."

"I forgive you for asking, Verdialos. And I forgive you your ambition. You do know that you will succeed me as Serenity, when I finally"—he smiled—"achieve the goal?"

"I had supposed I was one of those in line."

"Good. One should not face death with false modesty." He glanced at the paper, then crumpled it. "If the woman should return, another dose of your usual kind firmness, eh, Dialo?"

Verdialos nodded as the Serenity went out.

It was in fact a busy day for Verdialos; the mob had done quite a bit of superficial damage to the House, especially the gardens, and the repairs had to be supervised and accounted. They were, Verdialos thought, very often an order of bookkeepers and tally-counters, and he wondered if perhaps the work they did for the House bound them to it, created exactly the responsibilities they were supposed to be severing in their quest for the regretless death.

And then again, he thought with a stifled chuckle, neither the tomatoes nor the tomato worms would feel guilt at the gardeners' passing.

It was quite late when the last note had been written on the garden charts, the last cracked window mended against the night air. There was nothing artistic about any death that involved sneezing.

Verdialos ate a light dinner, a chop from the rioters' poor pig, and began a discussion with his wife concerning the healer and the Serenity. She ended it shortly by saying quietly, "Asking for an extra opinion never killed anyone." Verdialos laughed and kissed her warmly. Then he put on a cap and cloak of neutral gray (because prudence in troubled times had never killed anyone, either) and went out to talk to a City Guard.

He was directed to the Guard office in the Palace itself, and finally to Jemuel, who was studying reports and drinking kaf thick as syrup—"It's not supposed to taste good," she said, "it's supposed to keep me standing."

Verdialos told her about the day's events. "I am troubled by all of it," he said, "both the healer's interest in us, and the Serenity's interest in her."

Jemuel said, "It bothers me, too. I want to have a talk with your Serenity."

They shared a footcab back to the House, and climbed the stairs to Gorodain's chambers. Verdialos knocked on the door.

"Come in," said a voice that was not Gorodain's. Verdialos opened the door. His eyes widened. Captain Jemuel said, *"You."*

The Magician sat in a wicker chair, looking at a table with an etched-glass top. There was no one else in the room.

"May I ask," Verdialos said, "how you come to be so far from your usual, um . . ."

"A fool's errand," The Magician said. "I came to talk a priest out of his faith. But I arrived too late; he has already gone."

Jemuel said to Verdialos, "I have the right to commandeer the fastest horse in the neighborhood. I hope you have it."

"I have a faster horse," The Magician said, "and we all may ride. Open the window, please."

"Trav—the Serenity—"

"Is a branch of the Old Green Faith," The Magician said. "Those Who Assume Responsibility."

"Yes. I had been rather afraid of that. In our defense, he was never allowed to—well. Nothing to say now, is there." Verdialos opened the window.

Arianai had been dozing, nearly dreaming, when the knock came at her front door. It was a faint tap, hesitant. Shaking herself awake, she rushed to answer it, swung the door open. "Qua—" she said, before seeing anything in the dark, and only gurgled the rest.

Gorodain's hands were crossed in the grip called the Butterfly; they closed easily around Arianai's neck, fingertips thrusting into the hollows at the base of her skull, tightening, lifting. She lost the power of speech and movement at once. Her toes scraped the doorstep. Gorodain held her for several heartbeats, wishing that there were time for something more elaborate. So often he felt like a master chef who knew a thousand exotic recipes and was forced to prepare a single bland pudding for a toothless stomach patient.

Then, he thought, minimal art was still art, and this was the brushstroke that would complete his masterpiece, to confound a metaphor. And there simply was not time. Gorodain flexed his wrists, and there was a single sharp *crack* from Arianai's neck.

He lowered her, turning her on her back so that she lay across the threshhold of her front door, her head draped—quite elegantly, Gorodain thought—over the edge of the step. It might well be taken for an accident. Not that it mattered what it was taken for. Then, on impulse, he knelt beside her, stretched out a hand, tapped into his luck. The green glow would be simple enough to induce. Closure, that was what a work of art needed, a bright green line to link all the deaths.

There was a cold pressure at the back of Gorodain's neck. For a moment he thought it might be Quard—but the time was not right, it was still most of an hour until midnight. Then the touch resolved itself into pistol barrels. Gorodain looked up, saw Verdialos approaching, and with him The Magician—himself, out of his house!

The gun pressed hard against him, and a woman's voice said, "Just move, you dirtwad; just do us all a favor and make one little move."

"Don't, Jemuel," The Magician said, in that irritating prettyboy voice of his. "The favor would only be to Gorodain."

Gorodain grinned involuntarily. The Magician was right. There was nothing they could do now, any of them. Death would come for his dead lover, and to save her he would be forced to admit that he was truly Death, take the power that could not be controlled. In less than an hour, Imbre's son would be loosed upon Liavek; before dawn, Liavek would be Necropolis. He wondered if the glow of all the dead would shine out upon the sea, like a green dawn.

Quard was sitting on the floor of the toyshop, arms and legs at odd angles, like a marionette cast aside.

He had intended to go away. He had started to pack a bag with everything that was meaningful to him, and then realized that such a bag would be empty. He had been sitting on the floor for most of the day now, waiting for night, for midnight, the hour of his birth and his power. There was nothing for him in Liavek but Death, but there wasn't anything more for him anywhere else.

So he would stay, and when next someone came into his shop they would find him on the floor, green.

The door swung open and Theleme came in. "Master, master! You have to come, master!" She rushed to him, and without thinking he opened his arms and hugged her.

"What is it, Theleme? What's wrong? Where's Anni?"

"Anni's sick, master, sick. The green man. You have to come. You have to ride the camel for Anni."

Quard's throat tightened. He tried twice to speak and failed. On the third try he said, "Where is she, Theleme?"

"Home," Theleme said. "Come, master. Captain Jem will take us."

"Who . . . ?" Quard stood up, walked with Theleme to the door.

Just outside was a woman in Guard officer's uniform. Her face was pretty, but hard as a cliff. She had a pistol out, casually ready. "Good evening, Toymaker," she said, in a cold voice. "I've been wanting to meet you. But we've got some other business first."

Quard walked mechanically down the stairs. The Guard captain pointed at the toyshop door. "Aren't you going to lock up?"

"Why?" he said. "There's nothing in there that isn't mine."

It was not far to Arianai's house. There was a sphere of lucklight illuminating the scene, in the grainy, unreal fashion of magic.

Arianai was lying on the doorstep, half-in, half-out. The healer Marithana Govan was there, kneeling next to Arianai. Quard looked around at the rest of them: The Magician, Verdialos the Green priest . . . Gorodain.

"Welcome, son of Imbre," Gorodain said, and pressed his palms to his forehead. No one paid any attention.

Jemuel took Theleme inside. Quard said quietly, "Give her something to make her sleep," and Marithana went inside as well. The others stood out in the cold, around the body.

When the two women came out again, Jemuel said, "Well?"

"Her neck's cleanly broken," Marithana said. "She didn't suffer."

"I am an adept of my order," Gorodain said.

In a tightly controlled voice, Jemuel said, "If you speak out of turn one more time I will surely shoot your balls off."

"Can you mend the break?" Quard said abruptly.

Marithana said, "Young man, she's—"

The Magician said, "I can mend the bones, with guidance from Mistress Govan. Marithana, if they're splinted by magic, will they knit?"

"Trav, she's *dead*."

"If that changed?" The Magician said, and all of them stared at him, except for Gorodain and Quard, who looked at one another with unreadable expressions.

"In time," Marithana said. "Perhaps more than a year. Your birth time . . ."

"If it takes that long, Gogo can renew the spell."

"You're serious."

Quard said, "More than you know. Do it."

The Magician said, "Marithana, concentrate on the bones as they should be. We'll do it together."

Marithana Govan put her hands on Arianai's throat, straightening it, massaging it. There was a faint sound of grinding, crunching. Verdialos looked worried, Jemuel impassive, Gorodain positively merry.

The healer and the wizard moved back. Quard stepped forward. He said to The Magician, "If something goes wrong—if I come back before she does, it'll mean that—"

"I'll do what I can," Trav said.

Quard knelt by the dead woman. Gorodain was speaking again; Quard shut him out, looked up. Full moon at the top of the sky. Close enough to the crease of midnight. Quard stared at the moon, feeling the weight of luck tug at his heart, the tides of fortune raising his salt blood.

He stepped from his flesh and into his birthright.

Around him was still Liavek, still streets, houses, windows, rooftops, still just as lovely and hideous as any other Liavek; if anything, perhaps a little more precisely defined, cleaner of line and truer of angle, small where it should be small and grand where grandness was deserved. For it is not true that the dead know all things—indeed the dead know nothing that the living do not. But the dead have perspective.

Quard was surrounded by wraiths, human figures in translucently pale shades of green: not the dead but the living, dwelling here in their minds as they wished for death, in the degree of those hopes. Marithana Govan and Jemuel were barely even visible, delicate as soap bubbles. Verdialos was nearly solid, but without luminance; certain but not eager.

Quard looked at The Magician, who stood there with one hand

already in the quiet world; Quard examined the rest of The Magician, studied his wish, and almost laughed. He did not: laughter and tears were things of the full world.

Quard looked with interest at Gorodain, who flickered, wavering to and from oblivion. Quard reached out and touched Gorodain's shade. Its eyes opened wide, and the figure knelt out of Quard's way, growing fainter as it did so. As ever with the voyeur, Quard thought, recoiling at the actual touch. He walked by.

There was no source of light in the city: it was uniformly dim, dull perhaps, though the effect was not drab but soothing. And there was no glass in the windows, nor glasses on the walls, nor puddles on the ground—nothing at all that might cast a reflection.

He moved easily on the dustlessly clean streets, passing among the shades of the still living, looking up at windows luminous with their death wishes. "I felt Death breathe on me," their living selves would be saying, in the full world; "someone is walking on my grave." Quard could see easily through the windows, or the walls for that matter, and no door was closed to him: even Wizard's Row would be present, should he desire to travel it. Nor did he have to walk; others rode, he supposed, or flew, but walking was the one way he knew.

Quard paused at a house on Cordwainers' Street: in an upstairs room, a crowd of shades stood around a man on a bed. The supine figure was deep green, and his shade was very thick.

Quard held out his hand. "Come if you are coming," he said, and there was a sound somewhere between a sigh and the pop of a cork, and the shade on the bed was suddenly a body dressed in clothes of subdued color. The man rose up and followed Quard, as the shades they left behind—some fading, some thickening—threw themselves upon the empty bed.

There were others after that, the sick, the old, the murdered and suicided, a Vavasor who had eaten a spoiled fish, and nine sailors drowned off Eel Island. Some of their bodies were young and robust, some old and elegant in appearance, but they all walked steadily, and there was among them no mark of decay, no wound, no lesion, bloat, nor worm.

They all followed Quard, winding through the streets of that other Liavek like a streak of smoke, pointing and touching and talking among themselves in a low murmur, passing through the green shades of the wishful living without notice—as indeed they could not see them. That was for Quard alone.

Finally, after he had fulfilled his duties among the lastingly dead, he returned to find Arianai, in her house, searching through the rooms cluttered with what she loved. "Theleme," she said, "Theleme, where are you?" She ran her hands over Theleme's bed, touching, seeing nothing.

Quard saw Theleme, asleep on the bed even as Arianai's hands passed through her shade. Theleme clutched the cloth camel and rider to herself, and her wish shone in the cool-colored room. Quard shook his head and took Arianai by the wrist.

She looked at Quard, and in an instant she understood. Quard did not know what the dead saw in him, and there were no mirrors to show him. He led her from the house, to the street where the column of dead waited. Arianai saw them, standing patiently and calm, but looked right through the shades of the living clustered around her, each of them waiting for some kind of miracle.

Quard knew there were no miracles.

Arianai said, "You came to bring me back."

Quard said, "This is not the story you think it is. I did not charm you free from here. There was an exchange."

"Who? Not Theleme!"

Quard was silent.

"Is it Theleme? Or is it you? I won't accept such a trade."

"You are dead," Quard said, "and have no choice in the matter."

"If someone will die in my place, surely I have the right to know."

Quard said, "No knowledge is ever taken from this world." He pointed at the street, where he could see the shade of Marithana Govan kneeling. "Go, if you are going. We have a final destination, and you may not see it."

Arianai looked at the column trailing behind Quard. She seemed to be trying to recognize individual faces, but Quard gestured again, and she lay down on the ground. The air shuddered, and in place of the solid Arianai there was now a shade, even less substantial than Marithana's.

He had not lied to her. Gods never lie, even if they then change the world to suit their words. He had struck the bargain with himself.

Quard turned and left the square, the dead in quiet files behind him.

"Is he dead?" Jemuel said.

Marithana held a bit of polished metal to Quard's nostrils. "To the best of my ability to tell." She looked down. "Dear Lady around us," she said. "Anni's breathing."

Jemuel said, "He *could* do it, then."

Gorodain said, "Ah, but that is only the beginning."

"Shut up," Jemuel snapped at him, than looked at Quard, crouched motionless over Arianai, who was now only sleeping peacefully. "Gods, how are we going to tell her?"

"I'll tell her what needs to be said," Quard said, unfolding and stretching his limbs.

Marithana said, "You were—"

"I slept. I sleep very deeply."

Gorodain said, astonished, "You *return*—"

"You are a complete fool, Gorodain," Quard said, in a voice that made Gorodain step back from him. "You wished for Death to take the whole world down with you. But Death serves no man's wish, nor does it wear one face. Death is particular to all it touches."

The Magician nodded. Then Quard turned to face him. "And you sigh with relief, Magician, because your guess was right, because the city did not die for your miscalculation? What of my mother, who was tortured for nothing? Of my father, who died for nothing? Of the other five?"

The Magician looked Quard in the eyes, and nodded again. "But Anni and Theleme live," he said, without any force. "And I suppose I shall, too."

"Kind of a shame," Jemuel said, poking at Gorodain with her pistol, "all those other wizards dead, and not this green toad."

Quard said "I am . . . what I am. Justice is another thing entirely."

Jemuel said, "Fair enough. We'll see to justice," and pointed at Gorodain. "I know a nice little cell just your size."

Gorodain shifted his hands. The Magician said quietly, "Don't trust to luck." Something appeared between his fingers, and was as quickly palmed.

Gorodain smiled grimly, shrugged, lowered his hands. "Do you think," he said to Verdialos as if the others were not there, "that you could provide me with one of those little green skulls the youth are so fascinated with? Think of it as your first task as a Serenity."

"Pharn take that," Jemuel said. "You'll die on Crab Isle."

"True enough," Gorodain said, "for I am old, and once you destroy my magic—as you must—I will be older still. Better that Death come quickly for me."

Quard began to laugh. Gorodain looked at him, and went very pale. Quard threw his head back and laughed from the bottom of his lungs. Gorodain put his hands to his mouth, and his eyes were wide and black. Jemuel looked bewildered, Verdialos turned away, and The Magician was simply gone. Quard just kept laughing as he picked up Arianai in his wiry arms and carried her into the house.

Arianai woke damp with sweat, her neck stiff and sore as if she had slept with it twisted. Her scalp prickled, and she struggled to recall what her dream had been, but it had melted and run away.

She rolled over, pulling free of the sweaty sheets. Quard was on the floor across the room, cradling Theleme in his arms. Theleme shifted a bit, giggled in her sleep. Quard didn't move.

Quard didn't stir at all. He just sat, eyes shut, pale limbs wrapped around the child.

Arianai felt a chill touch her eyes, her spine. Draping a sheet over herself, she went to Quard's side, crouched, touched his shoulder. His skin was quite cold. She bit her lip and tightened her grip.

Quard's eyes snapped open. Arianai nearly screamed.

"Hello," Quard said softly. He shivered. Theleme stirred, but Quard rocked her to sleep again, then put her gently down, her head pillowed on the toy camel.

"You scared me," Arianai said.

Quard's face was mostly in shadow, but two little reflections stared her straight in the eyes. "Well. The world is full of possibilities this morning."

He got to his feet, and they went out of the room, with a last look at Theleme asleep and dreaming sweetly.

Arianai turned up the lamp in the office. Quard blinked in the light then said, "Is that really what you want to be doing?" and looked down at the soft, thick carpet.

She chuckled. "Then you've no other appointments."

"Not this midnight," he said, in a different voice, and looked her in the eyes again: in the better light she could see that his eyes, which had been hazel and clear as water, were now the color of green olives.

She turned out the light before she could see anything more. She felt Quard embrace her, felt him stir.

"You're like fire," he said, and pressed his cold lips to hers.

Only mortals look back, she thought, and knew that she was mortal.

He pushed her away to arm's length, said distantly, "How can you love me?"

"Day by day," she said, "until the end of the world," and pulled him close again. She felt Quard's tears, freezing down her cheeks, and prayed she would not wake up counting the days.

Paint the Meadows with Delight

by Pamela Dean

IT WAS GOING to be spring in Liavek; the month of Rain was
dissipating on a high wind. People became restless, or hopeful,
or lunatical, as their natures dictated; and in the temples of those
religions that regarded the turn of the seasons, the priests began
their preparations. Three thousand miles away in Acrivain, two
feet of solid snow held the countryside prisoner. The priests of
Acrilat, its one mad god, counted (those who could count) the
days until the equinox; and shrugged; and rolled the dice again.

Jehane Benedicti, who had left Acrivain for Liavek when she
was six, was contemplating going back again. In pursuit of this
course, she took her obligatory escort, made him put on a cape,
flung a shawl over her own head, and set off to visit the best
wizard of her acquaintance.

It was spring on the Street of Trees. The new needles of the
cypresses poked their yellow points out along every thin green
twig, and the strong bright shoots of crocus and tulip and arianis
stood up everywhere, already showing slips of purple and gold
and red. It had been a mild winter, even for Liavek, but surely
this was more than natural. Jehane wondered what Wizard's Row
looked like. She fortified the escort, who was Tichenese and only
ten, with a handful of dates, and left him sitting on a knee of the
western cypress. Cinnamon looked rueful but resigned, and had
stuffed three dates into his mouth before she turned to go on.

Granny Carry's azaleas had come out madly in enormous
shiny leaves, and those that flowered before the leaves were even
open were covered with blazing-pink clusters of long flowers.
Jehane inhaled their faint pale scent and considered the consequences of impatience. Then she shrugged and marched up the
walk to the little neat house, and hit its door as hard as she could.
Two brown cats leaped out of the whitegrass on her right and
took up stations under the door handle.

Jehane got down on her knees and spoke to them, and received a crack in the forehead from the opening door.

"What an auspicious beginning," said the dry, strong voice over her head. Jehane suddenly remembered that she had not been here for almost a year. She stood up, putting a hand to her forehead half in pain and half in greeting.

She was two hands taller than Granny, but it never helped in the least.

"You're getting lines around your eyes," said the old woman, who was not only wrinkled herself, but quite brown as well, and who had been used to laugh at Jehane's sister Isobel for worrying about her appearance. "Don't you go near that loom," she added, looking down. The two cats padded over the lintel and across the floor in the manner of a Tichenese procession, lacking only the bells. Jehane grinned.

"And you're not getting them by smiling," said Granny, standing aside. "You'd better come and tell me how."

Sharing a long red cushion with an orange cat, with a cup of extremely strong tea growing cold between her clutching hands, Jehane arranged her family in chronological order, and told her. "Marigand's baby died last summer," she said, "and she's as thin as a birch tree and never smiles."

"Marigand?" said Granny. "I'd expect her to be carrying another one by now; she's the only one of the lot of you with no imagination."

"Isobel hates everybody," said Jehane. Isobel, originally blessed with a sardonic wit and a heart like an overripe mango, never opened her mouth now except to say something hurtful. "And Livia pesters Mama and Father day and night to be allowed to go about freely like a Liavekan. She must be in love with someone unsuitable; I know the signs. And she's sillier than I was when I was her age. She's bound to do something stupid at any moment."

Granny frowned at this analysis and said, "That child hasn't the courage."

"That's what I thought," said Jehane. "But she asks Mama every day at dinner, in exactly the same words. And smiles. And *Gillo,* the only one of the boys I thought had any sense, just sold his winery and took up with a group of sailors. Givanni is going to start going about with them, too; he always does what Gillo does."

"That won't hurt Givanni," said the old woman, pushing an inquisitive kitten away from her teacup. "But I thought Gillo got seasick?"

"He does." Jehane rubbed the orange cat behind the ears. "And then there's Nissy."

"Nerissa has always been the odd one."

"This is more than odd. You know Floradazul—her cat— died last spring? Well, she sat up in the attic for three days; and then she went out and found the ugliest kitten in Liavek and named it Floradazul, and she acts exactly as if it *were* Floradazul."

"Nothing crazy in that," said Granny. "I gave her Floradazul, and she was a spanking-new cat."

Granny had always been a little strange on the subject of cats. Jehane said, "Nissy wears green all the time and she's gone all day."

"What does your mother have to say about that?"

"Nothing," said Jehane, "and she doesn't say anything to Livia about going on and on when she's been told no once, or anything to Isobel for scolding like a tavern keeper, or anything to Gillo for wasting all the money Father gave him for the winery."

"That," said Granny, "is very odd indeed. And your father?"

Their father went to political meetings every Luckday, as he had done for twenty years; but now he drank just enough beer to make him gloomy, and came home to read poetry until dawn.

"Poetry," said Granny, actually staring. "Giliam Benedicti reading poetry?" She put her empty cup down on the floor, and the orange cat jumped out of Jehane's lap, tipped the cup on its side, and lapped at the dregs. "Well," said Granny, "no doubt it'll do him good."

"It won't do *us* any good," said Jehane, divining after a moment that Granny meant her father, not the cat. "The money is running out." Since the rest of the exiles went back to Acrivain, no more money had come out of it for the Benedictis, not the income from their land, managed by one of the few revolutionaries who had not been caught or betrayed, and not the money for fomenting in Liavek any event that might be detrimental to the rulers of Acrivain. "I'm afraid," said Jehane, "that we have all been living on Livia's dowry this year, and we're probably about to start on mine."

"Just as well," said Granny.

"Yes," said Jehane, grimly. "There's nobody here we could marry."

"That wasn't precisely what I meant. What about—"

"So that," said Jehane, daring to interrupt her because the last thing she wanted was a lecture on the merits of marrying Liave-kans, "is why I have lines around my eyes. And I think it's Acrilat."

"Nonsense," said Granny, absently, as if it might be Acrilat but that was not the point. "It's the natural perversity of the Benedictis, exacerbated by the time of year and long dwelling in an uncongenial culture. What do you mean to do about it?"

Jehane stared at her. Granny had greeted her with a variety of peculiar remarks over the years, but she had never sounded like one of Father's history books. "Well," she said, "I think we should go back to Acrivain."

"You could shoot yourselves here, and save the passage money," said Granny.

She seemed to be waiting intently for Jehane's answer, as if hoping Jehane might be angry; but Jehane was amused, and Granny should have known she would be.

"I don't think I can engineer a revolution in Acrivain," she said, "but Father could, if somebody would make him. Mama used to try. But *I* have to find Deleon. Mama will never let us leave without him."

Granny stood up, scattering three tortoiseshell kittens and with them the kindliness and cheer of her expression. *"When did you lose him?"*

Jehane closed her mouth and met, with some effort, the clear black eyes of the old woman. "Mama didn't tell you," she said. A consciousness of ruin and betrayal was demanding her attention. She went on looking at Granny. "Eight years ago," she said. "He ran away on his twelfth birthday."

"The thirteenth of Snow," said Granny. "Did anybody look for him? Did she call the City Guard?"

"No, of course not," said Jehane. Granny always had some outrageous suggestion; no wonder Mama had not told her anything. *"We* looked for him, all the families."

"Of course." Granny sat down, and two of the three kittens bounced up into her lap again. "Maybe it *is* Acrilat," she said. "I don't think that even the proverbial foolishness of the Benedictis could quite account for this. Young woman, you came to see me in Rain of 3310 and talked to me at some length about a young man you wished to marry. You didn't say a word about your brother."

They looked at one another. Granny must know perfectly well who had told Jehane not to discuss the matter. "Could you find out if it's Acrilat?" said Jehane; that ought to be a more intriguing

subject than Mama's remissness. "And can you read this?" She
untied the cloth purse from her belt and tugged the blank book
out of it. "It might help."

"Why can't you read it yourself?"

"It's in Old Acrivannish," said Jehane. "It's Nissy's diary, and
it's got Deleon's name in it." She paged through it, looking for
the first occurrence, and only slowly became aware of the quality
of the silence.

"Camel-loving sons of jackals," said Jehane, with great force.
It didn't help. Cinnamon had been teaching her to swear; but
Cinnamon was Tichenese, and the Tichenese got angry slowly
and deliberately. Jehane wanted something explosive to say when
she was furious, not a beautiful string of elaborate and poetic
insult. She turned what she had just said over in her mind, working out the logical consequences of it, and suddenly giggled.
Angry people were always funny.

Except for Granny. She had not been funny in the least. Jehane dug her hands into the pockets of her skirt in just the way
she had been taught not to, and clenched them fiercely over the
linen. Once you thought about it, Granny was of course right.
You didn't keep the sudden disappearance of your little brother
from somebody who over the years had taken such a kindly interest in your family; you didn't read your sister's diary; you certainly didn't take your sister's diary to somebody else to read;
you did not, in short, pry or tattle or bribe or manipulate as you
had been doing these twenty years, since you were six, since you
came to Liavek.

You didn't, that is, if you lived with normal or reasonable
people. But Jehane did not. That was her defense, which Granny
knew perfectly well already. But Jehane was accustomed not to
consider this central fact, and she refused to say it to Granny.
Because that was another thing you did not do. They were her
family, and it was Acrilat, abandoned and furious, that had
twisted them all until they were afraid to speak the truth to one
another.

She should have realized that long ago. There was no provi-
sion in law or history for worshiping Acrilat across three thousand miles of ocean in a foreign city. Being accustomed to better
treatment, It no doubt felt insulted; and being mad, It would fail
to consider that they had been helpless in the matter. Jehane
doubted that, in the fear and confusion of their abrupt flight,
anybody had thought to ask a priest for advice. The priests were

all crazy anyway, so one's chances of getting a coherent answer to such a practical question were remote.

Jehane trudged grimly along the Street of Trees, Cinnamon trailing her in a sticky silence. As she came out of the shade of the last cypress and walked into the Two-Copper Bazaar, the sunlight faded.

"It's going to rain," said Cinnamon.

She needed a wizard. Father needed a wizard. That was the solution to the whole problem. A wizard could deal with Acrilat; a wizard could conquer the distance between Liavek and Acrivain; a wizard could even, perhaps, impress enough Liavekans to make an army. And a wizard could find Deleon. Granny wouldn't help, not now; but Jehane had heard of somebody who would do anything if you paid him enough. She would find out if she had enough. She shook out her crumpled skirt. "You won't melt," she said to Cinnamon.

Cinnamon was looking wary. He said, "Where are we going, mistress?"

"To Wizard's Row," said Jehane. She caught the gleam in his eye, and added, "*You* are going to stay outside."

"In the rain?"

"Maybe they'll have awnings," said Jehane, heartlessly, and quickened her pace.

It was winter on Wizard's Row. A small rain fell slanting along the thin western wind and made new runnels in the mud. All the houses were thick and solid, sandstone or fieldstone or marble, and they were all barred and shuttered and closed tight; except for Number 17. It was solid enough, a square two-story house of yellow brick with leaded-glass windows and its number on an enameled sign by the doorway arch. But the door was ajar. From inside Jehane heard a woman sing, not quite on key,

> *"When daisies pied and violets blue*
> *And ladysmocks all silver-white*
> *And cuckoobuds of yellow hue*
> *Do paint the meadows with delight*
> *The cuckoo then, on every tree*
> *Mocks married men, for thus sings he."*

A man's voice joined and overrode hers. "Tu-who, Tu-whit, tu-who, a merry note."

The song broke up in laughter. Jehane stood and looked very carefully at the sign. Number 17. Maybe this was not Wizard's Row, but something harmless to occupy the gap left when Wizard's Row, as was its reputed habit, was elsewhere. Well, she could ask.

"You stand under this tree," she said to Cinnamon. He looked stricken, which was a thing he did very well. It was a very large yew tree, with a circle of dry dust around it four feet in radius. But it was chilly here, much more so than it had been outside Granny's house. Jehane pulled off her shawl and popped it over Cinnamon's head. "And don't get it muddy."

She went up the walk and tapped on the doorframe.

A tiny and exquisite woman came down a long hall lined with doors. She was such a form as Hrothvekan jewelers make, her skin like copper and her hair like brass and her eyes as green as emeralds. She wore a stark white tunic and a smile like sunrise. Jehane closed her mouth and smiled back.

"Nerissa," said the woman, on a note of pleased inquiry. Then her gaze sharpened, and she looked a great deal more like a piece of jewelry.

"I'm her sister," said Jehane, too astonished to say more.

"You'd better come in," said the woman. She did not sound at all like someone who had just been singing.

Jehane followed her down the long hall and out another door into a covered walk that opened on a courtyard. Grouped along the wall were a brazier of charcoal, two hammock-chairs, and a little bamboo table with a tray of tea on it. In the nearer chair lay a brown-haired man in a red robe. He sat up as they came close, and the brass bracelets he wore caught orange sparks from the brazier. Jehane blinked, and missed his expression.

"Gogo?" he said.

"This is Mistress Benedicti," said the brass woman, placidly. "Mistress, The Magician."

The Magician contrived to bow without standing up. Jehane could not blame him overmuch; he had a silver kitten asleep in his lap. In the empty chair a round ginger cat was just settling itself in the warmth Gogo had presumably left. The third cat, a long brown one with blue eyes, had established itself under the brazier and tucked all its feet in so that it resembled a loaf of almost-burned bread.

"Which Benedicti are you?" said The Magician.

You could not like someone just because he kept cats. In any case, the brown one was far too thin, without being so dark that you could put its boniness down to age. Jehane said, "Jehane, my lord. How do you know my sister?"

"I suggest," said The Magician, in a mild voice that raised the hair on Jehane's neck, "that you ask her."

Wizards were all alike, it seemed. It was easy for them to talk about fair dealing.

"It doesn't matter," said Jehane. "I'm looking for my brother. If that's what Nissy wanted you to do, my lord, I don't want to spend the money twice."

The Magician opened his mouth, and the silver kitten sprang out of his lap. The ginger cat shot off its chair and disappeared into the dripping shrubbery. The brown cat unfolded itself and made a long noise suggestive of an unoiled gate. Jehane turned around to see what had prompted all this.

Nissy's black cat, no longer the ugliest in Liavek but still very gangly and peculiar-looking, was sitting on the flagstones, her spiky fur flattened with rain. The kitten danced up to her with the happy confidence of the young, and tapped her head with a paw. Nissy's cat took no notice.

"It's all right, Shin," said Gogo. "Disorder, do you want your silly ears chewed flat to your skull?"

The brown cat turned its back on them. The kitten fell over and looked expectant. The fat ginger cat stayed in the shrubbery.

"I'm sorry," said Jehane. "I didn't know she'd followed me. I can take her outside and give her to Cinnamon."

"Why don't you let me bring Cinnamon in?" said Gogo. "It's raining."

The Magician said, "I don't—"

"I'll take him to the kitchen and feed him," said Gogo.

"He likes snails," said Jehane.

Gogo grinned, and scooped up Nissy's cat, who let her do it. You couldn't like everybody a cat liked, either. The issue was not liking, anyway, but trust.

"Gogo," said The Magician. "I will never—"

"No," said Gogo, serenely, "I don't suppose you will."

"Will you sit down?" said The Magician, in resigned tones.

Jehane had black cat hair on her skirt already, so she sat gingerly on the abandoned hammock.

"If you're looking for a runaway," said The Magician, "I suggest you inquire at the House of Responsible Life. They keep track of such things—and they don't charge."

"He disappeared eight years ago," said Jehane, dubiously.

The Magician raised his eyebrows. *Don't you dare say anything,* thought Jehane, with unaccustomed ferocity.

"That makes it more difficult," said The Magician. "But you might try them first. You can always come back."

"I still need to hire a wizard," said Jehane.

"The Row is full of us," said The Magician. "Most of them come cheaper than I do."

"I've got money," said Jehane.

"Will you give me one levar to tell you why you should not spend it here?"

Jehane sat and looked at him for a considerable time, while the roof dripped gently onto the grass of the courtyard and the ginger cat came cautiously out of the shrubbery and stood by the brazier, shaking its feet. The brown cat growled at it. It moved six inches away and shook its feet again. Well, thought Jehane, she knew nothing now. If she paid him, she would know something, even if she did not understand what it was. You couldn't get to be The Magician unless you provided something of real value to those who came to you. He would probably give her a riddle. She was good at those. And he did keep cats.

"Yes," she said.

"I'd forgotten," said The Magician, ruefully. "The Acrivannish don't bargain. Very well. I have already done your family something of a disservice, and I hesitate to take on a commission that might constitute another. If your brother is well, or has met any normal fate, there are far less costly ways to find him. I tell you again, go to the House of Responsible Life. Runaways are their business, and their records go back considerably longer than eight years. They're on the Avenue of Five Mice, just off Neglectful Street. A very large, square, green building."

"What disservice, my lord?" said Jehane. "To whom? Nissy?"

"What did you want to hire a wizard for?"

"To make a revolution in Acrivain," said Jehane.

The Magician's head came up, and he laughed. "Another grand idea!" he said.

Jehane supposed the other had been Nissy's, but there was no point in asking. She wondered if it was what Nissy had done that had irked Acrilat. That would explain why her family had always been odd, but had taken to doing things contrary to their own oddity in the past year. Did consulting a foreign wizard constitute a betrayal of Acrilat? If so, she might be about to make It even angrier.

"I'm sorry," said The Magician, "but that's outside my field of privilege. I belong to Liavek."

"But if you won't concern yourself with Acrivain," said Jehane, "then what wizard will?"

"An Acrivannish one, I daresay," said The Magician.

Jehane drew in her breath to make a hot retort, and stopped, and looked at him thoughtfully. He looked back, out of nicely-shaped eyes of green with gold flecks in them. Jehane stood up. "You've been very good," she said, cautiously. "I'll have to send you the money."

The Magician stood up also. "A momentary weakness," he said. "This year is turning; put it down to that."

Jehane took this to mean that he would be less accommodating should she come again. "I'd better collect my cat," she said. She turned, and there was Gogo, with Cinnamon and Nissy's cat in tow. Shin growled again.

"Has the brown one been sick?" said Jehane, before she could stop herself.

"He's missing somebody," said Gogo, her bright eyes dwelling not on the brown cat but on The Magician.

Shin wailed like a Zhir singer and took two stiff steps forward.

"Thank you," said Jehane, quickly, moving past Gogo for the door. "Come on, Cinnamon." Cinnamon obeyed; Nissy's cat sat down. Jehane knew she would have to do it. "Floradazul!" she said. Nissy's cat got up and followed them, down the long hall and out into the misty street. The door shut firmly behind them.

Jehane looked at Cinnamon, who had a generous smear of butter on his chin and appeared blissful. "You smell of garlic," she said.

"Snails," said Cinnamon.

"Carry the cat, then; she'll lick your chin."

"She got some, too," said Cinnamon. But he picked up the cat, and they set off for the House of Responsible Life.

They were damp when they got there. The Avenue of Five Mice was wet and chilly, but in the gardens around a blocky green building on the street's eastern side, somebody had thought it safe to set out tomato and pepper and melon plants. Jehane didn't care for the look of the house. In sunshine it might have been cheerful, but in this weather it looked moldy. She walked down the street until she came to a pair of double wooden doors standing hospitably open, and went up three green-painted steps, followed by the slap of Cinnamon's sandals.

They came into a large airy hall, smelling pleasantly of bees-wax and books. To their right was a very wide wooden staircase; before them a set of swinging doors of the sort that usually lead to a kitchen; to their left a wooden table behind which sat a young man and a young woman, identically dressed in vivid green tunics and baggy white trousers. They had before them on the table a scattering of books and papers, and a little green glass skull. They were arguing, but broke off when Cinnamon sneezed. Jehane hoped she was not giving him a fever, dragging him all over the city in this weather. After so long in Liavek it seemed cold today even to her; and all these foreigners were as thin-skinned as apples.

"Good day to you," said the young woman, in a very odd accent. "May we answer your questions?"

"I'm looking for a runaway," said Jehane, "and Cinnamon and the cat just need somewhere to sit out of the wet."

"I'll take them back to the kitchen and give them some milk," said the young man, standing up. His Liavekan was quite normal.

Jehane nodded to Cinnamon, and he followed the young man through the swinging doors. A warm gust smelling of bread and kaf and ginger swept out and engulfed the hall. Jehane thought irritably that nobody seemed to want to feed *her*.

"A runaway?" said the young woman. "You'll want to see Mistress Etriae." She opened a green-covered book the size of a tea tray, ran her thumb down a line of writing, and looked up at Jehane. "Up the stairs, the fourth door to your right."

Jehane went up the stairs, treading on a runner of green carpet, passing walls painted pale green; emerged into a hall tiled in green and white; counted off the doors with their green glass knobs; and stopped before the fourth one on the right, wondering what was responsible about green.

Mistress Etriae was almost as tall as Jehane, and extremely dark, and very serious. She had another wooden table, a great many shelves full of scrolls, a little set of leather-bound printed books, and a tidy line of four dead mice leaking unpleasantly onto a stack of clean paper.

"Good day to you," said Etriae, with the same odd inflection the young woman had used. She laid a sheet covered with scribbled numerals over the dead mice.

Jehane, who knew all about the embarrassment caused by cats, refrained from smiling and explained her problem.

"Eight years?" said Etriae. She raised her voice. "Dialo! Ancient history!"

A small man who needed a haircut emerged from behind a bookshelf, his arms full of scrolls. He wore a green robe that had seen better days. When he saw Jehane, his brown eyes grew extremely large. He put the scrolls down on Etriae's table, as far from the mouse-pile as possible, and bowed to Jehane. "I'm Verdialos," he said. "How may I assist you?"

"She's looking for her brother," said Etriae, in a tone that seemed to contain some warning. "Deleon Benedicti."

"Thank you, Et," said Verdialos, without taking his eyes off Jehane. She was used to being stared at by Liavekans, who seemed to think that yellow hair was somehow supernatural; but there was something different in his regard. His voice, however, was mostly without expression. "Mistress Benedicti, if you'll come with me."

Jehane followed him next door into a much smaller room full of printed books, all bound in green. He did at least have a rag rug on the floor with a few streaks of red and white in it. "May I offer you some tea?" said Verdialos, pausing on the rug. "It's a long walk to the house of Responsible Life."

"Please," said Jehane, too grateful to ponder his tone of voice or to worry about the fact that, although it was a long way from where she had been, it was not a long way from everywhere. Verdialos went back out, and Jehane sat down on a wooden bench, irritably shoving aside the green cushions.

He was a long time getting the tea. When the door finally opened, Jehane looked up smiling, and was rewarded with the sight of her little sister Nerissa, dressed in an old green dress of Jehane's, in her arms a thick stack of paper and on her face a look of such huge surprise that Jehane's first impulse was to laugh.

"Why are you here?"

"I'm looking for Deleon," said Jehane, baldly.

It was unwise to speak of Deleon to Nerissa; but this time a relief even huger than the surprise swept over her face. "That's very clever of you," she said.

"Why are *you* here?" said Jehane, warily. Nissy was not free with her compliments.

"I work here," said Nerissa, smiling.

"Nissy, Father will—" *Or Acrilat has.*

"Not if you don't tell him." There was no particular plea in her voice; but then, there never was.

"What were you doing at Number Seventeen Wizard's Row?" said Jehane.

Nerissa dropped the stack of paper, the top half of which separated itself and swept gracefully over the floor.

"And what were *you* doing there? I won't tell if you won't," she said, standing there with her arms hanging at her sides and the thick yellow hair uncurling itself from its green ribbon and sticking to her neck.

"Not this time," said Jehane. "This time, you tell me, and I tell you, and neither of us tells anybody else."

The black cat trotted into the room and made an inquiring noise. Nerissa scooped her up absently; then her eyes widened and she swung on Jehane. *"You stole my diary!"*

That this was true did not change the fact that Nerissa had no evidence from which to have deduced it. "I didn't read it," said Jehane. She hadn't even been looking for the diary; she hadn't known that Nissy kept one. Nissy had spent two days walking around like a cat with a mouse in its mouth, momentarily uncomfortable but essentially pleased, which meant she had written a story. Jehane had wanted to read that.

"No virtue in that; you couldn't." Nerissa smoothed the cat's ears and stared blankly out the little window. Jehane looked too, but saw only streaks of rain and a luminous gray sky. *"I'll kill you!"* said Nerissa.

"What's the matter with you?" said Jehane, beginning to be frightened.

"How dare you go to Granny! How dare you go to Wizard's Row! Spying and tattling; what did you give The Magician to tell you where I was?"

"He didn't tell me anything; and I wasn't looking for you," said Jehane. "I was looking for Deleon."

"Much you care for him! Where were you eight years ago?"

"I looked for him! You were the one who hid in your room and howled."

Nerissa was extremely pale and looked quite likely to be sick any moment. Jehane had never seen her so wrought up. Jehane had answered her as she might answer Isobel or Livia; but she and Nerissa had never until now had anything resembling a quarrel. Nissy didn't argue; it wasn't her way.

Nerissa leaned her cheek against the top of the cat's head, and scowled hard. Anybody would think the cat was telling her things. "I don't believe it. You're as bad as the rest of them," said Nerissa, quite flatly.

"All I wanted to do," said Jehane, losing her temper with a will to cover the stab of regret that statement caused in her, "was to read your story. Don't try to tell me you haven't written a story. You always hide them in the same places, and you know I always find them. I can't help it if you don't hide your diary better."

"Why can't you leave me alone!"

"I like your stories," said Jehane, as calmly as she could manage.

"I suppose you think that helps?"

"Does it hurt?"

The cat mewed vigorously; Nerissa set it down without looking at it; and Verdialos came through the door and put a tray with cups, a pot, a plate of melon silces, and a basket of little golden cakes down on the table. Jehane found time to be relieved that the food was not green, though the porcelain was.

"*You!*" said Nerissa to the back of his head. "You knew she was here!"

Verdialos leaned on the table and looked at her expectantly, and Nerissa turned her head aside and knelt to pick up the scattered papers. Verdialos poured three cups of tea—green, Jehane saw with regret—and handed her one. She didn't want it now, but the warmth was useful.

"Is Nerissa your responsibility?" Verdialos asked her.

"Apparently not," said Jehane, who was still angry.

"I'm not looking for appearances," said Verdialos. He dragged the wooden chair out from behind the table and sat down in it. "Nerissa, your tea is getting cold."

Nerissa went on picking up the papers.

"She has been my responsibility," said Jehane. "Since Deleon left. But she's almost seventeen, and she won't talk to me."

"And is Deleon your responsibility?"

"He was," said Jehane.

"And you come seeking him now, when he is eight years absent?"

"They're *all* my responsibility," said Jehane, capitulating, "and something's got to be done about them now."

"What do you propose to do?"

"Get them back to Acrivain."

"I won't go," said Nerissa from under the table.

Jehane opened her mouth in a fury; Verdialos leaned forward sharply, spilling his tea, and shook his head hard. Jehane cursed the entire family, added a venomous thought in the direction of Acrilat, and said, "I can't make anybody go. But everybody must have the choice."

"Mother won't go without Deleon," said Nerissa, in that same flat voice.

So much for tact. Jehane looked again at Verdialos, who pushed the long hair off his forehead and said, "Nerissa, come out from under the table."

"Why?"

"Because when you hear what I have to say you will jump and hit your head."

Nerissa crawled out from under the table, stood up, neatened her stack of papers, slapped it down on the tabletop, and leaned against it, looking at the floor.

"Your brother is safe," said Verdialos, "and happy, and not at all inclined to join us."

Nerissa looked at him swiftly. "Mother said he'd outgrow it."

"Where is he?" said Jehane, wondering why it was she who had to say it. What was wrong with Nissy? How could she say she had loved Deleon and take Verdialos's news so calmly? Where had she learned that judicious tone, that still consideration?

"I think," said Verdialos, gently, "that that is the least of your problems. What do you return to, in Acrivain?"

"The Magician said—"

"He sent you?"

"Yes. He said you found runaways. And he implied that you had an Acrivannish wizard who could engineer a revolution in Acrivain, so that we could go back safely."

Verdialos opened his eyes very wide, as he had done when he first saw Jehane. "We have no wizards at all," he said, with considerable emphasis. "And I don't know of an Acrivannish wizard in the entire city. Are you sure—"

"Reasonably," said Jehane. "Do you know what he's like?"

"Oh, yes," said Verdialos. He handed the cooling cup of tea to Nerissa. "Sit down, my dear."

Nerissa sat on the floor and tucked her feet under her, precisely as she had been taught not to.

"I wonder," said Verdialos, holding the plate of cakes out to Jehane. He began to smile. "Silvertop," he said.

"An Acrivannish wizard?"

"He's a Farlander of some sort," said Verdialos, still smiling, "and he's certainly a wizard. He lives on the Street of the Dreamers."

"Thank you," said Jehane. She looked at her sister.

"I think," said Verdialos, very softly, "that you had better let her go."

Nerissa lifted the cup to her mouth and lowered it again without drinking. She would not look at Jehane.

"And my brother?"

"He knows where you live," said Verdialos.

"But he doesn't know we're going back to Acrivain. And it's been eight years; he might try to see if things have changed—"

"It seems to me," said Verdialos, again softly, "that they have not changed in the least."

"But if we do arrange to go back—"

"I'll see that he knows," said Verdialos.

"All right," said Jehane, not to Verdialos but to the top of Nerissa's head. "I won't tell if you won't." Nerissa didn't move. Jehane got up and bent her knee to Verdialos, and went down the stairs to collect Cinnamon.

It was late afternoon and still raining when they came to the Street of the Dreamers. They were both drenched. The first person they spoke to knew where Silvertop lived; the second person they spoke to, on the narrow stair leading to Silvertop's rooms, told them Silvertop wasn't in, but to try the Tiger's Eye. The Tiger's Eye was a bad place to walk dripping into, but Jehane was too tired not do to what she had already planned. They walked around the corner and splashed up to the building, brilliant white in the early twilight, where Snake had her shop. The firethorn had not bloomed yet. The orange clusters of its berries in their dark oval leaves were as bright as jewels in the gray light. Somebody inside was just lighting the lamps. Jehane pushed the door open and entered in a cascade of bells. It was warm inside and smelled of jasmine, of cinnamon, of sandalwood, of tiger-flowers.

There were three people behind the counter, arguing. There was a tall slim woman with a cloud of black hair shot with red; a smaller, darker girl with tight wiry hair and a skeptical expression; and the Acrivannish wizard. He was smaller than the girl, and narrower in the shoulders; he had skin like milk and features like the ivory carving of the Mountain Empress that Mama kept in the library, delicate as snow sculpture; he had a cap of pale hair that caught the lamplight even better than Nerissa's butter-yellow.

He was turning a thin band of silver over in his quick fingers. He spoke, and Jehane jumped. He had a voice like the wrath of Acrilat on the icefield, terrible as an army with banners. That was the voice. The words did not precisely match it.

"Snake, it's just what I need," he said. "It's perfect."

"Yes," said the taller woman. "It is perfect. And it is staying right here where some discerning customer can discover its perfection and pay for it and take it away and cherish it."

"I'll bring it back tomorrow."

"It will be green," said Snake. "It will be misshapen. It will be covered with cobwebs. That is, if it doesn't disintegrate altogether and coat your lungs with silver and kill you and make Thyan impossible to live with. No. You can't have it."

"All right, all right. How much?"

"No, you don't," said Thyan.

Snake looked at her over Silvertop's head, and shrugged.

"Too much, Silver," she said. "If you will tell me precisely what is perfect about it, perhaps we can find you something else?"

Jehane leaned back and pulled the door open again; the bells rang airily, and this time all three of them looked at her.

"Hello, Nerissa," said Thyan.

"It's Jehane," said Jehane, resignedly.

"I'm sorry. We haven't seen any of you for some time. Is your family well?"

Jehane grinned ferociously and said, "Yes, thank you."

"Come farther in," said Snake. "What can we help you with?"

"I'm wet," said Jehane.

"I just waxed the floor," said Thyan. "But don't drip on the new brocade."

Jehane dripped across the shining floor to the counter, Cinnamon dogging her footsteps.

"Would the little boy like to come help me unpack some bells?" said Thyan.

"You can feed me," said Cinnamon. "That keeps me quiet."

"I'll feed him," said Snake, coming around the counter. "This way, young one."

They disappeared through a door in the back of the shop, and Thyan turned back to Jehane.

"I'm sorry to be a trouble," said Jehane. "I don't actually want to buy anything. I was told Master Silvertop might be here?"

"Yes, he is," said Thyan, looking at the young man. Silvertop had abandoned the silver bracelet for a pair of earrings; he piled them in one palm and stirred them around with the fingers of his other hand, and red and green sparks leaped out.

"Silvertop," said Thyan.

Silvertop shook the earrings; they jingled pleasingly, and their delicate tremblers became an inextricable tangle.

"Hey!" said Thyan, shaking his shoulder. Silvertop leaned comfortably into her arm and went on shaking the earrings.

"Bubblehead!" said Thyan, at the top of her voice.

"Hmmm?"

"This is Mistress Benedicti, and she wants to speak to you."

Silvertop looked out of the circle of her arm at Jehane, with an expression of vague but cheerful inquiry. He had gray eyes, not the sometimes-gray sometimes-blue of Livia's, but gray and pure as the rainy sky. Jehane, wet, footsore, bewildered, and tired to death, stared at him and said in her heart the ritual she had not had occasion to use these twenty years. *Acrilat, thou art crueler to thy servants than to thine enemies; those who hate thee prosper and those who love thee suffer entanglements of the spirit.* He was even more unsuitable than the young man she had gone to talk to Granny about.

She cleared her throat. "I need to hire a wizard," she said.

"What for?" said Silvertop.

"To make a revolution in Acrivain."

"Acrivain!" said Thyan. "That's hundreds of miles away."

"Three thousand," said Jehane.

"Is it?" said Silvertop, intrigued. "That would be an interesting problem."

"Aren't you Acrivannish?"

"I might be," said Silvertop.

"You've never been there?"

"I might have been."

"You don't remember? You wouldn't want to go back?"

"Wizards," said Thyan, with an indecipherable expression, "can't cross water."

"Go there?" said Silvertop, disregarding this extraordinary statement. "Anybody could go there. I'd like to see it from here. Why a revolution?"

"The ruling powers are enemies of my family, and we want to go home."

"I'm not sure about a revolution. I might be able to make them abandon their duties; for a little while, anyway. How long does it take to get to Acrivain?"

"Four months," said Jehane.

"No . . . I could muddle their minds just before your arrival. I think the timing would be difficult, though."

"What about an earthquake?" said Jehane, who was suffering a serious disillusionment about the nature and power of wizards.

"Well, if—"

"That might kill somebody," said Thyan.

"So it might," said Silvertop, sounding disappointed.

Jehane said, "So would a revolution."

"Yes, I guess it would. We'd better think of something else, hadn't we? Thyan? What happened to those brass bowls?"

"I sold them," said Thyan, in an extremely grim voice.

Jehane looked down at her quickly. Thyan stared her straight in the face. Snake came back into the room, and Thyan immediately caught her eyes.

"He fell asleep," Snake said. "What's this about brass bowls?"

"Mistress Benedicti wants to hire Silvertop's services as a wizard," said Thyan.

"Good; you two can use the money."

"To make a revolution in Acrivain."

"Can Silvertop do that?" said Snake. Her eyes had not left Thyan's; they were carrying on another conversation entirely.

"He doesn't think so."

"But he wants my brass bowls?"

Thyan shrugged.

"I could send illusions," said Silvertop. "Of earthquakes, or revolution, or whatever you like. Would that cause enough confusion, do you think?"

"It might," said Jehane, cautiously. "I don't know much about the situation in Acrivain." They had no soldiers; but if Silvertop could send illusions of those, also, then perhaps—"

"Well, *that's* easy to find out," said Silvertop. "I've been wanting to try something like that. Then you can decide what you want done. You'd better come home with me."

"You can work here," said Thyan.

"He can?" said Snake.

Silvertop seemed pleased but dubious. "I'll need a lot of stuff from my rooms—"

"We'll help you carry it."

"Thyan!" said Snake.

"We'll use the roof."

"In this weather?" said Snake.

"We'll rig an awning. His roof leaks anyhow."

"Thyan," said Snake.

"I won't let him bring the peacock," said Thyan. Once again, they were conducting another conversation entirely separate from this one. There was a pause, and then Snake shrugged again.

"Don't you go *near* that acacia," she said.

"Word of honor," said Thyan.

"Silvertop," said Snake.

"Hmmm?"

"This doesn't seem very sound to me. It seems, in fact, politically naive in the extreme."

"First we'll find out what's going on over there," said Silvertop. "Then we'll see what to do about it. That's cautious, isn't it?"

"For you," said Snake.

"How much will you want?" said Jehane.

"I'll know after I've done it," said Silvertop, picking up the bracelet again.

"No," Snake told him.

"You can give two levars to Snake," said Thyan. "She'll need it if we're going to do this on the roof."

"I hope not," said Snake. "For two levars I could retile the entire roof and buy another acacia."

"Yes, you could," said Thyan.

"I'll bring the money tomorrow," said Jehane.

"I hope you're wrong," said Snake to Thyan. "All right, children, run along. Take jackets."

Jehane got home just before midnight, lugging a somnolent Cinnamon. Livia, of course, had left the little side door open for her; and Livia, of course, interrogated her vigorously, if sleepily, when she came into their room. Granny, Livia said, had come and talked to Mother for a very long while, and Livia had heard Jehane's name several times, though she had unaccountably failed to understand the gist of the conversation. But Jehane had been outwitting Livia for twenty-two years; and at breakfast the next morning, to which Jehane went sickly braced for an enormous battle with those whom she could not outwit, nobody said a word about it.

A little consideration and some reluctant listening at doors made Jehane aware that both her parents were far too worried about her two remaining brothers to spare half a thought for any of their daughters. This made her task the more urgent, but also made it far easier to accomplish. She could come and go as she pleased, without dragging poor Cinnamon all over Liavek and making him fat into the bargain. She took a few hours the first morning after she hired Silvertop to follow Livia to an assignation, confront her, and extract, in exchange for her own silence, Livia's promise not to tell their parents about Jehane's absences and not to do anything stupid with or about the young man for at least a fiveday. She also apologized to Nerissa, whose diary Granny had returned, no doubt unread. Nerissa, as usual, shut her mouth and went away; but she smiled first.

Jehane spent the next three days on Snake's roof. It took Silvertop two of them to assemble what he wanted. Jehane began to feel like a pack camel. Snake or Thyan usually came along, and seldom carried very much. Silvertop seemed pleased to have them. In between collecting and arranging his pots of paint and his brass bowls and his mildewed draperies and dead branches and jars of early tadpoles, he asked Jehane hundreds of incomprehensible questions.

For these two days, also, it rained. Jehane felt a great deal more as if she were playing with Nerissa and Deleon than as if she were accomplishing something; but she could think of nothing else to do, and The Magician and Verdialos, neither of whom appeared either mad or foolish, had sent her to Silvertop. She would see what he could do. And she appreciated having an excuse to see him.

On the third morning the sun came out weakly. Jehane, still feeling a little strange at being out and about all by herself, bought a jug of kaf from a little stall on the Street of the Dreamers and carried it along to the Tiger's Eye. Snake had made a sardonic remark about how much of hers they were drinking; and that really meant Thyan, who after all lived there, and Jehane, who didn't. Silvertop did not drink kaf; he just periodically spilled it and drew diagrams on Snake's roof with it. Thyan said despairingly that he was making an open-air spot smell exactly like his rooms. If his rooms smelled of equal parts of mildew, kaf, damp soil, and paint, she was right.

"Good morning," said Snake from behind the counter. She was always kind and courteous in the morning and became steadily more irate. Jehane could not blame her.

"Thyan and Silvertop are up there already," said Snake. "He seems to think that today may be his first attempt."

"I hope so," said Jehane. "It's urgent; and I'm sure you want us off your roof."

Snake bent over and extracted a shah board from under the counter. Then she yelped. "Does he have my soapstone shah pieces up there?"

"Thyan told him he couldn't have them," said Jehane.

"As well tell a camel not to spit," said Snake. "Tell him to give them back or I'll come up there and take them."

Silvertop received this threat unmoved. "She can have *most* of them, but I need the shahs."

"Silvertop, she's very unhappy."

"I'll go talk to her," said Thyan. She grabbed up a double handful of pieces and departed.

"You got blue paint on them," said Jehane.

"Hold this, please," said Silvertop.

"Silver, why is everything you use so *wet?*"

"I have to see over three thousand miles of ocean," said Silvertop, mildly put out. "And just as well, with all this rain."

The apparatus looked far worse in the sunlight. Jehane couldn't believe it was really like that. Every time she looked at it she thought that either her eyes or her mind were failing her. She expressed this dilemma to Silvertop, trying to disregard the filthy tangle of string he had handed her.

"Some of it isn't exactly there," said Silvertop, tying a knot and biting the end off neatly. Jehane feared for his health. "So it's hard for you to see it."

"Bubblehead," said Thyan, arriving at the top of the ladder. "Snake says today is the last day you spend on her roof, rifling her shop. She says this comes down tonight at moonrise."

"That's plenty of time," said Silvertop, "if I can have one more mirror. That ebony-backed one in the window would do. I need the comb, too."

Thyan came across the roof to them and patted him on the head. His hair was the color Deleon's had been when he was a baby. Jehane looked away from them, first at the tangle of string, and then with a kind of tearful hilarity at the acacia tree in its huge tub, lavishly smothered in blurry yellow flowers: unaltered, but not especially comforting.

Thyan said, "I'll get you the mirror and comb from my room."

"That's silver," said Silvertop, dribbling blue paint onto his knot and frowning. "I need something that was alive."

"It's ivory," said Thyan. "Are you going to put blue paint on it?"

"No, of course not."

"Will ivory do?"

"Are there elephants in Acrivain?" said Silvertop to Jehane.

"No," said Jehane.

"All right, then," said Silvertop.

He tucked his head into the crook of Thyan's arm and began rapidly disassembling a shiribi puzzle that Snake had given him yesterday in exchange for the return of six red glass jars. Jehane knew that Thyan would stay there, and that half an hour or half a day from now, he would ask her where the comb and mirror were. Then she would tell him what she thought of him, and he would be alert for about a quarter of an hour. It was a wonder Snake hadn't murdered them both.

At the third hour after noon, with a strong spring sun blazing
down on their awning and making the concatenation of smells
under it peculiar beyond belief, Silvertop professed himself ready
to begin.

They sat down in a row, Thyan, Silvertop, Jehane. Thyan held
in her lap an incredible clutter of objects she was supposed to
hand to Silvertop when he asked for them. Jehane had a pen and
a jar of ink and a pile of pages from Snake's ledger on which
Thyan, or possibly Snake, had made mistakes in arithmetic. Silvertop seemed to think that using the blank sides of those would
be better than using new paper. Jehane had no idea what she was
supposed to write down, so it hardly mattered.

Silvertop propped Thyan's ivory mirror up against a brass
chamberpot full of feathers. The comb had long since disappeared. Thyan had refused to give him the brush.

"Don't listen to this if you can help it," said Silvertop. "I
don't want to send *you* to Acrivain."

Thyan muttered something on which Jehane chose to practice
not listening.

Silvertop put his hands on his knees and began to speak. His
deep, rough-edged voice rolled out over the insane structure he
had made like a concourse of bronze bells. He was speaking
Acrivannish, or something like it. It was nursery rhymes, thought
Jehane, forgetting not to listen. No, it was tables of multiplica-
tion; no, lists of trees and flowers and rocks and birds. Her hand
wanted to write them down. She turned one of her pages over and
read silently, "Four lengths of red silk, six brass sundials, two
packets of jasmine, dried, four packets of jasmine flowers, preserved, twelve strings of wooden beads."

"There!" said Silvertop. "Jehane, what's this?"

Jehane looked at him. He was looking at the mirror. A pale
blue light washed out of it, like the full moon on a field of snow.
It gave his delicate face an unearthly and entirely too appropriate
beauty.

Jehane leaned over his shoulder, and saw in the mirror a long
hall paved in white and hung with blue. It had high narrow windows along its length, through which came the blue light. Outside snow fell glittering from a cloudless sky. There was no fire
in the hall. People in blue smocks and white trousers stood or sat
about. Some of them rolled what might have been dice. There
was no sound out of the mirror. Jehane could hear Thyan's
breathing, and the flap of the wind tugging at the awning, and a
finch singing far away.

"It's the tower of Acrilat," said Jehane, barely managing a whisper.

"Who?" said Thyan, considerably louder; Jehane admired her pluck.

"The god of Acrivain. It's mad. I don't think It wants you looking at It, Sil."

"What's It going to think about our messing with Acrivain?" said Thyan. "You didn't tell us about this."

"If you hadn't looked right in Its front door, It probably wouldn't have noticed," said Jehane.

"I looked right in Its front door," said Silvertop, without taking his eyes off the mirror, "because It's looking right into ours. It's working in Liavek." He held out his free hand to Thyan. "I need the peach."

Jehane never found out what he needed it for. The light from the mirror turned red, and then a hot white. Silvertop yelped and dropped the mirror. Jehane thrust her hand under it to prevent its breaking on the rooftop, and it seared the back of her hand like a splash of hot oil. Silvertop snatched at her wrist, the mirror fell and broke in a shower of glass and ivory, and Silvertop's entire apparatus cracked and fluttered and flung itself about in the air.

Nothing hit any of them. Almost everything landed right side up, and in considerably better order than in the apparatus itself. The exceptions were the awning and the blue paint. The awning drifted down onto the roof tiles like a sheet being spread over a bed—which in fact it had been, before Silvertop confiscated it— and the blue paint showered down over all of it and half Snake's roof as well.

The cacophony of brass and silver and wood falling dwindled and died; the paint pot fell straight down and cracked into two pieces; and Snake put her head over the edge of the roof.

Her first sentence was violently spoken and incomprehensible to Jehane; Thyan appeared to understand it.

"I know," she said.

"What happened?"

All three of them looked at Silvertop. Silvertop looked at Jehane. "Does Acrilat speak to you?" he said.

"No," said Jehane. He was still holding her wrist, and it was an even contention between that and the throb of her burned hand, which was the more distracting.

"If It did, It would have stopped," said Silvertop.

Jehane consulted her interior, and blinked. She was accustomed to feeling oppressed, and to overcoming it. There was nothing now to overcome.

"Did you send Acrilat out of Liavek?"

"No," said Silvertop. "But It's out of Liavek now."

"What is this all over my roof?" said Snake, in a deadly tone.

Jehane felt reasonably certain that Snake had wished to begin, immediately, an extensive inquiry into just what had gone on here, and had decided against it. Being in no mood for either wrath or philosophical inquiry, she blessed Snake, insofar as that was possible without applying to any particular god.

Silvertop let go of Jehane and looked at the sheet and the roof with their intricate sweeps of blue. "It's a map of Acrivain," he said. "It's much larger than I intended. You should have let me keep those glass jars."

Snake struggled, visibly, with some furious remark, and won. "Are you finished up here?"

Silvertop sighed. "Not nearly. All we found out is that the apparatus works. We'll have to build it again. If you'll just give me the jars and the shah pieces, next time—"

"Snake, don't," said Thyan, although Snake was only standing perfectly still and staring at Silvertop.

"No, wait," said Jehane, fighting a light-headed tendency to shriek with laughter and dance around the acacia. "If you sent Acrilat out of Liavek, maybe we don't have to go home."

"I didn't send It."

"But It's gone?"

"Yes."

Jehane suspected that he had sent It away without knowing what he was doing. "It's all right, then. Never mind the revolution."

"Snake?" said Thyan. "Who's minding the store?"

"You and Jehane," said Snake. "I am going to watch Silvertop clean up this roof."

Jehane sat on her unmade bed and reviewed in her mind, contentedly enough, the moment when Silvertop had grabbed her wrist. There was only so much to review, however, and her subsequent thoughts were less pleasant. The touch of Acrilat on all their lives might indeed have been removed; but Its mark remained. Marigand's baby was still dead; Deleon had still been gone for eight years; Nissy still worked as a clerk for a most peculiar organization, and pretended that one cat was another; Livia was still silly and Isobel still malicious; their mother was preoccupied and their father depressed. Liavek was still alien and bewildering. There was still no one for any of them to marry. Silvertop was neither suitable nor possible. He was a bubblehead and he belonged to Thyan.

She was not so engrossed that the opening of the door startled her. She prepared to deal with Livia's remarks about her slovenly habits; but it was not Livia. Nerissa came in, wearing green, with the black cat in her wake.

"Hello, Floradazul," said Jehane.

Nerissa held out to her a little blank book about the size of a skirt pocket. "Here's the story," she said.

"So you did write one."

"You always know," said Nerissa, smiling. She sat down on Livia's tidy bed, smooth as a field of snow.

"And I always have to steal them."

"I've been feeling better," said Nerissa. She fixed a judicious blue stare on her sister. "You look as if you've been feeling worse."

"How long have you been feeling better?"

"Oh, six months or so."

"The House of Responsible Life must be good for you."

"Yes," said Nerissa, with no particular expression.

Jehane abandoned any thought of further discussing the House of Responsible Life. She got no reward for this kind restraint. Nerissa said, "Why do you feel worse?"

Jehane looked at her for a moment and decided to risk it. "I'm in love," said Jehane. "It will pass."

Nerissa looked at her for about the same length of time. "Verdialos is married," she said.

Jehane began to feel indignant, and then realized what she had been told. "He's too old for you," she said.

"Silvertop," said Nerissa, "is too young for you."

"He's twenty-six."

"Going on sixteen."

"Going on sixty, I think."

"Too old *and* too young," said Nerissa.

Jehane grinned; it was perfectly true. She leaned forward and bounced the little book on her palm. "I can't read this if you're watching."

"I'll go in a minute. I wanted to ask you something. Do you think Silvertop *killed* Acrilat?"

"Silvertop says he didn't do anything," said Jehane. "He said that whoever did do something didn't destroy Acrilat, just told It in no uncertain terms to stay away from Liavek and everybody in

Liavek. Or at least, that's what he thinks."

"On Moondays," said Nerissa.

"No, it's not that," said Jehane. "He says that the available evidence supports any of three separate theories of how it happened; but what happened's quite certain."

"I don't feel quite certain," said Nerissa.

They looked at one another. "We could go and ask The Magician," said Jehane. "He told me that his field of privilege is Liavek, so perhaps he did it. And I owe him some money."

Nerissa nodded. "I sent him a letter," she said, "but it came back."

"Why?"

"It said, 'Removed. Left No Address,'" said Nerissa.

Jehane snorted; Nerissa giggled; they leaned their heads into their hands and laughed as they had not done since Deleon went away; and then they were no longer laughing.

They were still a little damp and red-eyed when they came along Healer's Street in the kindly sunlight and saw the long line of square white dusty houses that was Wizard's Row. They turned the corner cautiously and trudged through the dust.

"It looked nothing like this when I was last here," said Jehane, in hushed tones.

"I think," said Nerissa, "that this is its *habitual* aspect, and when it's different you can tell something of the mood of the inhabitants."

"But what?"

"I've no idea," said Nerissa, in a dry voice extremely reminiscent of their mother's.

Number 17 had a cracked green walk. The yew tree was still there. The ground around it was crowded with purple crocus and white and gold arianis.

"He's expecting me," said Nerissa, staring at the yew tree; she sounded half pleased and half frightened. She pulled the tongue of the brass gargoyle.

"Where's your cat?" it said musically.

"Didn't she cause enough trouble the last time?" said Jehane.

"What?" said Nerissa, in resigned tones.

"You'd better come in," said the gargoyle, and the door swung silently wide. They walked along the hall and went through the only open door, into a bare room with a fountain in the middle and long white benches. The Magician was sitting on one of them, dressed as he had been when Jehane last saw him. There were no cats.

"I'm sorry your letter was returned," said The Magician. "I prefer to commit very little to writing."

"It's good of you to receive us," said Jehane. She handed him the two half-levar coins. She supposed that Granny would not approve of her having stolen them, even from her own dowry, and she would have to replace them somehow.

"I hope," said The Magician, "that it is the last time I receive you, or any other member of the Benedicti family."

"Was it so much trouble to put Acrilat in Its place?" said Jehane.

"I did not put Acrilat in Its place," said The Magician. "Nobody having offered to pay me for doing so."

"Who did, then?"

"Your Granny Carry."

Nerissa sat down abruptly on a bench. Jehane was somewhat less startled, but she was alarmed. "Because I asked her to?"

The Magician shrugged slightly.

Jehane stood quite still. She had asked Granny to find out if it was Acrilat that was making her family so odd; she had never, after that thundering scold, expected Granny to do it. But she had asked; and Granny had done it. Acrilat had been in Liavek, in whatever way mad gods did these things; and Granny had sent It about Its business, no doubt in precisely the way she always did these things; and it was Jehane's fault. They could never go home now. Acrilat would be waiting for them.

Jehane swallowed hard, and looked up into The Magician's tired and knowing eyes.

"Don't trouble yourself," said The Magician. "You can all live in Liavek if you will make the attempt. And, if I may, don't try to make every one of your family happy. You cannot always paint the meadows with delight."

"Don't tell her that," said Nerissa, in a voice Jehane had never heard from her. "It's her best talent."

Jehane looked at her. "What *were* you doing at Number Seventeen Wizard's Row?"

"It's a very long story," said Nerissa.

"I'll tell you," said Jehane, "if you'll tell me."

The Magician saw them out. They walked to the end of Wizard's Row, not talking, not yet, and turned into Healer's Street. Some breath of wind, some wavering of the light, made them look around. Wizard's Row had departed.

In Acrivain, the snow lay nine inches deep until the middle of the month of Reaping. This happened one year in ten, and part of

the craziness of the First King was the making of incessant preparations for things that seldom happened. So nobody starved, but
there was a great deal of grumbling. The priests who could count
shook their heads philosophically, and rolled the dice again.

The World in the Rock

by Kara Dalkey

RAIN SPATTERED LIGHTLY on the window awnings, its patter barely audible inside the Tiger's Eye. Aritoli ola Silba glanced at the elegant gewgaws on display, pretending to himself that he was seriously in the market for a new luck piece. In actuality, he only sought a respite from a dreary day.

The week before had been disastrous to his feelings of self-worth. A poor but promising artist from Hrothvek had come to the city at Aritoli's assurance that a good commission awaited him. Then the noble offering the job reneged, and the artist had to return home with only Aritoli's apologies and levars as consolation. A message had arrived from Aritoli's sister at Silversea, urgently requesting his presence and advice on a matter of property negotiations. Aritoli had dismissed it with a curt reply, saying that if it was an offer to buy it was doubtless fraudulent, and a request to sell he would not deign to consider. It turned out to have been a discussion of the proposed rail line from Saltigos to Liavek (the delicacy of the politics involved had prevented her from telling him this), and she had been obliged to handle her side of the discussion from an impossible position. And the last lover he had hoped to please—Aritoli closed his mind against that embarrassing memory.

All considered, Aritoli felt quite useless and downhearted. His optimism now only reached as far as the half-hope of gazing upon the lovely, if formidable, features of the Tiger's Eye's proprietor. However, on this day, as his luck would have it, the shop was tended instead by her equally formidable young apprentice, Thyan. And Thyan was not forthcoming as to when her mistress would return.

So Aritoli lingered, looking over a set of enormous, bejeweled belt buckles. Before long, he was startled out of his musings by the chimes from the front of the store.

Aritoli looked up expectantly, but instead of Snake there entered a small, bedraggled figure. It was a girl no more than twelve years old, wet and muddy from the rain, and in her arms she carried a heavy object that was about the size of a goat's head. Aritoli watched as the child lugged the object down the central aisle of the shop to place it with a *thunk* upon the polished wood countertop before the appalled Thyan.

"What are you doing? I just dusted that—"

"Want to sell," said the little girl. She had an accent that Aritoli identified as Zhir. "How much for rock?"

Thyan picked clods of mud off the object. Curious, Aritoli approached to see what she would uncover. But after much picking and wiping, it proved to be only a rock. In fact, it was the ugliest lump of stone Aritoli had ever seen.

"We can't give you anything for this!" said Thyan. "It's just a rock!"

"But it's precious!" protested the girl. "The world is in the rock!"

"Huh," Thyan scoffed. She gave the girl a measuring look, then slowly took two copper coins from under the counter and slid them across to the girl. "Here. But from now on, do your begging outside."

Aritoli felt an odd, sudden urge toward philanthropy—as if whatever gods were watching had suggested, "Here is a chance to redeem yourself."

"One moment," said Aritoli, walking up to the counter. "My dear," he said to the girl, "if this rock means so much to you, are you sure you ought to be selling it?"

The girl frowned very seriously, as if considering a new and somewhat disturbing possibility. "Need coins," she said at last. "Had no more coins and am hungry."

Looking her over, Aritoli noticed that her short tunic, though worn and muddy, was well made. And the dirt on her skin was not the deep grime acquired through years of life on the streets.

"*Ke jwazlas ti?*" he asked the girl in Zhir. "What is your name? *Jwalengi* Aritoli."

"Tay-li."

"I am pleased to meet you, Tay-li. Where did you come from?"

"From house of iv Ning. But he send me away. Can no longer keep me."

"I've heard of him," Thyan said. "There were rumors that he got on the wrong side of a good wizard who enchanted him to make bad financial decisions. Last I heard, iv Ning was losing a fortune importing fish."

Aritoli gave a low whistle. "That was some enchanted iv Ning. So now he can no longer support servants, eh? What sort of work did you do for him, Tay-li?"

The girl shrugged. "Cleaning, errands, sort of thing."

"Well, Tay-li, perhaps today is your luck day. I happen to know of an establishment or two that could use a clever girl, and they would pay you more coins and meals than your precious rock could fetch. Come along with me and I'll see what we can do."

Thyan shot Aritoli an evil glare.

"Oh, come now," Aritoli snapped, "my tastes may be varied, but I've no interest in cradle-snatching. I suggest you remove your mind from the gutter before the rain washes it away." Aritoli gently took Tay-li's arm.

But she shook herself free a moment and reverently picked up the ugly stone. Hugging it to herself, she said, "Now I will go."

Outside, the rain had become a misty drizzle that clung to their clothing. Aritoli said, "May I carry that for you, Tay-li? It must be very heavy."

But Tay-li shook her head. "Not heavy. The world is in the rock."

Aritoli smiled awkwardly. "What do you mean by that? 'The world is in the rock'?"

"When you look at it, you will see."

As they walked down Cat Street, Aritoli wondered. Tay-li was far too young to have invested her luck yet, so it was unlikely that the rock was a vessel of magic. Could it be that the stone was all that was left of her "world"? All that was familiar to her? Aritoli turned his mind from such sad thoughts to the task of considering where he might find employment for her.

Before long, they arrived at Aritoli's townhome on Temple Way, where Tay-li was delivered into the capable hands of Aritoli's elderly manservant, Maljun.

"Please draw a bath for her, and see if you can find her something cleaner to wear."

Maljun looked with concern at the Zhir girl. "Suitable for . . . evening attire, master?"

Aritoli scowled back. "Suitable for an employment interview, if you please."

"Very good, sir." Maljun sketched what seemed to be a relieved bow. Gently, he coaxed Tay-li into relinquishing her rock, which he placed upon a table in Aritoli's study before leading her away.

Aritoli, meanwhile, sat at his desk and composed a short note that he gave to Maljun to deliver. That accomplished, he inexplicably found his attention drawn again to the rock.

He sat on the floor next to the table and studied the stone. It was a chaotic conglomeration of pebbles and granite and odd-colored veins, smooth in some places, rough in others. "A lapidarist's nightmare," Aritoli murmured, shaking his head.

"You like rock?" said Tay-li from the doorway.

Aritoli looked up. She stood fresh-scrubbed and smiling, wearing a cotton tunic of Aritoli's that had shrunk, tied with a woven belt. Except for the fact that she wore no sandals, she could be any well-to-do merchant's daughter.

"The rock? It's, er, very pretty, Tay-li."

"You see?" she said with a smile like bright sunshine. She walked up to the rock and knelt beside it. "You see the world?"

"The world? Well, not exactly, though there seem to be many kinds of stone represented here."

"Not just stones! Look!" She tumbled the stone this way and that, peering at it intently. Then she stopped and her little fingers traced a jagged gray ridge. "Here are Silverspine Mountains." She searched more and ran her fingers along a narrow ribbon of mica. "Here is Cat River." She rolled the rock over and touched a group of bumpy pebbles. "Here is camel." She pointed at an area of bluish rock with black specks. "Here are Kil in Sea of Luck." Again and again her nimble hands turned the rock over and touched on different shapes that Tay-li identified as places, animals, people, and so on.

Aritoli found himself caught up in her game. "Look, Tay-li, here is a dog's head," he said, pointing at a particular bump.

Tay-li studied the feature very seriously. "No. Is horse."

"As you say." Aritoli smiled gently. "But this is a pine branch, don't you think?" He pointed at a group of tiny green crystals.

"Yes! And here is cone that fell from branch!" Tay-li caressed a little brown lump beside the crystals.

"And here is a tea flower and leaf," said Aritoli.

"And there is cup that tea will be drunk from!"

They laughed together. The more Aritoli looked for things to point out to Tay-li, the more he saw. There seemed to be endless variation, and often a particular feature was part of different discoveries. Aritoli felt strangely pleased at each new thing he found, and Tay-li was enjoying herself immensely. "You see! You see!" she would say, and clap her hands with glee.

Aritoli did not know how much time was spent in this happy

pastime, but it seemed too soon when Maljun entered the study and said, "Mistress Pashantu from the House of Orange Blossoms has arrived, master."

"What? Oh, yes, Maljun, show her in." Aritoli leaned toward Tay-li. "This woman may have a job to offer you."

Maljun admitted a plump young woman wearing a many-layered dress of bright colors. "Ari, dear! How good to see you!" she said. "It has been too long since you graced the doorstep of our House." She gave an exaggerated bow in the Tichenese manner.

"Indeed it has. Welcome, dear Pashantu. May I introduce the prospective employee I mentioned? This is Tay-li, of the now-dispersed household of iv Ning. Tay-li, may I present Mistress Pashantu."

Tay-li gave a little bow and smiled shyly.

Pashantu bustled over to the girl and took her hands, holding her arms out straight. "Ah, is this the girl? My, what a healthy-looking one you are, Tay-li. I understand you've done cleaning work?"

Tay-li nodded.

"Have you ever worked in a kitchen?"

"Some."

"Bezwani fa Ka Zhir?"

"Wiya! Kolojali se sanaa jedu—"

"That's enough, dear, my Zhir is rusty. What languages do you read?"

Tay-li shrugged. "Zhir. Some 'Vekan."

"Well, Tay-li, here is what we can offer. The work is hard . . . for there is much linen and clothing to be cleaned, and many rooms to be washed and tidied. But we will feed and house you. And we will give you lessons in languages, geography, music, and etiquette. Then, in a few years, if you choose, you may join the older children in their work and take lessons in finance, political science, and, um, entertainment. But if you decide not to stay with us, we will find you a good position wherever you wish in Liavek. Does this sound acceptable to you, Tay-li?"

The girl was silent for a few moments. Then she looked up and smiled. *"Wiya.* Accept."

"Well, good! We'll be happy to have you with us. Come along and I'll take you to your new home."

"I'll walk you to the gate," Aritoli said, standing up. He felt a little sad to see Tay-li go.

Outside, the rain clouds were breaking apart and bright rays of sunlight streamed through. The air smelled fresh and Aritoli felt as though he were experiencing the wind and the sunlight for the first time.

He bent down and took Tay-li's hand. "Please feel free to visit me when you like. I've greatly enjoyed meeting you and seeing your rock . . . your rock! Wait a moment!" Aritoli ran back into the study. Scooping the rock under his arm, Aritoli returned to Tay-li and held it out to her. "We almost forgot your precious rock, Tay-li."

Tay-li smiled and shook her head. "No. You keep. Is just a rock."

"But . . . but the world is in this rock. You showed me!"

"Yes! You see! You keep rock. I find another. Bye-bye."

As Tay-li and Pashantu walked away, Aritoli looked after them in confusion. Then realization came. He looked down at the stone in his arms and for a moment it was again just an ugly, lumpy mass. Then he saw once more the face of the dog/horse and Aritoli knew everything they had found together was still there. Aritoli chuckled and walked into his forecourt garden, where he unceremoniously dropped the rock in a space of cleared ground.

"A new addition to the garden, master?" Maljun asked behind him.

Aritoli stood back and regarded the rock a moment. "It rather resembles a sand-skimmer on the Great Desert, don't you think?"

"Eh?"

"Or, perhaps, a collection of dawn spooks rising from a Hrothvekan swamp. No doubt tomorrow it will resemble something entirely different." He looked back at Maljun, who wore an expression of patient bewilderment. Aritoli laughed. "No, my dear fellow, my mind hasn't cracked completely. Just enough to let a little light in. Now tell me what delicious dishes you've prepared for supper."

Baker's Dozen

by Bradley Denton

MARDIS GLANCED QUICKLY around the Happy Swine's dingy public room as she and Karel entered, and was relieved to see that the only other customer was a drunk sleeping off last night's binge at a table by the hearth. Maybe this celebration wouldn't be as bad as last year's.

They were just sitting down when a horrendous crashing-and-splashing noise blasted from the kitchen doorway, followed immediately by a masculine bellow.

"Noooooo!" the voice cried. "Twelve months of tradition ruined!"

"It's your own fault!" a woman answered shrilly. "If I've told you once, I've told you a thousand times—never put a live pig into the pot-boil!"

An argument commenced, punctuated by the occasional clatter of a thrown saucepan and the squeals of the pig.

Mardis hesitated, hovering in a half-crouch over her chair. "Maybe we should go somewhere else this year," she said, and winced as the pig shot out of the kitchen and escaped through the main entrance.

Karel gave her a wry smile as the Happy Swine's burly, broth-spattered owner stumbled past their table in pursuit of the pig. "Wouldn't be a good idea, Mardie," he said when the innkeeper was gone. "This is the only place in all of Liavek where we can have your birthday breakfast without anyone noticing the chaos. Just don't order the pot-boil."

Mardis sighed and poured herself a mug of lukewarm kaf from a ceramic pot that had apparently been on the table for a few days already. The stuff tasted awful, but at least its smell overpowered some of the inn's other odors.

Karel and his damned "birthday breakfast" tradition. It was bad enough that she had to endure a birthday, let alone in public. She was eighteen today. If the trend of the previous seventeen disasters continued, this year's birth hours would be the worst ever.

Not that her luck had *always* resulted in calamity. Without it, she might never have met Karel.

"After all," he had said once, his grin a white gleam under his broad nose, "it's not every day that I ogle a pretty girl and have the sack of flour I'm carrying explode in my face."

Mardis smiled at the memory, which was almost enough to make her forget the taste of the stale kaf. She had stopped to help Karel up from the street, and then had gone home with him to verify to his parents that the loss of the flour had been unavoidable . . . without, of course, actually telling them that she was responsible.

That was the day she had discovered her talent for pastry baking, and Karel's parents had hired her, and—

Karel clinked his mug against hers, bringing her out of her reverie. "Here's to the woman with the most beautiful eyes, most delicious sweet rolls, and most rotten luck of anyone I've ever met."

"How would you like a pot of bad kaf dumped on your new pants?"

Karel waggled his eyebrows. "I can think of better fates for my pants, but I'll take whatever I can get."

Mardis rolled her eyes. "Why else would you stay near me today, knowing what's likely to happen?"

He shrugged. "If you didn't want me around, the time to say so was three years ago. Trusting me with your secret was part of what made me love you, you know."

"I was trying to warn you away, stupid. I thought that anyone a year older than me had to be smart, but I was obviously wrong."

Karel's eyes became uncharacteristically serious, and Mardis was afraid that she'd gone too far.

He seemed about to speak again when the innkeeper came back inside, the recaptured pig struggling in his arms.

"Would master and mistress care for breakfast?" the innkeeper asked, grunting as the pig kicked him in the throat.

Mardis saw the mischievous sparkle come back into Karel's eyes, and was glad. For a moment, he had looked like someone else.

"A little bacon might be nice," Karel said.

Mardis stifled a giggle.

The innkeeper didn't seem to catch the joke. "I'll see if we've any left," he said, and disappeared into the kitchen with the pig flailing vigorously.

Mardis and Karel looked at each other for a few seconds before letting out the laughter they'd been holding. The drunk by the hearth jerked awake, then swore and put his head down on his table again.

When Karel stopped laughing, Mardis saw that his eyes had become serious again.

"There's something we need to talk about," he said.

Mardis shifted on the rough chair. *So he knows. But how? I'm not even sure myself yet.*

"Listen, Karel," she began, almost whispering, "I should've told you—"

Karel covered his ears. "I've got to get through this all at once, Mardie," he said, "or I might not be able to get started again. Whatever you have to say can wait a bit, can't it?"

She nodded, and he lowered his hands.

Then he reached into his brown baker's smock and withdrew a slim silver bracelet. Taking Mardis's right hand in his left, he pushed the metal circle onto her wrist.

"It almost fits," he said, sounding nervous.

Mardis stared down at the bracelet—which was *not* what she'd been expecting—and marveled at the intricacy of its engraved loops and crisscrosses.

"This must've cost five or six levars," she said, thinking aloud.

Karel shrugged again. "I've been saving. Mother and Father are paying good wages."

"Not to me, they aren't."

"Ah, well, you're not family yet."

Mardis eyed Karel skeptically. "'Yet'?"

Karel looked exasperated. "Rikiki's nuts, Mardie! This is a family custom, like the birthday breakfast. We present a gift when offering marriage. I've heard Mother tell you so a hundred times. She had you marked as her daughter-in-law before *I* did."

Mardis touched the bracelet with the fingers of her left hand. The metal felt cool and elegant.

"If I refuse you," she said, "can I keep it anyway?"

Karel lunged in a mock attempt to grab it back.

Mardis leaned out of his reach and put her hands behind her head, gripping two of her four dark braids as if they were handles.

"Well, if that's the case," she said, feigning disinterest, "I'll force myself to go through with it."

"You're accepting me?"

"I just said so, didn't I?"

Karel put his hands behind his head, mocking her, and grinned. "Hah! It only cost *three* levars."

"I'm only worth two," Mardis said. "So there."

She felt better than she had on any other birthday. There was no need to risk spoiling it by telling Karel her news.

Not right away, at least.

Later, after breakfast had been served, Mardis realized that Karel would probably take what she had to tell him far better than her mother would take their betrothal.

"To say that Mother's going to be disappointed," she mused, chewing on a slice of gristly bacon, "is like comparing the Great War with Saltigos to a kitten-fight."

Karel shrugged a third time. "Rashell's in a state of *perpetual* disappointment," he said. "You could be marrying a margrave, and she'd find something about him that wasn't to her liking. So the fact that she doesn't like *me* isn't going to trouble my sleep."

Mardis made a face. "It's not you she doesn't like. It's that I'm not fulfilling her dream of having a wealthy wizard for a daughter. She's been pestering me to invest my luck for the past seven years."

Karel snorted. "You can't eat luck."

Mardis swallowed the bacon and pushed her plate away. "Or this stuff, either," she said. "But you don't need to convince me. I'd make a rotten magician, if for no other reason than that the only lessons I've had have been from that fool Thardik. Mother can't accept that, though, and I've run out of ways of telling her. All she knows is that she paid Thardik good money to magically prolong my birth hours, and that I'm ungrateful."

Karel wiped his hands on his smock. "Why should you be anything else? Thirteen hours is nothing to do somersaults over."

"Well, it beats the seven hours you've got."

"It does, does it?" Karel waved his hand in a gesture that took in the entire room. "If Rashell did you such a great favor, why are we celebrating your birthday in this bull-wallow?"

Mardis began to feel angry. She was of the firm opinion that her mother was a dunderhead, but she didn't appreciate it when Karel made it clear that he agreed with her.

"Maybe I just haven't been trying hard enough," she said. "Maybe I could still become a wizard if I wanted to."

Karel reached to the table behind him and brought back a

yellowish candle in a tin cup. "All right, Mardis the Magician," he said, setting the candle in the center of their table. "Rashell's forced you to take lessons for how many years? Eleven? Twelve?"

Mardis began to wish that she hadn't indulged the automatic urge to defend her own flesh and blood. "Fourteen," she said unhappily. "Since I was four."

"My mistake. All right, then—fourteen years of study, and now here you are in the second of your thirteen birth hours. A perfect opportunity to find out whether Thardik's taught you well."

Mardis sighed for the second time that morning. "Stop it, Karel. I don't want to be a wizard. I want to be a good, honest baker married to a slightly less good, slightly less honest baker. I don't want to play this game."

"But I do, Mardie," Karel said. "I don't want to wake up someday and find myself alone because you're chasing a dream I interrupted. So if your dream is magic, we'd better find out." He pointed at the candle. "Light it."

She shook her head. "You know what'll happen."

"No, I don't, and neither do you. Light it."

Mardis gave up and began to stare at the blackened wick. Maybe she did want to be a wizard, at that. Maybe her mother wasn't completely foolish. Maybe . . .

A huge spike of orange flame blasted from the fireplace and set the drunk's table ablaze. The scruffy man leaped up and ran out of the inn screaming, his smoldering coat leaving wisps of smoke behind to mark his path.

Mardis cringed. "A baker," she whispered as the innkeeper scurried from the kitchen and began beating at the flames with a greasy apron. "I want to be a baker."

Karel, looking shaken, took a few coppers from his smock and dropped them beside his plate to pay for their meal. "I'm glad," he said, standing. "Shall we go see whether we've any work waiting for us today? It's too warm in here."

They were only a few doors away from the bakery when Mardis saw her mother and the wizard Thardik approaching from the opposite direction at a fast waddle.

"Wonderful," she muttered. "Close enough to smell the dough rising, and now this."

Karel grasped her elbow. "Maybe we can run inside before they get their hooks into you."

They almost made it. Rashell reached the doorway two steps ahead of them and blocked it with her short, substantial frame.

"What do you think you're doing, child?" she demanded.

"I'm going to work, Mother," Mardis said, thinking that it must be the ten-thousandth time she'd said the words.

"On a Luckday? Don't this pup's parents believe in resting their slaves at the end of the week?"

Mardis glanced sidelong at Karel. "Well, 'pup'?"

"Woof," Karel replied.

Rashell scowled. "You're both terribly funny. Now, as you can see, Mardis, Thardik has returned from visiting his family in Cabri, and I've persuaded him to give you a lesson. I'll not have you wasting the opportunity."

Thardik, a blotchy-faced man with feathery tufts of white hair sticking up at random over his scalp, cleared his throat nervously. "Well, um, actually," he said, "a lesson wasn't exactly why I c-came looking for Mardis today."

Rashell turned her face toward the sky and clapped her hands to her temples. "Oh, gods, I knew it. My ungrateful daughter has finally alienated her only teacher, her only champion. What did I *ever* do to deserve this?"

Mardis felt her abdominal muscles contracting into a familiar knot. Sometimes her mother made her so angry that she wanted to burst . . .

Across the street, a cartload of early apples exploded, shooting geysers of pulp into the air. The vendor pushing the cart stopped short and gaped.

"You're letting her get to you," Karel whispered.

Mardis winced as a blob of applesauce landed on the back of her hand.

"You know what you did, Mother," she said angrily, shaking her hand to dislodge the blob. "You hired Thardik to prolong my birth hours—an act no *respectable* wizard would have even considered. And every birthday, this sort of thing"—she gestured at the mess across the street—"is the result."

Rashell brought her eyes down and stared at her daughter in horror. "Think before you talk!" she said hoarsely, jerking her head in Karel's direction.

"Mother, Karel's known my birth hours since we first met," Mardis said. "My birth luck is *why* we met."

Rashell took a step forward and grasped Mardis's shoulders. "What's wrong with you, child? A wizard never, *never* lets anyone know her birth hours!"

Thardik coughed. "Um, that's t-true, you know. . ."

"Well, I'm not a wizard," Mardis said, shaking herself free of her mother's grasp.

"Through no fault of mine!" Rashell cried to the sky.

The bakery door opened, and Karel's broad-shouldered father, Delfor, peered out warily.

"I *thought* I heard someone," he said when he saw Rashell.

"Nobody out here but us pups," Karel said. "Arf."

Delfor shrugged, looking much like his son. "Well, whatever you are, come get to work on a batch of crisp-buns. The Nins are having a reception this evening, and their regular baker's on holiday. If we do well, we may have our pick of wealthy clients. Mardis, I'd like you to make twelve dozen of those Zhir-style sweet rolls you're so good at."

Rashell looked up at Delfor with an expression of righteous indignation. "If you want Zhir rolls, baker, go hire a Zhir to make them. My daughter's Liavekan, and an apprentice wizard." She looked down at Mardis's baggy white Zhir pants, which matched Karel's. "Even if she does insist on dressing like a Gold Harbor prostitute."

Delfor raised an eyebrow. "Mardis is a good woman, son," he said to Karel in a low voice, "but are you sure you want this granddaughter of the Demon Camel for a mother-in-law?"

Rashell's face grew so red that Mardis was afraid the corpulent woman might suffer the same fate as the apples.

Stepping forward, she grasped her mother's arm and dragged her away from the doorway before Rashell could do more than sputter a few unintelligible curses.

"All right, Mother, all right," Mardis said in as soothing a voice as she could manage. "I'll come with you and take a lesson. For a few hours, anyway." She began pulling Rashell down the street toward their home, with Thardik hurrying on ahead.

"What about the sweet rolls?" Delfor asked.

"I'll only need three hours from dough to glazing," Mardis answered over her shoulder, "so I should return in time. If I don't, Karel can do a passable job."

"Considering what day this is," Karel called, "that might be a better idea anyway."

"Why?" Delfor asked. "What day is it?"

Mardis waved her right arm over her head. "Our betrothal day!"

She was brought to a halt as her mother became a dead weight.

Mardis rolled her eyes. "Help me carry her, Thardik. Make yourself useful."

The wizard waddled back to take Rashell's left arm, and then he and Mardis lugged the moaning woman down the street.

The gods only know how she'll react when I tell her I'm preg-nant, too, Mardis thought, and then remembered that she didn't yet know how Karel would react to that, either.

Mardis felt as though she'd been carrying her mother for a year by the time they reached Rashell's four-room house on Bregas Street. It wouldn't have been so bad if Rashell had made up her mind to either awaken or stay unconscious, but she had recovered and fainted, recovered and fainted, all the way home. With each recovery, she had given Mardis a pained look before collapsing again.

Rashell stood on her own as soon as they entered the house, which gave Thardik the opportunity to crumple into a sturdy wooden chair. His face had turned scarlet during the journey, and Mardis found herself thinking that if anyone were likely to *really* faint, it would be the overweight, puffing wizard.

"I am dizzy with grief," Rashell said dramatically, staggering across the room to the low couch that was her usual refuge during attacks of emotional turbulence.

Mardis leaned against a wall. "It's getting old, Mother," she said. "If I so much as suggest that I might someday move out and do what I like, you have a sudden illness. You might have sense enough not to do it on my birthday, though—if my wild luck made it real, a healer might not be able to help you."

"As if you would care!" Rashell wailed, sinking down onto the couch. "Besides, I'll never have need of a healer as long as Thardik is my friend."

Thardik, mopping his forehead with a shirtsleeve, wheezed and said, "M-my thanks for your confidence, mistress. May your judgment always be as sound as g-good wood."

"Hah!" Mardis said, trying to sound like Karel.

Thardik's chair crumbled to dust, and the wizard hit the floor with a loud thump.

"There was no need for that, child!" Rashell said. "You apolo-gize immediately, and then produce the coppers to replace that chair, which I've had since before you were born!"

Mardis spread her hands. "Do you think I did that on purpose?"

"You've studied under Thardik for fourteen years. It's well

within your skills to do such a thing during your birth hours."

Mardis let her hands drop. "You can't let yourself believe there's something wrong with me, can you? After all, then you'd have to consider the possibility that it was Thardik who did this to me in the first place."

Rashell raised herself on her elbows and glared. "What you're saying is that *I* did something wrong, when all I wanted was to fulfill your poor dead father's dream of siring a wizard. But do you care about honoring his memory? No!"

"I never even *knew* him!" Mardis shouted. "And he's not dead at all, or at least he wasn't when I was born—and even if he was, he didn't have any dreams for me! Everyone at the docks says he sailed to Gold Harbor with a dancer from Cheeky's as soon as he found out I was on the way!"

She hated herself as soon as the words were out of her mouth, because she saw the slackening in Rashell's face that she had only seen twice before. The histrionics were over for now, because real pain had set in.

"Oh, all right," Mardis said, trying to suppress her guilt and keep her voice defiant. "Let's go to my room and get it over with, wizard. I've got baking to do today."

Grunting with the effort, Thardik stood and began limping across the room.

Mardis turned to accompany him, but couldn't avoid seeing the wetness glistening in Rashell's eyes. For a moment, she almost decided that she would try to become a wizard after all, if only so that she would never have to see it again.

"So, great low-budget magician," Mardis said, sitting on her straw pallet. "Shall I levitate a vase and risk flinging the house into the sky? Or shall I learn a spell to boil water, and cook the city in the Cat River?"

Thardik sat down heavily on his accustomed stool in the far corner. "Um, no, my dear, I'm afraid I . . . I have no n-new spells to teach you."

Mardis crossed her arms tightly. "I wondered when we'd reach the limit of your knowledge, and I can't say I'm sorry it's happened. My birth luck is wilder every year, and I've always thought your labor-prolonging spell had something to do with it."

The wizard cleared his throat. "Well, I, um . . . you're r-right. I think."

Mardis glared at the pudgy man. "Are you *admitting* that you did this to me?"

Thardik was watching her as if afraid she would spring across the room and strangle him. "I've only just f-found out," he said. "Um, that is, I think I have . . ."

Mardis could feel her temper beginning to surge, and she struggled to suppress it. "How is it," she said slowly, "that a wizard would perform a spell without knowing all its effects?"

Thardik stood and shuffled to the room's only window, where he opened the sash and stood gazing out at the little yard.

"Let me t-tell the whole story before you judge me," he said, sounding incredibly old. "Wizards are scarce in the village of Cabri, so there isn't much chance for a young person to study the magical arts—particularly if he is of a poor family. So when a wizard from Liavek moved onto our street and offered to teach me . . . as you can imagine, I saw it as my way to a better life."

"No, I can't imagine," Mardis snapped. "There are many ways to improve oneself without resorting to magic. Better ways, in fact. As Karel says, 'You can't eat luck.'"

Thardik's shoulders sagged. "If you had been born into m-my family, you might have felt otherwise. In any case, I leaped at the chance to study under Allarin. I didn't think to question why he had left Liavek, or why he had moved to a village as poor as Cabri. I was too blinded by the promise of magic to see the oddness of such things."

The wizard paused for a long moment, and Mardis hugged herself still more tightly with her crossed arms. She didn't like hearing Thardik speak so softly and sadly, just barely stumbling over his words. It bothered her almost as much as her mother's tears had.

"I studied under Allarin for eleven years," Thardik continued, "b-buying a lesson whenever I had saved enough money from other labors. Then, having invested my luck, I came to Liavek to make my fortune . . . which turned out to be a few coppers a week for doing small tricks in the Levar's Park. What the pot-boil simmered down to, you see, was that I simply wasn't a very good wizard."

"I know," Mardis said, and was surprised at the sympathy in her own voice.

Thardik didn't seem to hear. "I lived that way for many years," he said. "Then, through a chance conversation with a midwife, I learned that Allarin had taught me a spell no other wizard in Liavek offered: a spell to l-lengthen labor, thus endowing a child with extra birth hours. I had never considered the spell a good one, because it prolonged pain; but the midwife assured me that some women's hopes for their children outweighed their dislike of pain."

"I know," Mardis said again.

This time the wizard turned toward her, though his eyes wouldn't meet hers. "Nevertheless," he said, "I found only one woman who was willing to risk it. Her husband had deserted her, but had left t-ten levars on the kitchen table. I took eight of them to perform the ritual.

"The task was difficult, and the results were not what I had hoped. Your birth hours were only slightly lengthened, and what luck you do have is, as you put it, wild. So I haven't performed the spell since."

"You're not telling me anything I haven't figured out for myself," Mardis said, trying to keep the bitterness out of her voice.

Thardik managed to look her in the eyes now. "Perhaps not," he said. "But there is one aspect of the spell that you d-do not yet know. While in Cabri last month, I learned that Allarin, who died twenty years ago, performed the spell as his final magical act. Apparently he was more skilled than I, for the labor lasted thirty hours."

At this, Mardis found herself intensely interested. She leaned forward, uncrossing her arms, and asked, "Did the child become a wizard, then?"

Thardik shook his head. "No. Her luck was wild, like yours, so rather than attempt investiture, she became a sailor. Then she married a shipmate and decided that she wanted a child of her own, and..."

The wizard's voice died to a whisper, and he turned to gaze out the window again.

Mardis stood and grasped his shoulder, digging her fingers into the flesh. "And *what?*" she demanded.

Thardik trembled and bowed his head. "The b-baby would have been fine, except... the labor lasted two days, and was violent... and she was at sea, and her shipmates couldn't help her..."

Mardis, feeling a chill spreading through her body, already knew what he was trying to say.

"They both died, didn't they?" she said. "That spell killed them."

"N-n-no," Thardik said, stuttering badly. "N-not the spell itself. It l-lasted only the length of the labor for which it was cast. But it d-did something to the sailor's luck, imprinted itself s-somehow, and when she herself became p-pregnant...

"P-perhaps as her contractions began, her baby's initial birth luck was channeled through her, which made it wild as well. Or p-perhaps Allarin's original spell actually caused a physical change in her body. It's impossible to know exactly what happened, because the true n-nature of luck itself is still a mystery. We know of certain ways t-to use it, but no one can say why those ways work and others fail—or what the effects of altering it m-might be. So all I'm sure of is that the sailor's l-labor was much too long, and that by the time her ship reached port, it was too late."

Thardik stopped talking, but his tremulous breathing continued to rasp at Mardis's skull.

She wanted to look at the problem as if it were only the sailor's, but a tiny, throbbing knot below her breastbone told her that she couldn't do that. She let her hand fall from Thardik's shoulder, then shuffled backward until she felt the edge of the pallet against the backs of her knees.

"Maybe the sailor's trouble had nothing to do with the spell," she whispered as she sank to the pallet. "Maybe she and her baby only died because she went into labor at sea, with no midwife or healer to help."

Thardik put his elbows on the windowsill and held his head in his hands. "I would l-like to believe so. But when I arrived b-back in Liavek yesterday, I searched for answers and found an old volume, a *Treatise on Undesirable Magical Practices,* in the Market. It discusses the spell, warning that 'p-pain and calamity will follow through generations' if anyone meddles with the nature of birth luck. It also says that using medicinal herbs, physical strength, or force of will to prolong labor will not have this effect, for such efforts d-don't alter the essential nature of a child's luck. A spell, however, is another matter."

Mardis felt pinpricks on her arms and legs, as if thousands of invisible insects were stinging her.

"I'm even worse off than I've always thought, aren't I?" she murmured.

The wizard, still holding his head in his hands, said, "Forgive me. I didn't know Allarin was an outcast. I didn't know that one of the spells he taught me had been forbidden. I just d-didn't know."

He gave a shuddering sigh and finally raised his head. "I d-don't expect you to accept that as an excuse. But whatever you may think of me, and whatever I m-may think of myself, neither of us can undo what has been done. You must live with your luck

once every year . . . and you must never become pregnant."

The prickling sensation became an intense burning all over Mardis's skin, and her throat and chest began to tighten so that she could hardly breathe. It felt as though the walls and ceiling were about to close in and crush her.

She jumped up from the pallet, shoving Thardik away from the window. She had to get outside before the house obeyed her thoughts. She had to breathe under the open sky, to get away—

Thardik grasped her right leg as she began to scramble over the sill. "Child, what are you—"

Mardis kicked back and struck the wizard in the chest. Then, with a convulsive effort, she wrenched herself outside and fell to the pebbled yard. The distance from the sill to the ground was less than Mardis's height, but the shock of the fall was enough to banish the tightness in her chest. As she stood, she was breathing more easily.

Looking back through the open window, she saw Thardik sitting on her pallet, clutching his chest with one hand and pulling at his sparse tufts of hair with the other.

"Are you hurt?" she asked.

The wizard looked out at her with eyes like an old, tired dog's. "N-not as m-much as I deserve," he said. "I know you will never be able to forgive m-me."

Mardis forced a smile. "You old goat-bag," she said with false cheerfulness. "I forgive you right now. I have to go to work, and my sweet rolls would sour if I made them while holding a grudge."

Thardik bowed slightly from his sitting position. "You are too k-kind, dear child."

Mardis lowered her eyes so that he couldn't see the look that had to be in them. "There's one thing I'm curious about, though," she said, trying to sound casual. "Did the book say anything about how the sailor might have avoided her 'pain and calamity'? What happened wasn't her fault. It doesn't seem fair."

Thardik remained silent for a long moment, and when he spoke, he didn't stutter. "Magic is under no compulsion to be fair . . . but the book does refer to one unlikely solution. If the sailor had invested her luck and then destroyed her luck piece, or if she had been sure to be more than three paces away from it when she went into labor, then the taint of her wild luck could not have been in her—and it was that taint, or perhaps the portion her infant inherited, that affected her labor. But investiture would have been impossible because of her luck's wildness. The ritual requires intense concentration, with no distractions."

Which meant that Mardis had no chance. When she concentrated during her birth hours, all she *got* were distractions. Exploding apples; bursts of fire; disintegrating chairs. If she attempted investiture, she would try to focus her will on her luck piece only to have it split into a hundred fragments.

She and her baby were going to die.

"Mother will be disappointed," she said.

Then she was running toward the bakery. Karel would be there, and she needed to see his grin more than she had ever needed to see anything in her life.

As she ran, she saw that the left leg of her new pants had torn in her fall. Blood welled from the bare knee, but she felt no pain, and didn't stop to see how badly she was hurt.

Ultimately, she knew, it didn't matter.

A crockful of lard melted and spilled onto the floor of the bakery kitchen as Mardis entered, and Delfor immediately slipped on it, releasing the sheet of unbaked buns he was carrying. Circles of dough smacked against the ceiling, a wall, and a hot oven just before the metal sheet clanged against the floor.

"How in the name of all the Levar's servants did *that* happen?" Delfor shouted. He looked up as if expecting an answer, and saw Mardis. "Good," he said, calming. "You can take over the sweet rolls while Karel cleans up this mess."

Karel, who had been working at a table across the room, came over and gave Mardis a kiss on the cheek.

"If anything else happens," he murmured, "you'd better leave. Father's so excited about the money we'll take in tonight that he's making enough mistakes without your luck to help him. Say, what happened to your knee?"

"It's nothing," Mardis said numbly, wishing that she hadn't come, but not knowing what else she could have done.

Karel grabbed a mop and smeared the spilled lard around the floor while his father gathered up the scraps of scattered dough. The two of them looked so normal, so perfectly like themselves, that Mardis wanted to cry.

Karel's mother, Brenn, came up and hugged Mardis with long, floury arms.

"So you said yes," Brenn said happily. "It's a good thing; Karel needs someone to serve as brains. If he starts acting like too much of a child, you let me know, and I'll bash his teeth in. Let's see the bracelet."

Mardis lifted her right arm, and the band of silver gleamed in the sunlight that shone in through the kitchen's three big windows.

"It's lovely," Brenn said. "But then, it should be. I hinted at which one to buy." She leaned closer and whispered into Mardis's ear. "I made sure he saved enough money for when the baby comes."

Mardis's muscles tightened, and a jar of sesame seeds shattered.

"All right, then!" Delfor shouted. "They'll be crisp-buns with sesame seeds!"

Brenn didn't even glance back at the noise. "Oh, don't worry," she whispered. "Karel doesn't know, so you can tell him when you like. But I've suspected for two weeks now, because you've been pausing in your work and touching your belly for no apparent reason. You *will* tell him before you begin to show, won't you?"

Mardis swallowed hard, then took a deep breath. The kitchen's air was sticky and sweet. "I'll tell him," she said. *But how can I, knowing what's going to happen?* "I'll tell him when I'm sure."

Brenn thumped her on the back. "Oh, you're sure. I can hear the terror in your voice. But there's nothing to be afraid of, dear. It hurts a little, but it's worth it. Even a knothead child can be a joy. Now, you'd better get to the sweet rolls, and I'd better check my loaves."

She gave Mardis another hug and then strode toward the ovens, being careful to avoid the lard-slick that Karel couldn't seem to get cleaned up.

Mardis walked across the room to the table where Karel had been mixing a batch of dough. If she could stay busy, she wouldn't have to think; and if she didn't have to think, maybe the problem would go away.

The sweet roll dough was too stiff. Karel always used too much flour and not enough milk or cinnamon. That was the trouble with some cooks; they followed recipes slavishly, without using any instinct for what was right, or what might be better.

That's the trouble with some wizards, too, a small voice inside her said.

As she thinned and reworked the dough that Karel had nearly ruined, the voice suggested that Thardik was only partially to blame for her dilemma. There was her mother, of course—but Rashell had only behaved in response to her father's desertion.

So it's really my father's fault . . . and Allarin's fault . . . and Thardik's fault . . .

She was cutting the resurrected dough into strips now, slashing at it as if it were the fools who were responsible for her impending death.

. . . and Karel's fault for getting me pregnant . . . and maybe even Delfor's fault for fathering Karel!

Two yelps behind her made Mardis turn her head, and she saw that Karel and Delfor were hanging upside-down in midair. As she watched, Karel's mop jumped up and slapped both of them in the face.

"What in the name of luck—" Brenn cried.

As if that were a magical signal, Karel, Delfor, and the mop all fell to the floor.

"That does it!" Delfor yelled, sitting up and rubbing his head. "Some wizard's got it in for the Nins' party and is taking it out on us! I don't care how much money's at stake—we're not filling the order!"

Karel gave Mardis a wry look.

She felt awful. If either one of them had been hurt—

"It wasn't a wizard," she blurted. "It's my birthday, and—sometimes things happen. I'm sorry."

Grimacing, Delfor picked himself up from the floor. "Sometimes things *happen?*" he cried. "By the gods, that's putting it mildly!" His expression softened as his eyes met Mardis's. "Well, you can't help it if that's your luck. But if we're to have any hope of getting this order ready in time, we can't have any more interruptions. You'd better take the rest of the day off. I'll pay you full wages."

Mardis gestured at the strips of sweet-roll dough. "But I haven't made the rolls, or mixed the glaze, or—"

Brenn put an arm around Mardis's shoulders and steered her toward the door. "We can take care of all that, dear. Karel, come kiss your wife-to-be and hurry up about it."

Karel left the kitchen with Mardis. As soon as they were alone in the front room, surrounded by display racks and trays, he held her close.

He smelled like lard, and Mardis pulled away.

Karel frowned. "Your birthday 'accidents' aren't really random, you know. That sack of flour exploded when we met because you didn't like me staring at you, and the fire this morning was the result of trying to light a candle. So I can't help wondering about what just happened to me and Father, and whether you're really sorry."

Mardis turned and headed for the main door.

"Are you angry with me about something?" Karel asked.

She paused with her hand on the latch. She wanted to turn back and look at Karel's face, but was afraid of what might happen if she did.

"Yes," she said. "And no."

Then the latch clicked open and she was running away again.

It was only many blocks later, when she was drenched with sweat and panting with effort, that it occurred to her: The fact that she had no idea of how to save herself and her child didn't mean that *nobody* did.

Foolish men had gotten her into trouble. Maybe a wise one could get her out of it.

Maybe she could find The Magician.

She forced her body into a sprint, dodging the few pedestrians and carts that had ventured out into the afternoon heat. The silver bracelet was brilliant on her wrist.

If he can help me, she thought, *I'll give him all I have—my money, my clothes, my hair, anything—except the bracelet. Even if it means my life, I won't give him that.*

It was a rash promise, but it made her feel better than she had thought possible. Despite her burning lungs, she began running faster than she had ever run in her life.

A pair of camels bolted away from their owner and charged down the street ahead of her, their ropes and halters flaming to powder.

Wizard's Row was gone. Mardis searched for it from every intersecting street and alley for three hours, retracing her steps over and over again, to no avail.

She wanted to curse, but was afraid to anger the gods, who already seemed to hate her. She had lived all eighteen years of her life only one street away from the Row, and had walked along it countless times—but now, the one time that she *had* to find it, it had vanished.

She supposed that she shouldn't be surprised. After all, it was a sunny Luckday, and every magician on Wizard's Row was probably on holiday. Besides, she was still in her birth hours, and there was no reason to expect her bad luck to improve just because she needed it to.

Finally, exhausted, she found herself behind her own home, and went inside to rest for a moment. Neither her mother nor Thardik was in the house, which was just as well as far as she was concerned. She went directly to her room and flopped down on the pallet.

Fatigue was good for her, she decided after a few minutes. It was hard to be panicky when she was dead tired. It was even hard to be simply afraid.

Fear had a nasty way of muddling up her mind so that she couldn't think clearly. She didn't like it, and she resolved that, no matter what her fate, she wouldn't be afraid anymore. It was pointless.

My baby and I are going to die, she thought, *and there's nothing I can do about it.*

Unless . . .

It was ridiculous even to think of it. There were only four hours left, which surely wasn't enough time for anyone, no matter how skilled, to perform investiture—let alone someone who couldn't concentrate for ten seconds without the walls crumbling around her.

And if she were to fail, as she surely would, she would sicken and die.

"I'm going to die in about eight months anyway," she said aloud. Her voice sounded weird and hollow, as if she were trapped in an empty cistern.

Still, those would be eight months that she would be able to spend with Karel.

But what kind of happiness could they have when her growing belly would serve as a constant reminder of the death that awaited her and her child?

On the other hand, perhaps they wouldn't die at all. Perhaps the labor would be normal, and . . .

"Perhaps" wasn't good enough.

She had to invest her luck.

Not here, though. Rashell might come home at any moment and ruin whatever minuscule chance Mardis might have at success.

Don't try to fool yourself, she thought as she hurried out of the house. *You aren't afraid that Mother will interrupt the ritual, because you know you've no chance anyway.*

You just don't want her to see you fail.

There was only one other place where she would feel comfortable enough to do what she had to do. Delfor, Brenn, and Karel

would be away at the Nin reception by now. She ran toward
Merchant's Way, and the bakery. Her legs felt as though they
were about to snap.

Windows shattered as she passed.

The door swung open before she could take her key from her
smock, and she had to blink the sweat out of her eyes to see who
was standing in the doorway.

It was Thardik. Rashell stood just behind him. Mardis had run
all the way from home to avoid them, and here they were.

*Well, I should at least say goodbye to my own mother,
shouldn't I?* she thought, and wished that there were some way to
see Karel again, too.

Thardik pulled her inside. "Where have you b-been?" he said,
his voice quaking. "We were s-sure you would be here, and
d-didn't know where to look when you weren't."

Rashell shoved the wizard aside and threw her arms around
Mardis. "My child, my child!" she cried. "Why didn't you tell
me you were going to have a baby? Why didn't you *tell* me?"

Mardis felt as though she were in the gray jelly of a dream.
"How did you know?" she heard herself ask.

Thardik shut the door. "I g-guessed it this afternoon," he said.
"After you asked m-me what the sailor could have done to save
herself, I saw that there could b-be only one reason why you
would seem so anxious to know."

Rashell was sobbing into Mardis's shoulder, mixing her tears
with her daughter's sweat. "I didn't know the spell would do this!
I didn't!"

Mardis stroked Rashell's tangled, graying hair, and felt a
strange calmness filling her with each stroke. "No one did," she
said. "But now that we do, I have to try to invest my luck."

Rashell shook her head violently. "There isn't time! I don't
even *want* you to anymore!"

Thardik stepped close. "She d-doesn't have a choice. Otherwise she won't l-live to see her next birthday."

"I only have a little over three hours," Mardis said, gently
pushing her mother away. "And I have to be alone, because—"
She paused and looked around the room, frowning. All of the
racks and trays had been pushed to the walls, and a circle was
chalked in the center of the floor. "I see you've tried to save me
some time."

Thardik shook his head. "That's for m-me."

Mardis stared at him. "Why?"

Thardik tugged at a tuft of white hair. "After you left, I t-told Rashell what I'd told you, and what I suspected, and r-realized you would have to invest your luck today. We tried to f-find Wizard's Row then, to ask for help, but it was g-gone. The only thing I could think of then was to buy a small bag of g-gold dust—"

"It cost us everything!" Rashell wailed. "All the money I had in the house, plus all that Thardik had saved from teaching!"

Thardik tugged harder at the tuft. "For all I know, any p-powder might work, but the spell as Allarin taught it to me specifies g-gold, sprinkled in a circle around the entire building."

Mardis tensed. "What spell?"

"One to suppress all m-magical activity inside the encircled building—*except* investiture—for as long as I c-can chant the ritual."

Mardis's calmness returned. "You intend to tame my wild luck, then," she said.

"But we sprinkled the dust before we realized you weren't already inside!" Rashell cried. "It's probably blown away by now!"

Thardik stepped into the chalked circle and sat down cross-legged, his joints popping. "M-maybe *believing* it's there will be enough."

Mardis looked at him with new respect. "Are you sure you're up to it?"

The wizard rubbed his knees. "I'll m-manage, as long as Rashell p-prevents anyone from coming in and b-breaking my concentration."

Rashell strode to the main door and stood before it with her fists knotted at her sides. "Let somebody try!"

Smiling, Mardis went to her mother and kissed her, then walked toward the kitchen door. Enough time had been wasted.

"One m-more thing," Thardik said. "You should know that the suppression spell won't help you w-with investiture itself."

"I understand," Mardis said, and paused at the kitchen door to turn and press her palms to her forehead. "My thanks."

Then she entered the kitchen. She no longer blamed anyone else for where the gods had brought her. If she died now, Rashell and Thardik would know that she bore them no grudge . . . and, in fact, loved them.

Karel, though, was another matter. She hadn't parted well

from him that afternoon, and if her investiture failed, he might go through the rest of his life wondering whether she had died angry with him.

For him, then—and for herself, and the baby—she had to succeed.

She went to the center of the room, where the lard had spilled earlier, and rehearsed the ritual in her mind. That was one thing, at least, that Thardik had taught her well.

And if Thardik succeeded, she thought, *Rikiki knows I should be able to. As long as I don't think about the time.*

Faintly, she heard the old man's voice begin to drone in the other room.

The kitchen was filled with soft, reddish light as the low sun shone through the windows, and Mardis's damp skin tingled with warmth. The brick ovens surrounded her like miniature castles, and the leftover smell of freshly baked bread filled her like a breathable liquid. The table beside her held a plate of three slightly overdone sweet rolls, and she took one of the soft, sticky pastries in her hand.

She brought it to her lips and touched her tongue to the glaze, then smiled. Karel had done a good, if not inspired, job.

At that thought, her gaze moved to the bracelet he had given her. It was solid, strong, and brilliant . . . perfect in its simple elegance.

She had forgotten to ask Thardik for his chalk, so she made a large circle on the stone floor with sifted flour.

Then she sat down inside the circle, concentrated on her chosen luck piece, and began to chant.

She had three hours. It couldn't be enough.

"Hah!" Mardis said contemptuously, and concentrated harder.

Her luck raged about her like a demon, snarling and spitting venom.

"You think you have me trapped in two circles," it hissed. "The one outside, keeping me from my fun; the one inside, holding me close. But I will fly away as soon as your hours have ended, and they are ending soon!"

Salt stung her eyes, but she couldn't let herself blink. She must keep gazing at her luck piece, must keep her parched tongue chanting the ritual.

"You have scorned me for the last time, weakling Mardis!" her luck cried. "You have made your circle too wide, and your

ally is too weak, and when I fly away, I shall be gone forever, and you will die!"

She felt a sudden dizziness, and her luck's wildness surged. Thardik was tiring, his spell slipping. Her luck cackled gleefully.

Her lips cracked, and she tasted blood.

But still she chanted, reaching, reaching, reaching to grasp the creature by the tail.

"Die!" her luck shrieked as she caught it. "You may think you have me, but I have fooled you again! I have shattered glass in your path, spilled lard on your head, rubbed flour into your bleeding knee! And just as you think I am trapped, I shall spring away and open the ovens, and the fires will leap out to boil your eyes from your head! What will happen to your baby then, when you're blind and in your grave?"

She tightened her grip, and still the thing tried to squirm away. If she were to falter for even an instant, it would be gone, and there would be no time left to catch it again.

She began to pull it down.

"Mardis!" her luck squealed. "It is not you who rule me! It is I who rule you! I am your master! Not your mother, your wizard, your husband, your child!"

"No," she said, her chanting finished at last. "I'm my own master. Always have been."

"You will die!" her luck screamed.

"Oh, shut up," she said.

And pushed it into the waiting vessel.

Her nose stinging with the stink of burnt flour, Mardis staggered out of the kitchen into the bakery's front room. The sun had set, and for a moment she thought she was alone in the dimness.

Then the faces of Rashell and Thardik came swimming toward her, and she tried to smile. She doubted that it looked right; she was probably incapable of any expression other than a grimace.

Rashell put her arms around her. "Child, you look terrible," she whispered, and squeezed.

Thardik was standing unsteadily in his circle, staring at them with big, watery eyes. "W-well?" he asked, wheezing. He looked almost as drained as Mardis felt.

Mardis tried to smile again. "It's all right," she said, and was surprised at how hoarse she was. "My luck's invested, and my baby's safe. Or will be as long as Mother doesn't break my ribs."

Rashell's grip loosened slightly. "I was so worried," she said, "and now I'm so proud. I can hardly believe you're finally a wizard."

Mardis disengaged herself from the older woman's embrace. "I've invested my luck, but only because I had to. The fact that I managed to do it--barely, and with help—doesn't make me a wizard." She managed a small chuckle. "Even you said that I look terrible. That's how well magic and I get along."

Mardis could feel her mother's relief turn to disappointment. "But you've a talent for it," Rashell said. "Only a natural-born wizard could manage to invest her luck in so short a time, under such pressure."

Mardis's chuckle became an outright laugh. "Desperation isn't talent. I actually started to see my luck as a monster, as an enemy. I don't think that's the right attitude for a wizard. If not for Thardik—"

Thardik coughed and stepped out of the circle. "Don't s-sell yourself short. M-my spell only subdued the distractions a l-little. Your mother's right: Only someone g-gifted could do what you've done. It would be a shame to throw that gift away."

Mardis rolled her eyes. She was too tired to argue.

"I'll make you a pact, Mother," she said. "Give me until my next birthday. If by then you can't agree that Mardis the Baker is as successful and respected as the average wizard, then I'll give magic a try. One year. That isn't too much to ask, is it?"

Rashell looked as though it *was* too much to ask, but Thardik said, "She needs to learn for herself what's b-best for her, Rashell. Besides, a truly great wizard, as she will be, is worth waiting f-for."

Rashell still didn't look as though she agreed, but she assented. "Very well," she said. "After all, it's your life, and you nearly lost it. I won't complain that you're wasting your skills . . . for one year."

Mardis leaned against a display rack and relaxed. She didn't believe the promise, but at least the battle was over for now.

"C-come then, wizard Mardis," Thardik said gallantly. "Allow m-me to escort you and your lovely mother back to your home. You are weary, and your b-bed awaits."

Mardis shook her head, and one of her braids stuck to her damp cheek. "I want to wait for Karel, to tell him the news."

"I'm sure he will be p-proud," Thardik said, taking Rashell's arm.

"The pup had *better* be proud," Rashell said as she went out to the street.

When they were gone, Mardis reentered the kitchen to find a candle. She was a little irritated that Thardik and Rashell had assumed the "news" she had for Karel was that she had invested her luck—as if that were the only thing in her life of any importance.

But then, they had probably also assumed that Karel was already aware of the news that had made the investiture necessary in the first place.

As Mardis had hoped, Brenn and Delfor went home to bed as soon as the reception was over, leaving Karel to cart the used serving trays and utensils to the bakery. And, as she had also hoped, he saw the light of her candle and came into the kitchen to investigate.

She was sitting on the floor, in her flour circle, with a sweet roll on a plate in front of her. She held up her bracelet as he entered.

"Do you want it back?" she asked.

Karel looked startled. "Rikiki's nuts, why would I?"

"Two reasons," Mardis said. "One, I've wanted a baby for a long time, so I've managed to get pregnant. I did it on purpose, without consulting you."

Karel sat down in the circle with her and grinned his usual grin. "I helped a little bit, didn't I?"

"You don't mind?"

"I mind if I didn't help."

"You helped."

His grin broadened. "Then I'm pleased as a boiling pot. Besides, I suspected as much. I figured you'd tell me when you got good and ready." He picked up the sweet roll and took a bite. "So, what other reason might I have for dumping you? Besides the fact that you ate two of the rolls I was saving for myself?"

Mardis put the bracelet back on her wrist. "They were delicious," she said.

Karel wrinkled his nose. "This one tastes a little funny. Now, come on—what makes you think I'd ever let you out of our deal?" He took a huge bite of sweet roll.

"Oh, it's not important now," Mardis said. "I just invested my luck, that's all." She scooted closer and put her arms around him.

Karel made a sour face. "You can't eat luck," he said around a last mouthful.

Mardis began to giggle, and then to laugh, and she couldn't stop, not even when Karel finished the pastry and began kissing her.

It *did* taste a little funny, at that.

Cenedwine Brocade

by Caroline Stevermer

JUST INSIDE THE door of Cheeky's, that Old Town bistro most famed for high prices, low entertainment, and scornful service, Dala stopped to blink. There was actually a waiter at his elbow, and a blandly polite waiter at that.

"Your table is ready, sir," the waiter murmured. Dala followed him in startled silence to a corner table, discreetly placed to afford a view of the dance floor and the other tables from a decent amount of shadow. His drink was already there, a double Dragonsmoke. Dala looked from the glass to the waiter suspiciously.

"Your host will join you in a moment," said the waiter, and held the chair.

Dala knew his place and took it. The Dragonsmoke was sublime, floating softly from his palate to his brain without the need to swallow. He swallowed anyway and drew in a reverent breath.

"You are prompt," said a deep voice at his elbow. "That's good."

He glanced up. A man in an ill-fitting mask of black velvet leaned over him, hooded cloak pulled close. "I came because Cheeky asked me to," Dala replied.

The man in the mask took the chair beside Dala, folded his hands on the table. "Much depends upon your cooperation."

Dala regarded the man's hands with displeasure. He disliked plump hands. "You want an appraisal."

"I do. A party of young people have reserved that large table. I will depart before they arrive. This mask is merely a precaution. I am interested in a red-haired woman, rather sickly looking, wearing a brocade robe. I wish your appraisal of that robe. I will meet you later this evening at the Two-Copper Bazaar, where I will give you your fee in return for your professional opinion of the robe."

Dala put his glass down. "An appraisal of a robe? While someone is wearing it? In a bar? Sorry." He pushed back his chair. Before he rose, the man's pudgy hand was palm down on

132

the table. When it moved, Dala saw a five-levar piece beside his glass. Dala picked his glass up.

"I want your opinion," said the man.

"Everyone has opinions," said Dala. "If that's what you pay for them, how can you afford to buy me a drink?"

"Just your opinion," replied the man, "nothing more. No curiosity, no interference, no rivalry."

Dala eyed the coin. It seemed to him the dim lamplight glinted along the coin's five-sided edge with particular beauty. "An opinion," he said. He put his palm down on the coin. "I'll meet you tomorrow and tell you what it is."

"At the Two-Copper Bazaar," said the man.

"By the snail booth," said Dala.

The masked man nodded and rose.

"It's still a lot of money for an opinion," said Dala.

The man paused to adjust his mask. "I think of it as an investment."

Ambrej Nallaneen swallowed and stared into her winecup with mingled astonishment and dismay. She'd expected the wine to be bad. It lay on her tongue with a metallic flavor at once singed and sour. What surprised her was the texture of the dregs. Evidently the management at Cheeky's topped off every cup of their best wine with a spoonful of sand. Aul Nin and his cousins did not seem to notice. They were drinking fast enough, she reflected, the sand probably didn't have the chance to settle. With a stifled sigh she put her cup down and turned her attention to the cat-dancer.

"Years of practice," Aul Nin said, leaning close to be heard over the din their party was making.

Ambrej nodded. "Looks dangerous," she offered, after a thoughtful pause. Aul leaned back in his seat looking pleased. He took a large sip of his wine. Ambrej averted her eyes.

It was well past midnight and the crowd at Cheeky's was a piquant mix of the sinister and the drunk. Everyone seemed to be having a wonderful time eyeing one another and glowering. Someone at her table had sent an order of drinks across the room to a pair of ruffians in red leather. The ruffians were conferring, evidently deciding whether or not to be insulted. The cat-dancer began his final series of swings, making a grand circuit of the tables closest to the dance floor. The merrymakers at Ambrej's table began to throw coppers.

"There's a heart ready to be broken," said Aul Nin.

Ambrej followed the direction of his gaze. At a table in the
corner sat a sallow young man in black, his eyes fixed on Ambrej. The moment her eyes met his, he looked away. Ambrej
frowned.

She had noticed him on their arrival. He had been the only
man in the place staring at an empty table—the table reserved for
her hosts. If he had a particular interest in her, she reflected, it
might be that her trip to trade Dragonsmoke for wine was finally
beginning to develop into something more promising. It had not
been easy to find a reason to leave Cenedwine. To prolong her
absence, she had accepted the wine merchant's invitation to attend his daughter's wedding this morning. The evening's amusement was one of the last she would be invited to share with Evor
Nin's son Aul and his cousins. Her time was limited. If the sallow man's interest was in her, she must make the most of her
chance. That his motives were mercenary, Ambrej could not
doubt. Even in Cenedwine her looks, red-haired and rangy, were
barely passable. Here in Liavek she seemed positively whey-
faced. More than once since her arrival she had heard the hiss
"ghost!" as she was mistaken for a Farlander.

"A skinny fellow," said Ambrej. Aul Nin simpered. Aul was
by no means a skinny fellow. Nor were his cousins, who com-
prised the rest of the party. Though well dressed, his cousins
were not well behaved, a fact that seemed finally to decide the
ruffians in red leather. They rose and crossed the dance floor
while the cat-dancer's boy was still scrambling after coppers.

"You with the feet," said the taller of the ruffians, "up."

Aul looked surprised, but not surprised enough to obey. The
ruffian reached down for him. A cousin intervened. With no apparent effort, the ruffian picked up the cousin and put him down
in the center of the table.

Ambrej got to her feet and took a step away from the fracas.

"Let's leave." The voice at her elbow made her jump. She
looked down at a small man with a scarred face and a very bored
expression.

"Nagual, I gave you the night off," said Ambrej.

Nagual shrugged. "Nothing else to do. Anyway, I know
Cheeky."

"I don't believe that for a second," Ambrej replied. "Where
have you been lurking?"

"Back there," said Nagual, with a vague gesture in the direction of the kitchens. "Let's get out of here."

"I don't want to leave until my hosts do," replied Ambrej. She glanced in the direction of the fracas. It had spread. She took a cautious step away, putting her back to the wall. "Come to think of it, there is something you can do."

Nagual looked a little less bored.

"The sallow man in black," said Ambrej, still watching the fracas carefully, "the one looking at me."

"The one looking at the robe," corrected Nagual, "I see him."

"When he leaves, follow him for me. I want to know what he does."

Nagual made no reply and when she glanced back at him, he was gone.

A cousin hurtled out of the melee, tossed by a ruffian. Ambrej glanced up in time to see him coming directly at her. She stood still. The cousin hit the wall an arm's length to her left. At the precise instant he did, six winecups at the nearest table shattered in unison. As he slid to the floor, Ambrej crossed her arms.

At the back of the room a door slammed.

Throughout the room heads lifted, customers strained to see. Late-night scuffles were part of the ambience at Cheeky's. An appearance by the owner herself was an unexpected honor.

"You inflict quite enough damage with the customary methods," said Cheeky, a slender young woman with a sleek mane of black hair, "no need to resort to magic."

Aul Nin propped himself on his elbows and found the breath to say, "Madam, this is an honor—my father will be delighted to hear you received my cousins and me personally."

Cheeky made a careless gesture with her left hand. Her attendants began to move methodically through the tangle of bodies now motionless on the dance floor. "Your joy at your sister's marriage is understandable. To bestow her disagreeable nature on some other family excuses much merriment. But I cannot abide disorder—and what I cannot abide, not even Evor Nin can afford."

Ambrej took a quick step away from her wall and busied herself brushing at Aul's shoulders.

Cheeky shook her head. "Comical," she said, her eyes on Ambrej's bland expression. "Get out before anything else breaks."

Aul and his cousins moved uncertainly toward the door. In the shadowed corners of the room, onlookers went back to their pursuits. The cat-dancer's rebeck player took up his instrument again and a tentative buzz of melody rose like a questing curl of smoke. As Ambrej walked, her hand under Aul's pudgy elbow, the lamplight picked out the untarnished silver in the brocade robe she wore. Quick and bright, she accompanied their halting progress out into the night. As they departed, the sallow man rose and followed.

Cheeky pushed a lock of black hair behind her ear and spoke to one of her attendants. "Have Rel total the damages and take the bill to Evor Nin's house before breakfast. With a house full of guests, he may neglect his son's affairs."

But Evor Nin was not at home at breakfast time the next morning. He was standing, heavily cloaked and masked, beside the snail stall in the Two-Copper Bazaar.

Dala bought a handful of snails and leaned against the stall while he worked at the first with a pin.

"Care for one?" he inquired politely. "No, I suppose not with gloves on."

Nin shook his head impatiently. "Well?"

"Ah, yes," Dala nodded, "my opinion." He pulled the snail from its shell, fragrant with garlic butter. He popped the snail in his mouth and went to work on the next.

Nin snorted his impatience and dropped a gleaming five-sided coin into the dust. Swift as a sand-wasp, Dala's booted foot shot out and came down firmly on the coin.

"Very well," said Dala. "In my opinion, the robe is a magical artifact."

Nin nodded. "Go on."

"You've heard of Cenedwine, perhaps?" Dala continued, handling the long pin with careless skill. "Ask anyone who's traveled the Silverspine. Worthless sort of place, good for oats and flax and a little barley. They distill Dragonsmoke and brew the worst beer ever tasted. They weave, sometimes brocade picked out with silver that they scrape from their mountains, and they conduct family fights. That robe is made in a Cenedwine pattern. The silver in the brocade is untarnished. A good guess is someone bound magic in it before it was old enough for the threads to tarnish. It was made for someone other than that woman—someone about five inches taller and far wider across the shoulders. The clans of Cenedwine are prone to heirlooms. Perhaps it is a relic of her house."

Nin nodded again. "Go on."

Dala lifted his dark brows. "I followed the party from Cheeky's—"

"I am not concerned with the woman or her companions," said Nin. "The robe, if you please."

Dala shrugged. "I've heard stories—those family fights they

conduct with such enthusiasm. But they're old stories. One of the family chiefs, Gavren Col, became a sort of sage. He wouldn't fight anymore but his clan listened to him anyway. He put a stop to the worst of the troubles. The tale is he invested his magic in his robe so he would be invulnerable to attack. That was why he was held to be a wise man, for no one could kill him. He lived a hundred years, the stories say. Only a tale. Probably." He extracted the last snail from its shell and licked his fingers.

"Gavren Col's robe"—Nin broke off to glance distractedly around the marketplace—"was silver brocade?"

"I have no idea," said Dala, "but since you pay so well for my opinion, I'll admit I think so. I saw something odd last night. And so did Cheeky."

Nin nodded until his jowls shook in the shadow of his hood. "Excellent. Just as I wished. You are worth your fee." He drew the cloak closer and set out through the market.

Dala bent down to retrieve his five-levar piece. "Anytime," he said as he straightened. "Tell your friends."

In the house of Nin the wine merchant, Ambrej Nallaneen pushed the last date across her plate with the tip of her finger. "Yes, Nagual," she said patiently, "very well done. But why did you follow Nin back here from the market? Dala might sell his opinions elsewhere."

"Do you care if he does?" asked Nagual. "I came back because I'm tired."

"I suppose not," said Ambrej, "as long as Nin has his guess confirmed."

"He skipped through the marketplace like a man with a good idea," said Nagual.

"Good," said Ambrej. She took a bite of the date. "I hope it is the same idea I have."

That night, midway through the meal, Evor Nin planted his elbows on the table and rested his chin in his hands. "Tell me," he asked his guest, plump hands on plump cheeks, "how is it that you travel with a bodyguard?"

Ambrej Nallaneen raked a glance at the faces ranged around the table, all relatives of Nin's. No one looked interested. She did not turn to look at Nagual, who stood behind her chair, as was his custom.

"He has been with me many years," she replied.

"Yet you wear a robe which spares you all such concerns,"

Nin said. "What need have you for such as he?"

"We all form habits," she replied. "The robe was a legacy. Nagual, I earned. And I've had him far longer than I've had the robe."

"You carry no weapon, even so far from Cenedwine," said Nin. "The robe makes such things unnecessary, I expect."

"Nagual makes it unnecessary," said Ambrej. "Your hospitality makes it unnecessary."

"May I abuse the honor of a host sufficiently to make an offer of a purely commercial nature? I would like to purchase that robe. You may suggest whatever price seems good to you." Nin leaned back in his chair and tented his fingertips.

"I regret I must refuse," Ambrej replied. "I may not sell this robe."

Nin dismissed her words with a brush of his hand. "We will reach terms satisfactory to both of us."

At Nin's gesture, a man in livery bearing a loaded crossbow entered the room and took his place beside Nin's chair.

"Nagual," said Ambrej, "I left a box in my room. I need it. You know the one, I think. The lid is lacquered red."

"I know the one," said Nagual, irritably.

"Fetch it."

Nagual uttered an aggrieved sigh and left the room.

"I understand your desire to authenticate the robe before you propose your terms," said Ambrej, "but must your entire family be present?"

"I think so," Nin replied. "After all, I want them to understand what the robe can mean. Any investment so substantial ought to be completely understood by all parties involved. And now, Madam Nallaneen, you will not take it amiss, I trust, if I tell my man to fire?"

"Would it stop you if I did?" asked Ambrej.

"No," said Nin. "Fire."

The crossbow bolt buried itself in the center of the table. The fruit bowl at Ambrej's elbow shattered, scattering grapes and figs across the table and onto the floor.

Aul Nin overset his chair as he sprang to his feet. "Father— he fired at your guest!"

"Be quiet," said Evor Nin. "She was never in the slightest danger."

From her place at the table Ambrej could reach the bolt. She gripped it and pulled with vigor. It did not budge.

Nagual returned, put a red lacquered box down in front of

Ambrej, and took up his station again.

"I think the demonstration is over, Nagual," said Ambrej. "Thank you." She opened the box and shook out its contents, five massy bits of metal, irregularly shaped, each as big as the last joint of a man's thumb. "Have you ever played knucklebones, Evor Nin? It is a very pleasant game. Universally popular. Even in Cenedwine." As she spoke she scooped up the pieces of metal, rattled them in her palm. With a deft snap of her wrist, she tossed the pieces, caught them on the back of her hand, tossed them again and allowed them to fall back into her palm.

Aul put his face in his hands. His father regarded him with impatience. "Our guest is not disturbed, why are you? She understands business. Now, pay attention. You might learn something."

"You understand the purpose of the robe," said Ambrej, shaking the knucklebones gently as she watched Evor Nin, "but perhaps you have some questions regarding its use. It is magic, as you guessed."

"Gavren Col invested his magic in it," replied Evor Nin. "He lived a hundred years, protected by it."

"Yet he died, in the end," said Ambrej. "Even the robe's owner must. It wouldn't grant you life eternal."

"It would grant me peace of mind," Nin replied, "physical protection from all possible threats."

"Well, all physical threats," said Ambrej. She lifted her free hand and let the silver brocade move and gleam in the light from the sconces ranged about the room. "It makes physical injury impossible. But there are laws even magic must obey. If a crossbow is fired at me, though physical injury is impossible, still the crossbow fires. And if it is impossible for the bolt to strike me, it is certain it must strike something. The robe is not very predictable. It can be inconvenient to people standing near."

"Hence your henchman's errand," said Nin. "Considerate of you."

"I am a responsible employer," replied Ambrej. "Now tell me. How will you compel me to give up the robe? You cannot threaten my life."

"Certainly not," Evor Nin agreed. "May I threaten your henchman?"

"I am merely Nagual's employer," Ambrej replied, "not his keeper. The robe's price goes beyond his life, I'm afraid."

"Then let me phrase this as gracefully as I may," Nin answered. "You have been an excellent guest. You have partaken of our entertainments with well-feigned enthusiasm. Allow me to invite you to extend your stay. I would like to arrange that your visit last—indefinitely."

"I decline," said Ambrej. She rattled the knucklebones. "Let me clarify the situation. The robe may not be sold. Cannot be mislaid, nor traded nor stolen—cannot, in short, fall into the hands of anyone but its owner. And even then it cannot be set aside. If I took off the robe, your henchman still could not put a bolt into me. Gavren Col was my grandfather. The robe was bequeathed to me—I cannot simply give it to you."

Nin's eyes narrowed. "Your counteroffer, then?"

"I propose to venture the robe as a gambling stake," Ambrej said, and rattled her knucklebones suggestively. "All due respect to your hospitality, but I do not mean to live and die in Liavek. I have family obligations."

"I agree," Evor Nin said. "We wager your robe against my hospitality."

Ambrej nodded and made her first throw.

The pair of them played turn about, Ambrej leading, Nin replying. Singles, doubles, triples, scatters, all went by in a desultory flash, then the variations began: Clicks, No Clicks, Over the Mountain, Rock the Cradle.

The rest of the diners continued their meal but they chewed with an absent air, eyes fixed on the flash of fingers, the sweep of swift hands.

Aul choked on an olive when one of Ambrej's pieces bounced into the gravy at Cross the Bridge. Ambrej played on, her concentration unimpaired. Evor Nin had difficulty at Hammer and Anvil, hitting his spoon as well as his target piece, but completed the turn in a rattle of scattered cutlery.

Ambrej pressed on, past Cat's Eye and Camels, then, at Thread the Needle, her hand grazed the soup tureen and her piece struck another with a flat, final click. Ambrej froze. The entire room was suddenly still.

"The end of an era," Nagual said.

Ambrej folded her arms and watched while Evor Nin gathered the pieces up into his pudgy hand. With great deliberation he made the first toss, then put up the throw stone. Serpent quick, he seized his piece and slid it through the others, snatched his hand back and caught the throw stone.

"I believe that," said Nin, setting the throw stone down with precision, "is that."

Ambrej rose and unclasped the robe, folded it, and laid it on the seat of her chair. In her linen trousers and jerkin, she seemed a little shorter suddenly, and a shimmer of red faded from her hair as she stood there. "The robe is yours," she said, and began sorting slowly through the disordered tableware to return the knucklebones to their lacquered box.

Nin pushed himself up from his place and moved around the corner of the table to reach for the robe. "A moment," he said, as he shook out the shining brocade and put his arms through the sleeves, "lest any of my family foolishly think the robe still protects you—"

He gestured.

The guard in livery put a second bolt to his bow and began to wind the crank that drew it taut.

Ambrej opened her mouth to protest. Before she could frame words, Nagual hit her hard between the shoulder blades. She went down. Nagual reached back, as though to scratch his neck, then brought his arm toward Nin in a wicked arc. Metal glimpsed the light, then Nagual dropped, too.

The wooden table vibrated as Nagual's knife struck beside the first crossbow bolt. With a chiming sound the silver soup tureen split in half and rolled off the table. The second bolt pierced the back of Ambrej's chair.

"That settles that," muttered Nagual, and began to make his way to the door on knees and elbows, a perilous journey through a maze of table legs, mashed fruit, and trickling soup.

"I think Nagual has made it very plain that the robe protects you now," Ambrej said, back on her feet. She picked up her lacquered box. "I have things I need to do in Cenedwine—and it's so hard to get people to listen if they think they'll be killed if they stand beside you."

The guard had brought out a third bolt and was cranking his bow industriously.

"Makes it hard to keep dependable staff, too," Ambrej said, and threw the gravy boat at Nin. It hit the guard instead and his bowstring snapped. The guard swore and nursed bruised knuckles.

Ambrej kept a wary eye on him as she worked Nagual's knife free of the table. "If you should try to gamble the robe away," she told Nin, "I recommend some game of skill. In games of pure chance the robe seems to, er, intervene."

The knife came free just as Nagual reached the door.

"And now," said Ambrej, following him, "we really must be going."

• • •

Next day, in the Two-Copper Bazaar, Dala found Evor Nin waiting beside the snail stall.

"They bought a camel and made straight for the Drinker's Gate," said Dala, when he had his fee. "There will be no catching them if they head for the foothills."

Evor Nin made a noise in the back of his throat. "I know they bought a camel. Her servant paid the trader half a silver soup tureen for it."

"It was a sound animal. I'm afraid she is beyond your reach. Still, it is a nice piece of brocade."

"Is it?" asked Nin bleakly. "My daughters laugh at it, my son is afraid of it, and every servant in the household has given notice as the result of a rumor it will kill them to stand near it."

"I hear it caused a little trouble in Cenedwine, too," said Dala, and started eating snails.

A Hypothetical Lizard

by Alan Moore

HALF HER FACE was porcelain.

Seated upon her balcony, absently chewing the anemic blue flowers she had plucked from her window garden, Som-Som regarded the courtyard of the House Without Clocks. Unadorned and circular, it lay beneath her like a shadowy and stagnant well. The black flagstones, polished to an impassive luster by the passage of many feet, looked more like still water than stone when viewed from above. The cracks and fissures that might have spoiled the effect were visible only where veins of moss followed their winding seams through the otherwise featureless jet. It could as easily have been a delicate lattice of pond scum that would shatter and disperse with the first splash, the first ripple . . .

When Som-Som was five her mother had noticed the aching beauty prefigured in her infant face and had brought the uncomprehending child through the yammering maze of nighttime Liavek until they reached the pastel house with its round black courtyard. Yielding to the tug of her mother's hand, Som-Som dragged across the midnight slabs with the echo of her shuffling footsteps whispering back to her from the high, curved wall that bounded all but a quarter of the enclosure. The concave facade of the House Without Clocks itself completed the circle, and into its broad arc were set seven doors, each of a different color. It was at the central door, the white one, that her mother knocked.

There was the sound of small and careful footsteps, followed by the brief muttering of a latch as the door was unlocked from the other side. It glided noiselessly open. Dressed all in white against the whiteness of the chambers beyond, a fifteen-year-old girl stared out into the dark at them, her eyes remote and unquestioning. The garment she wore was shaped to her body and colored like snow, with faint blue shadows pooling in its folds and creases. It covered her from head to toe, save for the openings that had been cut away to reveal her right breast, her left hand, and her impenetrable masklike face.

143

Staring up at the slim figure framed in its icy rectangle of light, Som-Som had at first assumed that the girl's visible flesh was reddened by the application of paint or powder. Looking closer, she realized with a thrill of fascination and horror that the skin was entirely covered by small yet legible words, tattooed in vivid crimson upon the smooth white canvas beneath. Finely worded sentences, ambiguous and suggestive, spiraled out from the maroon bud of her nipple. Verses of elegant and cryptic passion followed the orbit of her left eye before resolving themselves into a perfect metaphor beneath the shadow of her cheekbone. Her fingers dripped with poetry.

She looked first at Som-Som and then at her mother, and there was no judgment in her eyes. As if something had been agreed upon, she turned and walked with tiny, precise steps into the arctic dazzle of the House Without Clocks. After an instant, Som-Som and her mother followed, closing the white door behind them.

The girl (whose name, Som-Som later learned, was Book) led the two of them through spectrally perfumed corridors to a room that was at once gigantic and blinding. White light, refracted through lenses and faceted glassware, seemed to hang in the air like a ghostly cobweb, so that the shapes and forms within the room were softened. At the center of this foggy phosphorescence, a tall woman reclined upon polar furs, the cushions strewn about her feet embossed with intricate frost patterns. The glimmering blur of her surroundings erased the wrinkles from her skin and made her ageless, but when she spoke her voice was old. Her name was Ouish, and she was the mistress and proprietor of the House Without Clocks.

The conversation that passed between the two women was low and obscure, and Som-Som caught little of it. At one point, Mistress Ouish rose from her bed of white pelts and hobbled across to inspect the child. The old woman had taken Som-Som's face lightly between thumb and forefinger, turning the head in order to study the profile. Her touch was like crepe, but surprisingly warm in a room that gleamed with such unearthly coldness. Evidently satisfied, she turned and nodded once to the girl called Book before returning to the embrace of her furs.

The tattooed servant left the room, returning some moments later bearing a small pouch of bleached leather. It jingled faintly as she walked. She handed it to Som-Som's mother, who looked frightened and uncertain. Its weight seemed to reassure her, and she did not resist or complain as Book took her lightly by the arm and guided her out of the white chamber. Long minutes passed before Som-Som realized that her mother was not coming back.

The first three years of her service at the House Without Clocks had been pleasant and undemanding. Nothing seemed to be expected of her save for the running of an occasional errand, or the proferring of some small assistance with the pinning of hair and the painting of faces. Those who served in the brothel were kind without patronage, and as the months passed, Som-Som had come to know all of them.

There was Khafi, a nineteen-year-old dislocationist who, lying upon his stomach, could curl his body backward until the buttocks were seated comfortably upon the top of his head while his face smiled out from between the ankles. There was Delice, a woman in middle age who used fourteen needles to provoke inconceivable pleasures and torments, all without leaving the faintest mark. Mopetel, suspending her own heartbeat and breath, could approximate a corpse-like state for more than two hours. Jazu had fine black hair growing all over his body and would walk upon all fours and only communicate in growls. And there was Rushushi, and Hata, and unblinking Loba Pak . . .

Living amidst this menagerie of exotics, where the singular was worn down by repeated contact until it became the commonplace, Som-Som was afforded a certain objectivity. Without discrimination or favor, she spent the best part of her days observing the animate rarities about her, wondering which of them provided a template for what she was to become. Eavesdropping upon Mistress Ouish and her closest associates, patiently decoding their under-language of pauses and accentuated syllables, Som-Som had determined that she was being preserved for something special. Special even amid the gallery of specialties that was the House Without Clocks. Would she be instructed in the art of driving men and women to ecstasy with the vibrations of her voice, like Hata? Would Mopetel's talent of impermanent death become hers? Smiling as she accepted the candied fruits and marzipans offered by her indulgent elders, she would study their faces and consider.

Upon her ninth birthday, Som-Som was escorted by Book to the dazzling sanctum of Mistress Ouish. Her parched smile disquieting with its uncharacteristic warmth, Mistress Ouish had dismissed Book and then patted the wintery hides beside her, gesturing for Som-Som to sit. With what looked like someone else's expression stitched across her face, the proprietor of the House Without Clocks informed Som-Som of what might be her unique position within that establishment.

If she wished, she would become a whore of sorcerers, exclusive to their use. Henceforth, only those cunning hands that sculpted fortune itself would have access to the warm slopes of her substance. She would come to understand the abstracted lusts of those that moved the secret levers of the world, and she would be happy in her service.

Kneeling at the very edge of the bed of silver fur, Som-Som had felt the world shudder to a standstill as the old woman's words rolled about inside her head, crashing together like huge glass planets.

Sorcerers?

Often, sent to fetch some minor philter or remedy for the older inhabitants of the House Without Clocks, Som-Som's errands had taken her to Wizard's Row. The street itself, shifting and inconstant, full of small movements at the periphery of the vision, presented no clear and consistent image that she could summon from her memory. Some of its denizens, however, were unforgettable. Their eyes. Their terrible, knowing eyes . . .

She pictured herself naked before a gaze that had known the depths of the oceans of chance in which people are but fishes, a gaze that saw the secret wave-patterns in those unfathomable tides of circumstance. In her stomach, something more ambiguous than either fear or exhilaration began to extend its tendrils. Somewhere far away, in a white room filled with obscuring brilliance, Mistress Ouish was detailing a list of those conditions that must be fulfilled before Som-Som could commence her new duties.

Firstly, it seemed that many who dealt in the manipulation of luck would themselves leave nothing to chance. Before such a sorcerer would enter fully into physical congress with another being, the inflexible observation of certain precautions was demanded. Foremost amongst these were those safeguards pertaining to secrecy. The ecstasies of wizards were events of awesome and terrifying moment, during which their power was at its most capricious, its least contained.

It was not unknown for various phenomena to manifest spontaneously, or for the name of a luck-invested object to be murmured at the moment of release. In the world of the magicians, such indiscretions could be of lethal consequence. The most innocent of boudoir confidences, if relayed to an enemy of sufficient ruthlessness, might yield a dreadful harvest for the incautious thaumaturge. Perhaps he would be plucked from the night by cold hands with unblinking yellow eyes set into their palms, or perhaps a sore upon his neck would blossom into purple, babyish lips, whispering delirious obscenities into his ear until all reason was driven from him.

The intangible continent of fortune was a territory steeped in hazard, and she who would be the whore of sorcerers must also undertake to be the bride of Silence.

To this end, Som-Som would be taken to a specific residence in Wizard's Row, an address remarkable in that it could only be located upon the third and fifth days of the week. Here, the child would be given a small pickled worm, ocher in color, the chewing of which would render her unconscious and insensitive to pain. As she slept, her skull would be carefully opened, revealing the grayish pink mansion of her soul to the fingers of one who abided in that place, a physiomancer of great renown. At this juncture, the Silencing would commence.

Connecting the brain's hemispheres there existed a single gristly thread, the thoroughfare by which the urgent neural messages of the preverbal and intuitive right lobe might pass to its more rational and active counterpart upon the left. In Som-Som, this delicate bridge would be destroyed, severed by a sharp knife so as to permit no further communication between the two halves of the child's psyche.

Following her recovery from this surgery, the girl would be granted a year in which to adjust to her new perceptions. She would learn to balance and to pick up objects without the benefit of stereoscopic sight or depth of vision. After many bouts of tearful and frustrating paralysis, during which she would merely stand and tremble, making poignant half-completed gestures while her body remained torn between conflicting urges, she would finally achieve some measure of coordination and restored grace. Certainly, her movements would always possess a slow and sightly staggered quality, but if directed properly there was no reason why this dreamlike effect should not in itself be erotically enhancing. At the end of her year of readjustment, Som-Som would have a cast taken of her face, after which she would be fitted with the Broken Mask.

The Broken Mask was not so much broken as sliced cleanly in two. Made of porcelain and covering the entire head, it would be precisely bisected with a small, silver chisel, starting at the nape of the neck, traversing the cold and hairless cranium, descending the ridge of the nose to divide the expressionless lips forever. The left side of the mask would be taken away and crushed to a fine talcum before being thrown to the winds.

Prior to the fitting of the Broken Mask, Som-Som's head would be completely shaven, the scalp afterward rubbed with the foul-smelling mauve juices of a berry known to destroy the follicles of the hair so that there could be no regrowth. This would at least partially ensure her comfort during the next fifteen years, in which time the mask was not to be removed unless the slowly changing shape of the skull made it uncomfortable. In this eventuality, the mask would be taken from her and recast.

Covering the right side of her head, the flawless topography of the Broken Mask would be uninterrupted by any aperture for hearing or vision. The porcelain eye was opaque and white and blind. The porcelain ear heard nothing. Concealed beneath this shell, their organic counterparts would be similarly disadvantaged. Som-Som would see nothing with her right eye, and would be deaf in her right ear. Only in the uncovered half of her face would the perceptions be unimpaired.

By some paradoxical mirror-fluke of nature, those sensory impressions gleaned from the apparatus of the body's left side would be conveyed to the brain's right hemisphere. And there, due to the severing of the neural causeway that had connected both lobes, the information would remain. It would never reach those centers of cerebral activity that govern speech and communication, for they were situated in the left brain, a land now irretrievably lost beyond the surgically created chasm. Her eye would see, but her lips would know nothing of it. Conversation that her ear might gather would forever go unrepeated by a tongue ignorant of words it should shape.

She would not be blinded, not exactly. Her hearing would remain, after a fashion, and she would even be able to speak. But she would be Silenced.

Within the flattering opalescence of her white chamber, Mistress Ouish concluded her descriptions of the honors which awaited the stunned nine-year-old. She rang the tiny china bell that signaled Book to the room, terminating the audience. Stumbling over feet made suddenly too large by loss of circulation, Som-Som allowed the tattooed servant to lead her into the startling mundane daylight.

Poised upon the threshold, Book had turned to the blinking child beside her and smiled. It wrinkled the words written upon her cheeks, rendering them briefly illegible, and it was not a cruel smile.

"When you are Silenced and can reveal their conclusions to no one, I shall permit you to read all of my stories."

Her voice was uneven of pitch, as if she had long been unpracticed in its application. Raising her ungloved and crimson-speckled hand she touched the calligraphy upon her forehead, and then, lowering it, lightly brushed the lyric spiral of her breast. Smiling once more, she turned and went inside the house, closing the white door behind her, an ambulatory pornography.

It was the first time that Som-Som had ever heard her speak.

The following day, Som-Som was escorted to an elusive residence where a man with a comb of white hair that had been varnished into a stiff dorsal fin running back across his skull gave her a tiny, brownish worm to chew. She noted that it was withered and ugly, but probably no more so than it had been in life. She placed it upon her tongue, because that was expected of her, and she began to chew.

She awoke as two separate people, unspeaking strangers who shared the same skin without collaboration or conference. She was conveyed back to the House Without Clocks in a small cart lined with cushions. She rattled through the arched entranceway and across the gargantuan inkblot of the courtyard, and all that had been promised eventually came to pass.

Twelve years ago.

Seated upon her balcony, her half-visible lips stained blue by the juices of the masticated blossoms, Som-Som regarded the courtyard of the House Without Clocks. Unrippled by the afternoon breeze, the black pond stared back at her. Here and there upon the impenetrably dark water, fallen leaves were floating, motionless scraps of sepia against the blackness.

Surely, if she were to topple forward with delicious slowness toward the midnight well beneath her, surely she would come to no harm? Dropping like a pebble, she would splash through the impassive jet of the surface, a tumbling commotion of silver in the cold, ebony waters surrounding her.

Up above, the ripples would race outward like pulses of agony throbbing from a wound. They would break in black, lapping wavelets against the courtyard walls of the House Without Clocks, and then the waters would once more become as still as stone.

Down below, kicking out with clean, unfaltering strokes, she would swim away beneath the ground, out below the curved walls of the House Without Clocks, out under the City of Luck itself and into those uncharted, solid oceans that lay beyond. Diving deep, she would glide among the glittering veins of ore,

through the buried and forgotten strata. Darting upward, she
would flicker and twist through the warm shallows of the topsoil,
surfacing occasionally to leap in a shimmering arc through the
sunlight, droplets of soil beading in the air about her. Resub-
merging, she would strike out for the cool solitude of the clay and
sandstone, far, far beneath her . . .

Someone walked across the surface of the black water,
wooden sandals scuffing audibly against its suddenly hardened
substance, crunching through leaves that were quite dry. Unable
to sustain itself before such contradictions, the illusion melted
and was immediately beyond recall.

One side of Som-Som's face clouded in annoyance at this
intrusion upon her reverie, half her brow clenching into a petulant
frown while the other half remained uncreased and indifferent.
Her single visible eye, one from a pair of gems made more exquisite by the loss of its twin, glared down at the visitor passing
beneath her. Unnoticed upon her balcony, she studied the inter-
loper, struck suddenly by some quirk of gait or posture that
seemed familiar. Her left eye squinted slightly as she strained for
a better view, deforming the symmetry of her bisected face into a
mirthless wink.

The figure was slender and of medium height, swathed in
gorgeous bandages of red silk from crown to ankle so that only
the face, hands, and feet were left unwrapped. The delicate line
of the shoulder and arm seemed unmistakably female, but there
remained something masculine about the manner in which the
torso joined with the narrow, angular hips. Walking unhurriedly
across the courtyard, it paused before the pale yellow door that
lay at the rightmost extremity of the House Without Clocks.
There the figure hesitated, turning to survey the courtyard and
giving Som-Som her first clear glimpse of a painted face at once
strikingly alien and instantly recognizable.

The visitor's name was Rawra Chin, and She was a man.

During the years of her service within that drifting environ-
ment, her perceptions of the world limited both by her condition
and by the virtual confinement that was its effective result, Som-
Som had nonetheless contrived to reach a plateau of understanding, an internal vantage point overlooking the vast sphere of
human activity from which the Broken Mask had excluded her.
This perspective afforded her certain insights that were at once
acute and peculiar.

She understood, for example, that quite apart from being a
limitless ocean of fortune, the world was also a churning mael-

strom of sex. Establishments such as the House Without Clocks were islands within that current, where people were washed ashore by the tides of need and loneliness. Some would remain there forever, lodged upon the high-tide line. Most would be sucked away when the ebb of the waters came. Of these fragments reclaimed by the ocean, few would ever again reach land, and if they did it would not be in those latitudes.

Rawra Chin, it seemed, was an exception.

Som-Som remembered Her as a wide-boned and awkward boy of fourteen whose employment at the House Without Clocks had commenced when Som-Som was already in the fifth year of her service. Despite the flatness and breadth of Her face and the clumsiness of Her deportment, Rawra Chin had even then possessed some rare and indefinable essence of personality, animating the uneasy frame of the adolescent boy and lending Her a beauty that was disturbing in its effect.

Mistress Ouish, long skilled in detecting that pearl of the remarkable that is concealed within the oyster of the ordinary, had noticed Rawra Chin's distinct yet elusive charm when she decided to employ the youth. So, too, did the clientele of the House Without Clocks, with numerous merchants, fishermen, and soldiers proclaiming Her their especial favorite, asking after Her whenever they should chance to visit that establishment.

The common bond shared by all those who admired this charisma within Rawra Chin was that none of them could precisely identify it. It remained a mystery, concealed somewhere within the oddly disparate components of Her broad and starkly decorated face, hovering at some imaginary point of focus between Her hasty pencil-line of a mouth and Her widely-spaced eyes, overwhelmingly tangible, eternally ungraspable.

Som-Som, one of two people within the House who came to know Rawra Chin closely, had always been inclined to the belief that Her charms originated in the emotional depths of the nervous and hesitant lad Herself, rather than in some fluke of physique or physiognomy.

There was a restless melancholy that seemed to inform everything from the boy's stance to the way She brushed Her hair, long and soft, so golden it was almost white. There was also the occasional icicle glitter of fear in those eyes that had too great a distance between them for prettiness but just enough for beauty. These disparate threads of personality were woven into a design that gave the overwhelming impression of vulnerability. As to the precise nature of that vulnerability, Som-Som had no more idea than the most brief and casual of Rawra Chin's adoring customers.

Often, She had come to sit and drink tea with Som-Som upon her balcony to pass the time between engagements, a diversion popular with many of the inhabitants of the House Without Clocks. Due to the singularity of Som-Som's impairment, they could reveal their longings or resentments without fear. Rawra Chin had visited her often during the long, dull mornings, seeming to delight in the thin floral infusions and the opportunity for one-sided conversation.

It seemed to Som-Som that she had contributed little to these often intimate discussions, having no confidences that she was able to share. Since the side of her brain that governed speech had known nothing but darkness and silence for several years, the best that it could offer conversationally was a string of inappropriate and disconnected fragments, half-remembered impressions and anecdotes relating to the world that Som-Som had known before the Silencing.

Confusing matters further, Som-Som's verbal half could not hear and was forced to make interjections without knowing whether the other person had finished speaking. Thus, while Rawra Chin would be engaged in a vivid description of what She hoped to do once Her employment at the House Without Clocks was ended, Som-Som would startle Her by saying, "I remember that my mother was an unlikable woman who rushed everywhere to get her life over with the sooner," or something equally obscure, followed by a long silence during which she would stare politely at Rawra Chin and sip her floral infusion through the left corner of the mouth.

Though at first disoriented by these random pronunciations, Rawra Chin grew accustomed to them, waiting until Som-Som had finished her non sequitur before resuming. The continuing presence of these bizarre ejaculations did not seem to lessen Rawra Chin's enjoyment of their conversational interludes. Som-Som supposed that her real contribution to these talks had been her simple presence.

Her function was that of a receptacle for the aspirations and anxieties of others, although this fact never became oppressive. She enjoyed the exclusiveness of these glimpses into the way that ordinary life was conducted. The fact that people would relate to her things that went unvoiced even to their lovers gave Som-Som a perspective upon human nature more true and comprehensive than that enjoyed by many sages and philosophers.

This gave her a measure of personal power, and she took pride in her ability to unravel the many and varied personas that presented themselves to her, laying bare the essential characteristics that were concealed beneath their facades of affectation and self-deception. Rawra Chin had been Som-Som's only failure. Like everyone else, she had been unable to give a name to that rare and precious element upon which the bewilderingly attractive adolescent boy had founded Her identity.

On the other hand, Som-Som had been able to construct a relatively complete picture of Rawra Chin's aversions and ambitions, however superficial these appeared without an understanding of Her more fundamental motivations.

Som-Som knew, for example, that Rawra Chin did not intend to make a lifetime's vocation of prostitution. While she had heard similar avowals from most of the occupants of the House Without Clocks, Som-Som sensed a determination in Rawra Chin that was iron-hard, setting Her appraisal of the future apart from the rather sad and much-thumbed fantasies of Her fellows.

Rawra Chin, She often assured Som-Som, would one day be a great performer who would travel the globe, transporting Her art to the masses by way of a celebrated company of dramaticians such as the Torn Stocking Troupe, or Dimuk Paparian's Mnemonic Players. The less aesthetically demanding acts of pantomime that She was called upon to perform each day behind the pale yellow door of the House Without Clocks were merely a clumsy rehearsal for the innumerable thespian triumphs waiting somewhere in Her future.

The pale yellow door gave access to that part of the house that was given over to romantic pursuits of a more theatrical nature, its four floors each housing a single specialist in the erotic arts, linked by a polished wooden staircase that zigzagged up outside the house from courtyard level toward the gray slate incline of the roof.

In the topmost chamber lived Mopetel, the corpse-mime. Beneath her lived Loba Pak, whose flesh had a freakish consistency that enabled her to adjust her features into the semblance of almost any woman between the ages of fourteen and seventy. Rawra Chin lived upon the second floor, acting out mundane and unimaginative roles for Her eager male clientele but compensating for this with Her charisma. On the first floor, immediately beyond the pale yellow door, there lived a brilliant and savagely passionate male actor named Foral Yatt whose talent had been subverted into a plaything by the many female customers who enjoyed his company, and with whom Rawra Chin had become amorously entangled.

Foral Yatt was the subject of a great number of those balcony conversations, conducted through the motionless fog of warm vapor that hung above their tea bowls, with Rawra Chin talking animatedly upon one side while Som-Som sat listening upon the other, breaking her silence intermittently to remark that she remembered the color of a quilt her grandmother had made for her when she was an infant, or that a brother whose name she could no longer call to mind had once knocked over the pot-boil and badly scalded his legs.

The heart of Rawra Chin's anguish concerning Foral Yatt seemed to lie in Her knowledge that if She were to achieve Her ambition, She must leave the intense and darkly attractive young actor while She progressed to greater things. She confessed to Som-Som that though in private She and Foral Yatt would make their plans as if they would quit the House Without Clocks together, pursing parallel careers in the outside world, Rawra Chin knew that this was a fiction.

Despite the fact that Foral Yatt's raw talent dwarfed Her own to insignificance, he possessed neither the indefinable appeal of Rawra Chin or the remorseless drive that would propel him through the pale yellow door and into the pitch and swell of that better life that lay beyond. Adding masochistically to Her anguish, the wide-faced boy also felt troubled by the fact that She was using Her nearness to Foral Yatt to study the finer points of his superior craft, storing each nuance of characterization, each breathtakingly understated gesture, until that point in Her career-to-come when She might use them.

Having purged Herself for the moment of Her moral burden, Rawra Chin would sit and stare miserably at Som-Som, waiting for some acknowledgment of Her dilemma. Long moments would pass, measured in whatever units were appropriate within the House Without Clocks, until finally Som-Som would smile and say, "It was raining on the afternoon that I almost choked on a pebble," or "Her name was either Mur or Mar, and I think that she was my sister," after which Rawra Chin would finish Her tea and leave, feeling obscurely contented.

Despite Her tormented writhings, Rawra Chin had eventually summoned sufficient strength of character or sufficient callousness to inform Foral Yatt that She would be leaving him, having been offered a place in a small but critically acclaimed touring company by a customer who transpired to be the merchant without whose continuing financial support the company could not survive.

Som-Som could still remember the ugly playlet that the two estranged lovers had performed in the courtyard of the House on the morning that Rawra Chin was to leave. While the other inhabitants watched with boredom or amusement from their balconies, the players paced across the flat black stage, seemingly oblivious to the audience that watched from above as their angry accusals and sullen denials rang from the curving courtyard walls.

Foral Yatt pathetically followed Rawra Chin around the courtyard, almost staggering beneath the weight of that dreadful, unexpected betrayal. He was a tall, lean man with beautiful arms, his eyes dark and deep set, brimming with tears as he trailed behind Rawra Chin, an unwanted satellite still trapped within Her orbit by the irresistible gravity of Her mystique. The fact that he kept his skull shaven to a close stubble to facilitate the numerous changes of wig required by his customers only added to his air of desolation.

Rawra Chin remained a measured number of paces in front of him, occasionally directing some pained but dignified comment over Her shoulder while he ranted, incoherent with hurt, raging and confused. Som-Som suspected that She was in some oblique way enjoying this abuse from Her former lover, that She accepted his tirade as an inverted tribute to Her mesmeric influence over him.

Eventually, when desperation had driven Foral Yatt beyond all considerations of dignity, he threatened to kill himself. Pulling something from the small pouch that he wore at his belt, the distraught young actor held it aloft so that it glittered in the morning sunlight.

It was a miniature human skull, fashioned from green glass and holding no more than a mouthful of the clear, licorice-scented liquid that it had been designed to contain. No more than a mouthful was required. These suicidal trinkets could be purchased quite openly, and it was impossible to determine how many of Liavek's more pessimistically inclined citizens carried one of the death's-heads in anticipation of that day when life was no longer endurable.

His voice ragged with emotion, Foral Yatt swore that he would not be deserted in so casual a manner. He promised to end his life if Rawra Chin did not pick up Her baggage and carry it back through the pale yellow door to their chambers.

They stared at each other, and Som-Som had thought that she perceived a flicker of uncertainty dance across the widely-spaced eyes of the young boy as they moved from Foral Yatt's face to the skull-shaped bottle in his hand. The instant seemed to inflate into a massive balloon of silence, punctured by the sudden rattle of hooves and wheels from beyond the courtyard's arched entrance, signaling the arrival of the carriage that was to take Rawra Chin to join Her theater troupe. She darted one last glance at Foral Yatt and then, picking up Her baggage, turned and walked out through the archway.

Foral Yatt stood transfixed at the center of the huge black disc, still with one flawless arm raised, clutching its cold green fistful of oblivion. He stared blankly at the archway as if expecting Her to reappear and tell him it was all some ill-considered hoax. From beyond the encircling walls there came the jingle of reins followed by a slow clattering and the creaking of wood and leather as the carriage moved away down the winding streets of the City of Luck. After a pause during which it seemed that he would never move again, the actor slowly and falteringly lowered his arm.

Three floors above him, realizing the abandoned lover wouldn't kill himself, one of the denizens of the House Without Clocks pursed her shiny black lips discontentedly and made a clucking sound before retiring to her quarters. Hearing the sound, Foral Yatt tilted back his gray-stubbled skull and stared up at the watchers in surprise, as if previously unaware of their scrutiny. His eyes were full of miserable incomprehension, and it was a relief to Som-Som when he lowered them to the black tiles at his feet before walking slowly across the courtyard toward the pale yellow door, the glass skull now quite forgotten in his hand.

Scarcely a handful of months elapsed before news began to work its way back to the House Without Clocks of Rawra Chin's dizzying success. It seemed that Her elusive charisma was able to captivate audiences as easily as it had once enthralled Her individual customers. Her performance as the tragic and infertile Queen Gorda in Mossoc's *The Crib* was already the talk of Liavek's intelligentsia, and rumor had it that a special performance for His Scarlet Eminence was being considered.

Such talk was generally kept from the inconsolable Foral Yatt, but within the year Rawra Chin's fame had spread to the point where the embittered young actor was as aware of it as anyone. He seemed to take the news of Her stellar ascent with less resentment than might have been anticipated, once the initial despair of separation had lifted from him. Indeed, save for a coldness that would creep into his eyes at the mention of Her name, Foral Yatt made much of his indifference to his former lover's fortunes. He never spoke of Her, and those less insightful than Som-Som might have supposed that he had forgotten Her altogether.

Now, five years later, She had returned.

In the courtyard beneath Som-Som's balcony, Rawra Chin turned to face the pale yellow door, a resigned slump in Her shoulders. She lifted one hand to knock, and there was a sudden dazzling scintillation that seemed to play about Her fingers. It took Som-Som a moment to realize that the young man had chips of some reflective substance pasted to Her nails. The afternoon was hushed, as if holding its breath while it listened, and the sound of Rawra Chin's white knuckles upon the pale yellow wood was disproportionately loud.

Seated high above on her balcony, Som-Som found that she wanted desperately to call out, to warn Rawra Chin that it was a mistake to return to this place, that She should leave immediately. Silence, massive and absolute, surrounded her and would not permit her to make the smallest sound. She was embedded in silence, a tiny bubble of consciousness within an infinity of solid rock, mute and gray and endless. She struggled against it, willing her tongue to shape the vital words of warning, knowing as she did so that it was hopeless.

Below, someone unlocked the pale yellow door from inside and it creaked once, musically, as it opened. It was too late.

Som-Som's balcony was situated upon the third floor, the adjacent living area being one of four contained behind the violet door at the extreme left of the House Without Clocks' concave front. Thus, as she sat upon her balcony and gazed down at Rawra Chin she could not see who had opened the door. She supposed that it was Foral Yatt.

There was a surprisingly low exchange of words, following which the crimson-wrapped figure of the celebrated performer stepped inside the house and beyond Som-Som's vision. The pale yellow door closed with a sound like something sucking its teeth.

After that, there was only silence. Som-Som remained seated upon her balcony staring down at the pale yellow door with mute anguish in her one visible eye while the sky gradually darkened behind her. Finally, when the moment of her urgent need for a voice was long past, she spoke.

"I ran as fast as I could, but when I reached my mother's house the bird was already dead."

• • •

Since the closing of the yellow door, no word had been spoken in the rooms that lay immediately behind it. Foral Yatt sat in
a hard wooden chair beside the open fire, amber light flickering
across one side of his lean face. Rawra Chin stood by the window, Her vivid crimson darkening to a dull, scablike burgundy
against the failing light outside. Uncertain of how best to gauge
the distance that had arisen between them, She watched the play
of firelight upon the velvet of his shaven skull until the absence
of conversation was more than She could endure.

"I brought you a gift."

Foral Yatt slowly turned his head toward Her, away from the
fire, so that the shadow slid across his face, and his expression
was no longer visible. Rawra Chin immersed one chalk-white
hand in the black fur of the bag She carried, from whence it
emerged holding a small copper ball between the mirror-tipped
fingers. She held it out to him and, after a moment, he took it.

"What is it?"

She had forgotten how captivating his voice was, dry and deep
and hungry, quite unlike Her own. Calm and evenly modulated,
there remained a sense of something watchful and carnivorous
lurking just beyond it, pacing quietly behind the accents and in-
flections. Rawra Chin licked Her lips.

"It's a toy . . . a toy of the intellect. I'm told that it's very
relaxing. Many of the busiest merchants that I know find that it
calms them immeasurably after the bustle of commerce."

Foral Yatt turned the smooth copper sphere between his
fingers so that it gleamed red in the glow of the fire.

"What's special about it?"

Rawra Chin took a step away from the window, Her first tentative movement toward him since entering the House, and then
paused. She let Her black fur bag drop with a soft thud, like the
corpse of an enormous spider, onto the empty seat of the room's
other chair. A certain establishing of territory accompanied the
gesture, and Rawra Chin hoped She had not overstepped in Her
eagerness. Foral Yatt's face was still in shadow, but he did not
seem to react adversely to the wedge-end represented by the bag
upon the chair, now less like a dead spider than a sleeping cat
dozing before the hearth. Encouraged by this lack of obvious
rebuke, Rawra Chin smiled, albeit nervously, as She replied to
him.

"There might be a lizard asleep inside the ball, or there might
not. That's the puzzle."

His silence seemed to invite elaboration.

"The story goes that there exists a lizard capable of hibernating for years or even centuries without food or air or moisture, slowing its vital processes so that a dozen winters might pass between each beat of its heart. I am told that it is a very small creature, no bigger than the top joint of my thumb when it is curled up.

"The people who make these ornaments allegedly place one of the sleeping reptiles inside each ball before sealing it. If you look closely, you can see that there's a seam around the middle."

Foral Yatt declined to do so, remaining seated, his back toward the fire, holding the ball in his right hand and turning it so that molten highlights rolled across its surface. Though an impenetrable shadow still concealed his expression, Rawra Chin sensed that the quality of his silence had changed. She felt whatever slight advantage She had gained begin to slip away. Why wouldn't he speak? Unable to keep the edge of unease from Her voice, She resumed Her monologue.

"You can't open it, and, and you have to think about whether there really is a lizard inside it or not. It's to do with how we perceive the world around us, and when you think about it you start to see that it doesn't matter if there's a lizard inside there or not, and then you can think about what's real and what isn't real, and . . ."

Her voice trailed off, as if suddenly aware of its own incoherence.

". . . and it's said to be very relaxing," She concluded lamely, after a flat, dismal pause.

"Why did you come back?"

"I don't know."

"You don't know."

It was as if Her words had hit a mirror, rebounding back at Her full of new meanings and implications, warped out of true by some fluke of the glass. Rawra Chin's fragile composure began to crumble before that flat, disinterested voice.

"I . . . I don't mean that I don't know. I just mean . . ."

She looked down at Her pale, well-kept hands to find that She was wringing them together. They looked like crabs mating after having been kept in the dark for too long.

"I mean that there was no real reason for me to come back here. My work, my career, it's all perfect. I have a lot of money. I have friends. I've just completed my role as Bromar's eldest daughter in *The Lucksmith* and everybody will talk about me for months. For a while, I do not have to work. I can do whatever I want.

"I didn't have to come back here."

Foral Yatt remained silent, the firelight behind his shaven head edging his skull with a trim of blurred phosphorescence as it shone through the stubble. The copper ball turned between his fingers, a miniature planet rolling from day into night.

"It's just that . . . this place, this house, it has something. There's something inside this house, and it's something true. It isn't a good thing. It's just a true thing, and I don't know what the name of it is, and I don't even like it, but I know that it's true and I know that it's here and I felt, I don't know, I felt that I had to come back and look at it. It's like . . ."

Rawra Chin's hands seemed to pluck and squeeze the air before Her, as if the words She required were concealed beneath its skin, and that by probing She could guess at their shape. Separated now, the blanched crustacean lovers lay upon their backs, feebly waving their legs as they expired upon some unseen shoreline.

"It's like an accident I saw . . . a farmer, crushed beneath his cart. He was alive, but his ribs were broken and sticking through his side. I didn't know what they were at first, because it was all such a mess. There were a lot of people gathered 'round, but nobody could move the cart without hurting him even more than he was hurt already.

"It was summer, and there were a lot of flies. I remember him screaming and shouting for somebody to beat the flies away, and an old woman went out and did that for him, but until then nobody had moved, not until he screamed at them. It was horrible. I walked by as fast as I could because he was suffering and there was nothing anybody could do, except for the old woman who was beating the flies away with her apron.

"But I went back.

"I stopped just a little way down the road, and I went back. I couldn't help it. It was just that it was so real and so painful, that man, lying there under that terrible weight and screaming for his wife, his children, it was so real that it just cut through everything else in the world, all the things that my luck and my money have built up around me, and I knew that it meant something, and I went back there and I watched him drown on his own blood while the old woman told him not to worry, that his wife and children would be there soon.

"And that's why I came back to the House Without Clocks."

There was a long hyphen of silence. A copper world rotated between the fingers of a faceless and unanswering god.

"And I still love you."

Someone rapped twice upon the pale yellow door.

For a moment there was no movement within the room save for the illusion of motion engendered by the firelight. Then Foral Yatt rose from the hard wooden chair, still with the fire at his back and his face in eclipse. Crossing the room, ducking beneath the blackened beams that supported the low ceiling, he passed close enough for Her to raise Her hand and brush his arm, so that it would be thought an accident of passing. But She didn't.

Foral Yatt opened the door.

The figure on the other side of the threshold was perhaps forty years of age, a large and strong-boned woman with raw cheeks who wore a single garment like a tent of smoky gray fur. It covered the top of her head with a hole cut away to reveal the face, and then its striking, minimal lines dropped away to the floor. There was no opening in the fur through which she might extend her hands, which suggested to Rawra Chin that the woman must have servants to do everything for her, the feeding to her of meals not excluded. Even in the world that Rawra Chin had known over the previous five years, such arrogantly flaunted wealth was impressive.

As the inopportune visitor tilted back her head to speak, the flickering yellow light caught her face, and Rawra Chin noticed that the woman had an umber blemish, unpleasantly furry-looking, that almost entirely covered her left cheek. The woman had obviously attempted to conceal it beneath a thick coat of white powder with little success. The discoloration remained visible through the makeup as if it were a paper-thin flatfish that swam through her subcutaneous tissue, its dark shape discernible just below the clouded surface of her face.

When she spoke, her voice was distressingly loud, her tone strident and somehow abusive.

"Foral Yatt. Dear Foral Yatt, how long? How long has it been since I saw you last?"

Foral Yatt's reply was professionally polite, coolly inoffensive, and yet delivered at such volume that Rawra Chin winced involuntarily, even though She stood several paces behind him. It came to Her suddenly that the fur-draped woman must suffer from some defect of hearing.

"It has been two days since you were here, Donna Blerot. I have missed you."

A wave of hotness washed over Rawra Chin, cooling almost instantly to a leaden ingot in Her stomach. Foral Yatt had a customer, and She must leave him to his labors. Her disappointment was so big She could not admit that it was Hers. She resolved to leave immediately, hoping to keep it one step behind Her until She could reach Her own rooms in a lodging house on the far side of the City of Luck. Once She was safely behind closed doors She would let it have its way with Her, and then there would be tears. She was reaching for Her bag, sleeping there in its chair, when Foral Yatt spoke again.

"However, it is not convenient that I should see you tonight. A member of my family has come to visit"—here he gestured vaguely over his shoulder toward the stunned Rawra Chin—"and I regret that you and I must let our yearnings simmer untended for one more day. Please be patient, Donna Blerot. When finally we meet together, you know that our union will be the sweeter for this postponement."

Donna Blerot turned her head and gazed past Foral Yatt at the slim, crimson-swathed figure that stood in the flamelit room, almost like a flame Herself within the gaudy wrappings. The dame's eyes were frozen and merciless, boring into Rawra Chin for long instants before she turned them once more toward Foral Yatt, her expression softening.

"This is too bad, Foral Yatt. Simply too bad. But I shall forgive you. How could I ever do otherwise?"

She smiled, her teeth yellow and her lips too wide.

"Until tomorrow, then?"

"Until tomorrow, dearest Donna Blerot."

The woman turned from the door and Rawra Chin heard the slow, derisive clapping of her wooden sandals as she walked back across the black courtyard. Foral Yatt closed the door, sliding the bolt across. The sound of the bolt's passage, metal against metal, was electrifying in its implications, and Rawra Chin shuddered in resonance. The actor turned away from the closed portal and stared at Her, his face brazen in the fire glow.

His face seemed less chiseled and gaunt than She had remembered it. His eyes, conversely, were so riveting and intense that She knew Her recollection had not done them justice. Across a chamber so filled with swaying clots of darkness that it seemed like a ballroom for shadows, the two young men stared at each other. Neither spoke.

He walked toward Her, pausing only to set the small copper globe upon the polished white wood of his tabletop before continuing. His pace was so deliberate that Rawra Chin felt sure he must be aware of the tension that this deliciously prolonged approach kindled within Her. Unable to meet his gaze, She lowered Her lashes so that the quivering light of the room became streaks of incoherent brilliance. Her breathing grew shallow, and She trembled.

The warm, dry smell of his skin enveloped Her. She knew that he was standing just before Her, no more than a forearm's length away. Then he touched Her face. The shock of physical contact almost caused Her to jerk Her head back, but She controlled the impulse. Her heart rang like an anvil as his fingernail traced the line of Her jaw.

The ingenious arrangement of bandages that was Rawra Chin's costume had a single fastening, concealed behind a triangular black gem in a filigree surround that that She wore upon the right side of Her throat. The pin pricked Her neck as Foral Yatt withdrew it from the blood-red windings, but even this seemed almost unbearably pleasant to Her in that aching, oversensitized state. She lifted Her gaze and his eyes swallowed Her whole. With his hands moving in languid, confident circles, he began to unwind the long band of brightly dyed gauze, starting from Her head and spiraling downward.

Free of the confining wrap, Her thick hair tumbled down upon Her white shoulders. She gasped and shook Her head from side to side, but it was not an indication of denial. A wave of thrilling coolness crept down Her body as progressively more of Her skin was exposed to the drafts of the room. It moved across Her belly and down to the angular and jutting hips, over the shaven pudenda and past the jumping, half-erect penis. It continued down Her thighs and on toward the rush carpeting, where the unraveled wrappings gathered in a widening red puddle about Her feet, as if Her naked flesh bled from a dozen imperceptible wounds.

He nodded his head to Her once, still without a sound, and She knelt upon the floor at his feet, Her knees pressed against the tangle of fallen bandages so that they would leave a faint lattice of impressions upon Her skin. Closing Her eyes, She allowed Her head to sink forward until it came to rest against the seat of the chair in which She had placed Her bag an eternity before. Its luscious dark fur and the hard wood were equally cool against Her burning cheek.

Behind Her, a single brief chime, Foral Yatt's buckle dropped unceremoniously to the rush matting. Upon an impulse, She allowed Her eyes to open, their gaze drifting across the chamber, drinking in the moment in all its infinitesimal detail. On the other side of the room, the copper ball rested upon the tabletop where Foral Yatt had placed it. It was like the freshly gouged eye of a brazen speaking-head, such as certain personages in Wizard's Row were reputed to possess.

It stared back at Rawra Chin, glittering suggestively, and all that came to pass behind the pale yellow door was reflected impartially, in perfect miniature, upon the convex surface of that lifeless and unblinking orb.

Later, lying flat upon Her stomach with their mingled sweat drying in the hollow of Her back, Rawra Chin allowed Her awareness to float tethered upon the margins of wakefulness while Foral Yatt squatted naked by the fire, adding fresh coals to sustain a fading redness that had burned low during the preceding hour. The air was heavy with the intoxicating bouquet of semen, and each of Her muscles slumped in blissful exhaustion.

Still, something nagged at Her, even in the sublime depths of her sated torpor. There was yet something unresolved between the two of them, no matter how eloquent their lovemaking may have seemed. It was barely a real thing at all, more a disquieting absence than an intrusive presence, and She might have ignored it. This, however, proved more than She could bear. It was a cavity within Her that must be filled before She could be complete. Though reluctant to send ripples through the calm afterglow of their congress, eventually She found Her voice.

"Do you still love me?" This was followed, after a hesitant beat, by, "Despite what I did to you?"

She turned Her head so that the right side of Her face rested against the interwoven rushes. He crouched before the fire with his back toward Her as he carefully arranged cold black nuggets atop the bright embers. His skin glistened, a yellow smear of watercolor highlight running down the side toward the fire. She followed the line of his vertebrae with Her eyes to the plumbline-straight crease that bisected the hard buttocks, adoring him. He did not turn to Her as he replied.

"Is there a lizard asleep within the ball?"

Taking another piece of coal in a hand already blackened by dust, Foral Yatt placed a capstone atop the dark pyramid in the scaled-down hell of the fireplace. Nothing more was said behind the pale yellow door that night.

Upon the following morning, Rawra Chin visited Som-Som and took tea with her, as if the five-year hiatus in their ritual had never existed. She recounted a string of anecdotes from Her career, then paused to sip Her infusion while Som-Som informed Her that her mother had once closed a door, and that it had once been dark, and that once she had been unable to stop coughing. Rawra Chin's smooth reentry into the bizarre rhythms of their conversation did much to eradicate any distance between the two that might have flourished in their half decade of separation. Even so, it was not until the interlude approached its conclusion that the performer felt comfortable enough to broach the subject of Her resumed relationship with Foral Yatt.

"I won't be staying here forever, of course. In another month or so I must begin to consider my next role, and it would be impossible to do that here. But this time, when I leave, I believe I shall take him with me. I'm rich enough to keep him until he finds work of his own, and it seems ridiculous that someone with his talent should be wasting it upon . . ."

Her hands performed a curious movement that was part theatrical gesture and part genuine involuntary revulsion. It was as if they were retching with violent spasms that shuddered out from the slender throat of the wrist and on toward Her fingertips, where ten mirrors shivered in the cold morning sunlight.

". . . upon ugly, sick old women like that terrible Donna Blerot! He deserves so much better. I could look after him, I could find work for him, and then perhaps neither of us would need to come back to this place ever again, not even just to look at it. Don't you think that would be a good idea?"

Som-Som sipped her floral infusion through the corner of her mouth and said nothing.

"I think we can do it. I think that we can love each other and be together without anything going wrong between us. It was only my ambition that pushed us apart before, and I've fulfilled that now. Things can be just as they were, only somewhere else, in a better place than this."

Rawra Chin looked thoughtful, sucking the dazzling tip of Her right index finger so that it made a small and liquid popping sound when she pulled it from between Her lips. She did this twice. Behind Her, birds wheeled above the diverse skyline of Liavek. When She spoke again, Her voice had assumed a puzzled tone.

"Of course, he has changed. I suppose we've both changed. He's very quiet now, and very . . . very commanding. Yes, that's it exactly. Very commanding. It's wonderful, I'm not complaining at all. After all, those are his chambers and he's being kind enough to let me stay there for the next couple of months so that I don't need to keep up my rooms at the lodging house. I don't mind doing whatever he wants. I think, you know, I think it's good for me in a way, good for how I am as a person. Since my career broke out of the egg, nobody had told me what to do. I think that's spoiled me. It doesn't feel right, somehow. Not when people just defer to me all the time. I think I need someone to—"

"A sticky head looked out from between the cow's legs, and I screamed."

Som-Som's interjection was so startling that even Rawra Chin, accustomed to such utterances, was momentarily unnerved. Blinking, She waited to see if the half-masked woman intended to make any further comment before continuing.

"I'm having my clothes sent over from the lodging house. I have so many beautiful things it hardly seems fair. Foral Yatt says that he will store my wardrobe, but he does not want me to wear the more exotic creations while I am with him. He prefers plainer things."

Rawra Chin glanced down at the clothing She was dressed in. She wore a simple blouse of gray cotton and a skirt of similar material. Her white-gold hair swung about Her narrow shoulders and sparked life from the dusk-colored fabric with its contrast. It lay against Her blouse like wan torchlight reflected on wet, gray cobbles. Evidently satisfied with the novel restraint and subtlety of her costume, She raised Her lashes and smiled across the tea bowls at Som-Som.

"But enough of my affairs and vanities. Which side of luck have you yourself walked these five years gone?"

The divided face stared back at Her with its one live eye. No one spoke. Over the City of Luck, great scavenger birds dipped and shrieked, so that it sounded as if babies had been torn up from the earth and dragged wailing into the oppressive dome of the sky.

On the fifth day after Her arrival, Rawra Chin appeared upon Som-Som's balcony wearing breeches of leather with a stout length of rope looped about the waist as a belt. She did not refer to this reversal of Her sartorial tendencies, but after that Som-Som never again saw Her in a skirt and supposed that this was due to Foral Yatt's austere influence. The performer seemed also to forgo the application of face paint and the wearing of all jewelry save for a simple band of unadorned iron, which She wore upon the smallest finger of Her left hand. The ten slivers of mirror were long since vanished.

Two weeks after Her return, Foral Yatt persuaded Rawra Chin to shave off Her hair.

Sitting with Som-Som the following morning, She would break off from Her trail of conversation every few seconds and run one incredulous palm back from Her temple and across the stubble. Her talk had a forced gaiety, and there was something nervous and darting within Her eyes. Som-Som realized with some surprise that Rawra Chin no longer seemed attractive. It was as if Her charisma had leaked out of Her, or been sheared away as ruthlessly as the spun sunlight of Her hair.

"I think, I think I look better like this, don't you?"

Som-Som said nothing.

"I mean to say that it, well, it makes such a change. And I think it will do my hair a service, after it grows back. The colorings I use had made it so brittle, a new head of hair will be such a relief. And of course, Foral Yatt likes it this way."

The casual delivery of this last phrase was belied by an evasive glance and an air of restless self-consciousness.

"I mean, I understand how it must look, how it must look to people who don't know him, but . . ."

One hand rasped lightly across Her skull in a single, backward motion.

". . . but the way that I dress is important to him, the way I look, it's so important to him, the way that I look when we make love."

Som-Som cleared her throat and told the performer the name of the street where she had lived before the night when her mother had led her out by the hand, through the noise and toward the Silence. Rawra Chin continued Her monologue without acknowledging the interjection, Her eyes hollow and sleepless with their gaze still fixed on the grubby tiles.

"He's changed, you see. He wants different things now. And, and I don't mind. I love him. I don't mind what he wants me to do. I even like it, sometimes I like it for myself and not just for him. But the fact, the fact that I like it, that's something that frightens me. Not frightens me, really, but it's as if everything is changing and moving under my feet, and as if I'm changing too, and I feel as if I should be frightened, but I'm not. It's so easy, just slipping into it. It's so easy just to let it happen, and I don't mind. I love him and I don't mind."

From the dilated pupil of the courtyard, someone called Rawra Chin's name. Som-Som turned her gaze to the flagstones below, puzzling for a moment over the stranger that stood there before she was able to reconcile the familiar face with the unplaceable gait and manner, finally resolving these disparate impressions into Foral Yatt.

Rawra Chin had spoken the truth. Foral Yatt had changed.

Standing beneath them, looking up with one hand raised to shield his eyes from the sun, the bar of shadow cast across his features did not conceal the change that had come over them. The actor seemed less lean. Som-Som supposed that this was in part due to Rawra Chin's wealth supplementing his income and his diet.

His clothing, too, was noticeably different from the somber and functional raiment that he had appeared to favor. Foral Yatt wore a long tunic, its blue so deep and vibrant that it bordered upon iridescence. A wide orange sash was wound twice about his waist, and the billowing pants that he wore beneath were orange also, a fragile, mottled orange almost white in places. His feet were naked and exquisite, much smaller than Som-Som would have expected them to be. Something glittered, a sparkling fog about the toes.

"Rawra Chin? Our meal is almost prepared."

His voice had altered, too: lighter, a patina of melody imposed upon its assured tones. And there was something else, something which above all was responsible for the striking change in his aspect, something so obvious that it eluded her completely.

Rawra Chin murmured an apology as She made ready to leave, not bothering to tie up any loose ends remaining from Her conversation with Som-Som. As was Her custom, She reached out and squeezed Som-Som's wrist to let the half of her brain that was cut off from sight or sound know that her visitor was leaving. In response, the half-masked woman lifted her gaze until it met Rawra Chin's. When she spoke, her voice was filled with a sadness that seemed to have no bearing upon the content of her speech.

"I do not think that the food was so good, back then."

Rawra Chin's lips twitched once, a helpless little facial shrug, and then She turned and ran down the narrow wooden stairs that led to the courtyard below, where Foral Yatt awaited Her.

She joined him there and they exchanged a snatch of dialogue that was too low for Som-Som to hear before making their way toward the pale yellow door. Som-Som craned her neck to watch them go. Just before they passed from her sight, she identified the single glaring quirk that had so transformed the young actor.

Running along his brow in an uneven snow-line, curling around the topmost rim of his ears, Foral Yatt's hair was starting to grow out.

On the fifteenth night after Her arrival at the House Without Clocks, something occurred behind the pale yellow door that gave Rawra Chin Her first glimpse into the darkness that had been waiting for Her for five long years. She went indoors to share Her evening repast with Foral Yatt just as the sun was butchering the western horizon, and before morning She had seen the abyss. She was not to comprehend the immensity of the hungry void beneath Her for some three days further, but that first shattering look was the beginning. It was as if She dropped a pebble into the chasm that awaited Her and listened for the splash. When three days later the splash had still not come, She knew that the blackness was bottomless, and that there was no hope.

On the earlier evening, however, when She walked through the pale yellow door with the sunset at Her back and the rich aroma of the pot-boil hanging before Her, this shadow was yet to fall. It seemed to Her that all her anxieties were containable.

They ate their meal quickly, the two of them facing each other across the blanched wood of the table, and then Rawra Chin cleared away what debris there was while Foral Yatt retired to his bedchamber to prepare for the business of the evening ahead. Rawra Chin, scraping an obstinate scab of dried legume from the lip of his bowl, wondered idly what She would find to amuse Herself tonight during the hours when Her presence behind the pale yellow door was not required. On previous nights She had walked down to the harbor. Watching the moon's reflection in the iron-green water, She had tried to wring some cooling trickle of romance from Her situation.

With an abbreviated cry of pain and surprise She looked down to discover that She had split Her nail upon the nub of dried and hardened food. Her nails were a ruin, She thought, all of them bitten and uneven, many of them split or with raw pink about the quick. She wondered how long it would take for them to regain their former elegance, and as She did so She ran Her other hand back over Her razed scalp without being aware of the gesture.

Foral Yatt called to Her from the bedchamber and She went to see what he wanted, wiping Her hands upon the coarse gray fabric of Her shirt as She trudged across the rush matting.

Stepping through the door of the chamber, She was puzzled to discover that Foral Yatt had retired to bed, rather than preparing for the evening's duties. He lay upon the rough cotton of the sheets with his eyes half-closed and his hands resting limp upon the patches of dyed sackcloth that formed the counterpane.

"I cannot work this evening. I am ill."

Rawra Chin's brow knotted into a frown. He did not look discomforted, nor was his voice unsteady or less masterful, and yet he said that he was sick. It was as if he meant Her to understand that this was a lie but to respond as if it were irrefutable truth.

Searching within Herself She discovered, with only the briefest pang of surprise or disappointment, that She did not mind. She accommodated the fiction, because that was the easiest thing to do.

"But what of Mistress Ouish? There have been other nights lately when you have not worked. A room not in use is a drain on her resources. Others have been dismissed for as much."

Mistress Ouish, though now blind and close to death, was still the dominating presence at the House Without Clocks. Even Rawra Chin, who had not been employed at that establishment for five years, regarded the old woman with alloyed respect and fear. From his blatantly spurious sickbed, Foral Yatt spoke again.

"You are right. If no work is done here tonight, it will be the worse for me."

He raised his lowered lids and stared directly into Rawra Chin's eyes. He smiled, knowing that to smile altered nothing between them. The masquerade was accepted by mutual consent. His voice dry and measured, he continued.

"That is why you must do my work for me."

It was as if there were some sudden dysfunction within Rawra Chin's mind that rendered Her unable to glean any sense from Foral Yatt's words. "That," "must," "do," "work"—all of these sounded alien, so that She was almost convinced that the actor had coined them upon the spot. She ran the sentence through Her head again and again. "That is why you must do my work for me." "That is why you must do my work for me." What did it mean?

And then, recovering from the shock of the utterance, She knew.

She shook Her head and in Her horror still had room to be surprised by the absence of soft hair swinging against Her neck.

Barely audibly, She said "No," but it didn't mean "I will not." It meant "Please don't."

But he did.

Donna Blerot took Her hand (His hand?) and pulled it up beneath the fur tent so that it came to rest upon the dampness between the disfigured woman's thick legs. Beneath her single outer garment the dame was naked, flesh damp and solid like dough.

Later, burying Herself in the woman's body as Donna Blerot sprawled back across the table, gasping noiselessly like a fish upon a slab, Rawra Chin looked down at her and saw the abyss. The bell of gray fur had ridden up to reveal the body beneath, so that it now covered Donna Blerot's face, birthmark and all. For a lurching instant the woman looked like a drowned thing washed up on the coastline of the Sea of Luck, a sheet already covering the puffy, fish-eaten face.

Fighting nausea, Rawra Chin shifted Her glance so that it came to rest upon Her own body, luminous with sweat, plunging mechanically forward, jerking back, thrusting and withdrawing like a gauntlet-manikin worked by the hand of another. She regarded the jutting hardness that grew from Her own loins and wondered how it was that She could be doing this thing. She felt no desire, no lust for the deaf woman and her bucking, heaving desperation. She felt nothing but shame and horror. How could Her body sustain such ardor in the face of that abomination?

Later still, Donna Blerot kissed Rawra Chin and left, closing the pale yellow door behind her. The performer sat naked in one of the wooden chairs, elbows resting upon the tabletop before Her, face concealed behind Her hands as if behind the slammed doors of a church. The memory of the matron's kiss was still thick about Her lips. It had seemed as if a fat and bitter mollusk were attempting to crawl into Her mouth, leaving its glistening saliva trail across Her chin. This imagery slithered out of Her mind and down Her throat, from whence it dropped into Her stomach. There was a faint, warning spasm, and Rawra Chin tortured Herself with an image of their hastily devoured meal from earlier that evening. The gelatinous, half-melted skirt of fat trailing from the gray-pink fingers of meat . . .

Struggling silently to keep from vomiting, She did not hear Foral Yatt leave his bedchamber until he was standing just beside Her.

"There. Was that so bad?"

Startled by his voice, Rawra Chin moved one hand so that only half of Her face remained concealed, and opened Her eyes. She was looking down at the floor, and She could see nothing of Foral Yatt above the knee without moving Her head, which seemed an unendurable prospect.

His feet were as white as the flesh of almonds.

Fixed to each of the toenails was a tiny mirror. Suspended beneath the surface of ten miniature, glittering pools, Rawra Chin's reflections stared back at Her, insects drowning in quick-silver.

Rising unsteadily from Her seat and pushing past Foral Yatt, Rawra Chin staggered to that chamber set aside for bathing and the performance of one's toilet. Lava rose in Her throat, flooding Her mouth, and She was sobbing as She emptied Herself noisily into a chipped and yellowed handbasin. Drained, She gagged upon emptiness until the convulsions in Her gut subsided, and then raised Her head to look at the room about Her through a quivering lens of tears.

Something caught Her eye, a green blur twinkling from atop the chest where Foral Yatt kept his soaps and perfumes and oils. Rawra Chin wiped Her eyes with the blunt edge of one hand and tried to focus upon the distracting blot of emerald. It was a fixed point on which to anchor Her perceptions, still reeling in the wake of Her nausea. Gradually, the object swam into definition against the damp gloom of the washroom.

Tiny glass sockets stared at Her, unblinking. Behind them, within the translucent green brainpan, unguessable dreams mar-inated within cerebral juices that smelled of licorice.

Rawra Chin stared at the skull full of poison. It stared back at Her, its gaze concealing nothing.

Time passed in the House Without Clocks.

On the eighteenth night following Her arrival, Rawra Chin fell to the darkness. That which had only licked and tasted Her now distended its jaws and took Her at a bite.

She was drunk, although it would have happened had this not been the case. Miserable over the dinner table, She had taken an excess of wine in the hope of numbing the pangs of self-loathing. The alcohol served only to muddy Her anxieties, making them slippery, more difficult to apprehend. She stood framed in the open doorway with one hand upon the pale yellow wood, looking out at the deserted courtyard, drinking great ragged lungfuls of autumn air. It did nothing to still the buzzing that droned inside Her head, a dismal hive somewhere between her ears.

Gazing at the indifferent black flagstones, She understood that She must leave. Leave Foral Yatt. Leave at once and return to the soothing babble of Her wardrobe boys, the comforting dreariness of committing endless lines to Her memory. If She did not go immediately, She would be trapped forever, crushed beneath the hulking farm wagon of circumstance, screaming for someone to brush away the flies. If She did not go immediately...

From the chambers behind Her, Foral Yatt called Her name.

She looked up from the flagstones and there, on the opposite side of that wide obsidian pond, there reared the archway, with Liavek beyond it.

A note of mounting impatience discernible in his voice, Foral Yatt called again.

She turned and walked back into the house, closing the pale yellow door behind Her.

He was in the bedchamber, as had become customary since the evening when Rawra Chin had been called upon to service Donna Blerot, Her first knowledge of a woman. She supposed that Foral Yatt had summoned Her to order a repetition of that occasion, and for an instant She savored a fantasy of refusal, but for not longer than that.

"My love? Would you light the lantern for me? It is so dark in here."

Foral Yatt's voice, altering since Rawra Chin's arrival in that place, had moved into another stage of its metamorphosis. Softened to a deep velvet, it seduced rather than commanded.

Her fingers struggled with the flint for a second before the tinder caught, and then She lifted the flame to the wick of the lantern. A bubble of sulfurous yellow light expanded and contracted within the chamber, wavering until the flame grew still and its light clear. Rawra Chin turned from the lamp, white-hot maggots engraved upon Her retinas by the brilliance She had brought into being.

Foral Yatt lay upon his side on top of the patchwork counterpane, supporting himself upon one elbow, fingertips lost in the tight blond curls at his temples. A wide band of blue cosmetic color ran in a diagonal line across his face, overlaying the left side of his brow, sweeping down across the left eye, the bridge of the nose, the right cheek. A narrower band of red, little more than a single brushstroke, followed its upper edge over the ridges and hollows of his smooth, sculpted features, terminating beneath the right ear.

He was wearing one of Her costumes.

It was a gown, long and violet, gathered in extravagant ruffs at the shoulders so that the arms were bare. The collar was high, reaching to the point just above the bulge in Foral Yatt's throat, and below that the material was solid and opaque until it reached a demarcation line just beneath the breastbone. From there, the dress seemed to have been slashed into long strips that trailed down to the ankles, every second violet ribbon having been cut away and replaced by a panel of coral pink twine, knotted into snowflake patterns through which the skin beneath was visible. There were mirrors upon his toes and fingers.

Entering through a chink in the wall with a sound like a child blowing across the neck of a narrow jar, a breeze disturbed the perfumed air and caused the lantern flame to stutter. For a moment, armies of light and shadow rushed back and forth in quick-fire border disputes. The shadows gathered within Foral Yatt's eye sockets seemed to flow across his cheek like an overspill of tar before shrinking back to pool beneath the overhang of his brow. He smiled up at Her through lips fastidiously stained a rich indigo.

"I had to come back. I couldn't just leave you here."

The second word in each sentence was stressed in a lush and affected manner, so that even as Rawra Chin struggled to make sense of the actor's words, so too was She striving to identify that quirk of inflection, maddeningly familiar and yet beyond the grasp of her recall.

"But . . . what do you mean? You haven't been anywhere. You . . ."

Rawra Chin could feel something bearing down upon Her, coming toward Her with a hideous speed that froze the will and made evasion unthinkable. It was like stories She had heard concerning eclipses when men would see the giant moonshadow rushing toward them across the land, a vast planet of darkness rolling over the tiny fields and pastures with a speed that was only comparable to itself. Standing there in the scented chamber, She understood their terror. The shadow-world was almost upon Her. Another moment and She would be crushed beneath its endless, inescapable mass. From the bed, Foral Yatt spoke again. The pattern of emphasis within his speech continued to dance just beyond the fringes of recognition, mocking and unattainable.

"I left you. Don't you remember? I left you because it was so important to me that people should know my name. I know it must have seemed unfair to you, but you were only ordinary, and I am a special creature. I have something rare in me, a unique charm that men have not words to describe, and though I loved you deeply, deeply, it was my duty to expose the treasure that I am to the world and all its people. Surely this is not beyond your comprehension?"

Quite suddenly, Rawra Chin knew where She had heard the voice that Foral Yatt was using. The dark planet crashed upon Her, and She was lost.

"But all of that is done with now. Now, people everywhere know my name and are drawn like moths to the fire within me, whose nature only I can put a name to. Now I am complete, and I am free to love you once more. I adore you. I worship you. I love you, love you more than anything in the world save for celebrity. But . . ."

The parody was unspeakably vicious, undeniably accurate. Having identified the voice, Rawra Chin could do nothing more than accept the cruel mirror-image of the face that accompanied it. Nailed by the black weight of a phantom moon, She could only watch as Foral Yatt exposed all the conceits, the inanities, the small evasions that were the components of Her existence. The young man lounged upon the bed, touching a shimmering constellation of fingertips to the blue of his lower lip in a pantomime of anxiety and indecision. Looking up at Rawra Chin, his long lashes flashed an urgent semaphore pleading for sympathy while his jaw trembled beneath the burden of the words unspoken in the mouth above. Finally, when he had drawn out his melodramatic hesitation to the snapping-point of absurdity, the words spilled out in a breathless cascade.

". . . but do you still love me?"

He paused, blinking twice.

"Despite what I did to you?"

In one corner of the room the idiot child began to blow across the slender neck of its jar, and the patterns of light and shade within the chamber convulsed. Rawra Chin, adrift upon a lurching ocean of nightmare, heard a voice speak in the distance.

"Is there a lizard asleep within the ball?"

The voice was so deep and masculine that She assumed it must belong to Foral Yatt, except that Foral Yatt's voice wasn't like that anymore. Whose, then, could it be? When the answer came, Her senses were too brutalized to ring with more than the dullest peal of despair. It was Her voice. Of course it was Her voice.

On the bed, Foral Yatt smiled and flopped languidly onto his back. The smile he wore belonged to Foral Yatt rather than to his grotesque and pointed lampoon of Rawra Chin, but when he spoke it was with Her accents.

"Perhaps I am a ball. Perhaps the unfathomable quality that men perceive in me is a lizard, coiled within me, its material reality questionable, its effects upon the mind undisputed."

Their eyes were locked, their awareness of each other fixed in that moment of mutual understanding that has always existed between snakes and rabbits. Licking his indigo lips, Foral Yatt luxuriated in the taste of the long instant preceding the stroke of grace.

"Shall I tell you the name of my lizard? Shall I tell you the name of that thing that makes me vulnerable, makes me loved, worshiped, celebrated?"

Knowing the answer already, Rawra Chin shook Her head violently from side to side, but was unable to make the slightest sound.

"Guilt."

There. It had been said. He knew. The lantern flame quivered. The shadows charged and then fell back, regrouping for their next assault.

"You see, it is vital to what I am. It is the hurt that drives me, and without it I am nothing. Oh, my love, I feel so ashamed of all the misery that I have brought you."

Standing at the foot of the bed, swaying, the wine of their evening repast now bitter in Her belly, Rawra Chin became confused as the layers of meaning began to fold in upon each other, blossoming into new shapes like a toy of artfully creased paper. Was Foral Yatt describing feelings of his own or mimicking those agonies that he perceived in Her? Did he genuinely feel remorse for the venomous charade that he had perpetrated? At the center of the fear and confusion that tore through Rawra Chin like a hurricane, a nugget of resentment began to form, cold and bright in the still heart of the cyclone.

How dare he apologize? How dare he plead for understanding after this insufferable pageant of debasement? The anger grew within Rawra Chin as She gazed icily down at the figure upon the bed, the yielding and defenseless line of the body beneath the slatted violet gown gradually becoming as infuriating as the wheedling of that unbearable little-girl voice.

"Can you forgive me? Oh, my love, you seem so stern. How thoughtless I was to injure you in such a dreadful, careless fashion."

Foral Yatt sat up and reached toward Rawra Chin with imploring arms, pale as they emerged like swans' necks from the ruffs at the actor's shoulders. His eyes pleaded for release from the apparent agonies of self-flagellation that he was enduring, and his blue lips mouthed inaudible half-words of explanation and apology, puckering as if for a kiss of absolution.

With as much force as She could muster, Rawra Chin struck him across the mouth with the back of Her hand, smearing the blue lip dye over his cheek and Her knuckle.

The dry smack of the blow and the bark of pain from the actor rebounded back at them from the cold stone of the walls. Foral Yatt fell back, covering his face and rolling onto his side so that he lay curled upon the patchwork with his back to Rawra Chin.

Struck suddenly by the sight of his curving spine, visible through the disheveled violet fringes of his gown, Rawra Chin found that the anger in Her heart was matched by a sudden pressure at Her loins as a burgeoning erection reared against the restricting hide of Her ash-gray breeches. On the bed, Foral Yatt nursed his mouth and began to weep. Almost of their own volition, fingers that felt suddenly numb and overlarge moved toward the knot in Her rope belt, where it pressed in a hard fist of hemp against Rawra Chin's stomach.

She raped him twice, brutally, and there was no pleasure in it.

When it was done, She understood the damage that She had done to Herself and began to sob noiselessly, in the way that men do, sitting there upon the edge of the counterpane with Her shoulders shuddering in silence. Foral Yatt lay on the bed behind her, staring at the far wall. Rawra Chin's seed had dried in a small, irregular oval on the plucked alabaster flesh above his right knee, a tight puckering of the skin beneath the thin, clear varnish. He picked at it absently with mirrored nails and said nothing.

The wick of the lantern grew shorter, until finally it guttered and died. Thus could the passage of hours be measured, there in the House Without Clocks.

"I had no right. No right to treat you like that. . . ."

"Please. It doesn't matter."

"Will you stay? Will you stay here with me?"

"I can't."

"But . . . what am I to do if you go? There is no reason for you to leave."

"There's my work. My work and my career."

"But what about me? You're leaving me trapped here, don't you see? I'll never get away now. Please. I'll do anything you want, but don't leave me here."

"You should have thought of that before you took your revenge."

"Oh, please, I said that I was sorry. Can't you think of what we were to each other and forgive me?"

"It's too late, my love. It's far too late."

"I won't let you go. I won't let us be separated again."

"Please. I don't want a scene. What happened last time was so embarrassing."

"Oh, don't worry. Don't worry. I won't make any fuss at all."

"Good. Now, I must send one of the House-waifs to order my carriage for the morning and arrange to have my wardrobe moved back to the lodging house."

"Won't you leave me anything? Please. Let me keep the violet gown."

"No."

"Don't you see what you're doing to me? You're taking away everything! How has this happened?"

"Don't be naive. We are in the City of Luck."

"Here, you speak to me of luck? I am no longer sure that luck exists. Is there luck, or is there only circumstance without form or pattern, a senseless wave that obliterates all before it?"

"Is there a lizard asleep within the ball?"

Seated upon her balcony, absently chewing the anemic blue flowers she had plucked from her window garden, Som-Som regarded the courtyard of the House Without Clocks.

A carriage had arrived outside the curving walls with the first shafts of dawn, some short while ago. The half-masked woman had realized that Rawra Chin must be leaving the House to return to Her fabulous existence in the world beyond its seven variegated portals.

Since Rawra Chin had originally spoken of Her stay at the House in terms of months rather than weeks, Som-Som supposed that it was the dark undercurrents flowing between Her and Foral Yatt that had prompted this unannounced departure. She wondered if the performer would call upon her to say goodbye before

She left, and felt a pang of sadness at the thought of their separation.

Countering this regret, there was a tremendous relief. Som-Som was glad that Rawra Chin had not allowed Herself to become a prisoner of the terrible gravity that the House possessed, and for this reason alone she hoped that luck would take the performer far beyond those walls that curved like gray, embracing arms.

The sound of the pale yellow door opening was jewel-sharp in the silent morning, and Som-Som leaned out from her balcony a little to watch the elegant, crimson-bandaged figure step out onto the cold black flagstones, where the chill of the night had left a faint dusting of frost.

To Som-Som, who had not enjoyed the perception of depth since her ninth year, it seemed that a self-propelling droplet of blood had leaked from a pale yellow gash in the skin of the House to roll across the frost-flecked black disk of the courtyard, trickling slowly toward the arch on the opposite side. Occasionally, a two-dimensional white hand would become visible, depending upon the perspective, a cream petal bobbing briefly to the surface of the red blot before vanishing again.

As the bead of crimson progressed across the yard, it became something that a person without her affliction would recognize as a human being. The figure paused at a point halfway across the courtyard and turned, tilting back its head to gaze directly at Som-Som, as if it had been aware of the half-masked woman's scrutiny since first setting foot outside the pale yellow door. From out of the redness, a face swam into view.

Foral Yatt stared up into Som-Som's eyes, both the one that blinked and the one that could not.

His expression seemed furtive for an instant, tinged with a guilt that Som-Som found disturbingly familiar, and then he smiled. Long seconds passed unrecorded while their eyes remained locked, and then he turned and continued across the wide circle of jet, passing out through the high stone archway.

After a moment there came the sound of reins snapping, followed by a rattle of hoof upon cobblestone as the carriage horses roused themselves and cantered off down the winding thoroughfares of Liavek, where the scent of a hundred simmering breakfasts hung reassuringly between the huddled buildings.

Som-Som sat motionless upon her balcony, her gaze still fixed upon the point where Foral Yatt had stood when he turned and looked at her. His smile remained there, an afterimage in her mind's eye. It was a smile of a type that Som-Som had seen before, and which she recognized instantly.

It was a wizard's smile. It was the expression of a luck-shaper who had finally achieved a satisfaction long postponed. For an unquantifiable time, Som-Som did not move. A blank expression was frozen onto her face so that those divided features regained a semblance of unity, the living half transformed to porcelain by her bewilderment.

Standing suddenly, she upset her chair so that it toppled to the balcony floor behind her. She moved rapidly, with an odd jerkiness. All of the training and discipline that had disguised her difficulties of locomotion were cast aside as she ran down the narrow wooden steps and across the rounded yard.

The pale yellow door was not locked.

Rawra Chin was seated at the table, rigid and upright in one of the straight-backed chairs. She seemed to be staring at two objects that rested on the white wood of the tabletop, barely distinct in the smoky dawn light. Approaching the table, Som-Som peered closer, squinting the eye that still possessed the ability to do so.

One of the objects was a plain copper ball that meant nothing to her. The other item seemed more like an egg with the top cleanly sliced off.

Except that it was green.

Except that it had empty, staring sockets and a lipless smile.

She noticed the odor of licorice at the same moment that she realized Rawra Chin had not breathed since her arrival in the chamber.

It was not a physical horror that propelled Som-Som backward through the pale yellow door, gasping and stumbling, shoved out into the courtyard by the immensity of what lay within. Neither was it an aversion to the presence of the dead. The whore of sorcerers is witness to worse things than simple mortality during the course of her service, and suicides at the House Without Clocks were frequent enough to be unremarkable. Certainly too frequent to engender so violent a reaction in one whose customers had, upon occasion, transformed into beings of a different species or entities of churning white vapor at the moment of their greatest pleasure.

Neither was it entirely a horror that preyed upon the mind, nor wholly a revulsion of the spirit. It had no shape, no dimension at all that she could grasp, and that was the fullest horror of it. A monstrous crime had been committed, an atrocity of appalling magnitude and scale that somehow remained both abstract and intangible. Having no perceivable edges, its monstrosity was thus infinite, and it was this that sent Som-Som reeling out backward into the cold, black courtyard.

She wanted to scream at the indifferent windows of the House Without Clocks, still shuttered against the morning light while those beyond enjoyed whatever sleep they had earned the previous evening. She wanted to cry out and wake the City of Luck itself, alerting it to this abomination, perpetrated while Liavek looked the other way, unsuspecting.

But of course, she could say nothing. The enormity of what had occurred remained locked within her, something scaly and cold and repugnant inside her mind, which could never be seen, never be touched or spoken of to another. Curled in the unreachable dark behind the porcelain mask it basked, beyond proof, beyond refute.

Hardly there at all.

Training Ground

by Nancy Kress

THE OFFICER OF the City Guard halted, scowling, in the middle of the Levar's Park. Jen Demarion, hurrying up an ornamental hill, saw the Guard come into view scowl first, followed by shoulders with a corporal's insignia, followed by the rest of him—with Cav standing before him on the path. Jen had known from the moment she saw the officer halt that Cav would be what had halted him, and from the moment she saw the officer scowl that Cav would be what he scowled at. She hurried faster, trying to reach them before Cav could say much. Preferably, before Cav could say anything at all.

"What?" the officer said to Cav. "What did you say, boy?"

Cav said, "Have your clouds cast, sir?"

The Guard looked up. Jen did not need to look. No clouds, not even one, floated in the sky. Blue, hot, empty: no clouds. Jen groaned inwardly, and swung into action. There was no time for more than the fastest scrutiny of the soldier, but Jen knew she had a good eye.

"Cav!" she cried, and her voice was all silvery delight, a waterfall in sunshine. "There you are! I've been looking all over!"

The officer turned his scowl from the sky to Jen. She met it with an artless smile, but the scowl did not soften. Cav must have been particularly stupid or irritating. Not that he had to be stupid to irritate; sometimes all he had to do was *stand* there as he did now, a resistant doughy lump with an expression so blank it approached not being there at all.

Jen put a light hand on the officer's arm. "Thank you for helping me find my twin! You're so tall, it was easy to see you clear across the park!"

The corporal looked from Jen to Cav, and back again. *"You* two are twins?"

"Oh, yes! I'm Jenneret Demarion—Jen—and this is my brother Cav. My mother is looking all over for him!" She widened her eyes. "Cav isn't in any . . . trouble, is he, sir?"

"He—well, maybe he is. He was cloud casting, or soliciting to cloud cast, and a new—"

"Cav! You *were!*" Jen cried, with such intense delight that the Guard stopped talking. Cav said nothing. After a moment, Jen wrinkled her forehead. "But . . . but, Cav, there aren't any clouds today."

"Well, that's just it," the officer said, with a faint note of apology, which Jen did not think he heard himself. "That's why it looked suspicious. And there's a new decree from His Scarlet Eminence that—"

"Oh!" Jen cried. "Have you ever seen His Scarlet Eminence? Up *close?*"

"Well, I—"

"Of course, you must have!" Jen breathed. "What is he *like?*"

"He's tall, he—look, young mistress, this new decree—"

"Not as tall as you! He couldn't be! That tall?"

"Well, no, not that tall," the Guard said. He drew up his shoulders a little. "But then, I'm tall for a Liavekan. This decree—"

"You're tall for anyone," Jen said, and smiled dazzlingly. This time the soldier smiled back.

"Maybe. This new decree from His Scarlet Eminence says that within the Levar's Park all strolling entertainers must show a permit. So they can prove they've paid the new tax—"

"And the City Guard has to do the checking? Oh, what a lot of trouble for you to have to go to!" She moved slightly off the path; the officer turned his face toward hers, and away from Cav.

"It certainly is!" he said, and scowled again. "Not everybody seems to understand that!"

Jen said warmly, "That's not what you signed up for!" She moved his gaze a little farther from Cav.

"It sure isn't!"

"And you have to do this all over Liavek?"

"Only in the Levar's Park. Too many petty thieves, says His Scarlet Eminence."

"What a shame. You'd think a man of his height would recognize how many more valuable uses there are for a trained fighting Guard!"

"You'd think so!"

"Please forgive us for having put you to the trouble," Jen said. The officer made a small expansive gesture. "Not your fault."

"And certainly not *yours!*" Jen cried, and flashed her dimple at him. "Tell you what—I'll give you a free cloud casting for your trouble, on the very next cloudy day of this gorgeous weather. I promise!"

"I'll remember that," the soldier said. They smiled at each other, the warm smiles of old friends. Jen gave his hand a parting squeeze—affectionate and confiding—and waved. The soldier moved off in the direction of the wave, whistling a lighthearted tune; Cav no longer blocked his path in that direction. He even shuffled his polished boots a little on the stone walk, in honor of the gorgeous spring weather.

Jen moved fast. She and Cav were over the rise and gone before the officer could realize that he had seen no permit, or discover the copper missing from the sleeve pocket where her hand had trustingly squeezed his arm.

"How could you do that?" Jen hissed. *"How?"*

Cav answered nothing. His slack face did not change.

"Oh, Cav," Jen said despairingly. Her despair had the same vivid exaggeration as her smiles. Next to her Cav seemed even more lumpish, more passive. She put her arms around him and hissed into his ear.

"Now before we go in, listen to me. She's in a rotten mood, and she's going to ask you again what you want for a birthday gift to invest your luck in. This time, *tell* her something!"

"I don't want anything."

"Tell her something anyway!"

"I don't want to."

"Cav," Jen said. She gave him one last despairing squeeze and pushed open the door to the cheap rented house in the northeast section of Old Town. "I found him, Erlin! He was *working!*"

A tall woman turned from the hearth. "Working at what?"

"At cloud casting, of course!" Jen cried gaily, as if this were a given. "He was finding you a client!"

Erlin—she did not like her children to call her 'Mother,' it sounded staid—looked with skeptical suspicion at Cav. She wore a blue gown too youthful and too elaborate, the neckline kept barely decent by a hard-working ribbon with frayed edges. Her face, which had once been beautiful, had a kind of overwrought theatricality: Jen's vividness grown middle-aged.

"And where is this client?"

"He was very suddenly called away on business."

"Ah. And he will no doubt be returning later, won't he, Cav, my son?"

"Oh, yes," Jen said.

Erlin fiddled with the sleeves of her gown. Her voice was sweet. "I went outside to the flower seller's just a few minutes ago, Cav, isn't that a coincidence? My headache was better. And there were no clouds, none at all. How did you expect me to cast this mysterious vanished client's clouds without clouds, Cav, my son?"

"He just—"

"Let Cav answer, Jen."

"I don't know," Cav said. There was no strain in his voice; there was nothing in his voice.

"So you thought to bring this client here to me," Erlin went on, even more sweetly, "and let *me* explain how I would cast clouds without clouds. Did you hope to damage my reputation very much? Was it an important client?"

"Oh, no!" Jen cried. "Just a Guard, of low rank. Nobody at all!"

"So my son thinks the sort of client to match his mother's skill is nobody at all."

"No, he—"

"I *said* let Cav answer! Did you want to humiliate me, my son? Is that what you wanted to do?"

"No," Cav said, without inflection.

"What *did* you want to do?"

"I didn't want to do anything."

"Erlin, you *told* him to go out—" Jen began desperately. Erlin snatched a jar—it was a pot of rouge—from the table and hurled it. It missed everyone by several arm spans.

"I said be quiet! So you didn't want to do anything, Cav, my son. Only to humiliate me. Only to thwart every desire I ever had for you, every hope I scrimped and saved and worked my fingers to the—what gift do you want for your birthday?"

"I don't want anything."

"You must invest your luck in something!"

"I don't want to invest my luck."

"You will become a cloud caster! All the Demarions have been cloud casters, all of them, and I haven't wasted a fortune in hard-won levars in investiture lessons for nothing! You will become a cloud caster, you will you *will!*"

"I don't want to be a cloud caster."

"And just what in the name of Wizard's Row do you want? What do you ever want?" Erlin's voice scaled upward to a shriek; she grabbed her hair with two hands and wailed. Jen, who was afraid of her mother only before one of Erlin's dramatic rages began, stepped forward with sudden authority.

"That's enough, Mother. You'll get hoarse."

"I want to get hoarse!" Erlin shrieked. "At least I want *something!* But that lump, my son—*my son!*—he's too stupid to want anything! He never wants anything! You don't even want to leave my presence this minute, do you, Cav? You're too stupid to even want to leave the room when someone is screaming at you! Why don't you leave the room? Why don't you?"

"I don't want to," Cav said.

Someone knocked on the door. Jen, who was closest, seized the knob with palpable relief, flung open the door—and stepped back a pace. Her hand went to her mouth, and her eyes grew wide.

On the doorstep, which had wobbled for two years now, balanced a young man in magnificent scarlet livery. Black ringlets dripped to his shoulders; exquisite nostrils quivered with exquisite disdain; he held a letter of vellum so heavy his rouged hand curved languidly under the burden.

Instantly Erlin's fury vanished. She swept forward with immense dignity, and motioned the page inside. He stepped onto the plain stone floor as if it were dung.

"A summons, mistress, from my Lord Count Dashif."

Erlin opened the letter with studied weariness; her voice said that she received notes from lords every day. "A cloud casting. Yes. Well, I believe I can fit in one more tomorrow, at the time he suggests. But please inform your master that I may be a *few* moments late—it is possible that His Scarlet Eminence may not be quite done receiving my counsel."

The page grinned. Erlin raised her chin and looked down her nose. The page bowed—with only one finger held to his forehead, and still grinning. Erlin turned her back with a magnificent sweep of hem. The page backed through the doorway with exaggerated care that no thread of his livery touch the doorjamb. Erlin did not bother to close the door after him, no more than one would after a fly. The page, a half second off the wobbly doorstep, began to whistle a scurrilous tune from a recent half-copper rag. Erlin trailed haughtily into her bedroom, not deigning to hear him.

Jen figured the honors came out about even. She closed the door, and her eyes shone.

"Cav—a count! That could mean real money! Just think! Only"— she lowered her voice, glancing at the bedroom—"only why Mother? If a noble wanted a cloud casting, why not a 'caster from Wizard's Row? Why . . . her?"

Cav said nothing. Jen frowned and bent to pick up the rouge pot Erlin had thrown. Sticky pink smeared the stone. "You know, she would get less furious if you would fight back. Truly, Cav. It enrages her that you won't fight."

"I don't want to fight."

Jen made a despairing soft noise at the back of her throat and swiped at the pink smear. "Damn it, Cav, I almost think she's right! You don't want to be a cloud caster, you don't want to choose a luck piece for your investiture, you don't want to talk about this client, you don't want to stand up to Mother—what *do* you want?"

"I don't want anything."

The next day brought clouds. Erlin dressed in her best gown, a blue brocade of a startling style popular very briefly fifteen years earlier, in which she had once, before the twins' birth, cast clouds for a margrave. After this pinnacle, the brocade had been laid away in camphor, of which it smelled strongly. Jen watched the bodice seams with alarm as Erlin tugged the neckline lower and smiled at herself, flushed, in the fly-specked mirror.

"The thing, Jen—hand me that pin, no, the silver one—the thing is to watch the client, see what he wants. Everyone wants something, remember that, and a good cloud caster lets them see they can have it—if the clouds cast it that way, of course."

"Of course," Jen mumbled.

"You and Cav can learn a lot from how I handle this today, although it *would* have been nice to cast again at the palace . . . have I ever told you about the time the Margrave of—"

"Yes! Yes. You have."

"Well, you watch. And make Cav watch, too; he could certainly stand to learn from—Cav, where do you think you're going?"

"Out."

"No, you're not. You're going to stay and learn something! With your investiture only two weeks off. . . . Jen, why are you fidgeting? Where is that rouge pot? Caveril, don't you dare—where's the needle for that *seam?* No one ever tells you camphor can shrink brocade like this! Cav, Jen . . . oh, gods, there's the door. Answer it, Jen!"

Two men entered. Erlin straightened her shoulders and strolled toward them with the expression of a great painter in the presence of collectors who chose art by dominant color.

Count Dashif, tall and very dark, walked with a limp. Twin scars snaked down his cheeks. He wore a pair of double-barreled flintlock pistols thrust through his belt, and a very expensive jeweled bracelet on his left wrist. The bracelet rode loosely, so that the stones turned and glittered. Jen studied the clasp, glanced at the count's narrow eyes and livid scars, and regretfully took her eyes from the bracelet.

The other man wore plain clothes of good cloth. Scrawny and nervous, with limbs like the twiggy legs of small birds, he gave one startled glance at Erlin's neckline and thereafter kept his eyes on the wall. *Merchant,* thought Jen, eyeing him. *Afraid of magic.*

"Mistress," the count said, in the most musical voice Jen had ever heard, "I am Count Dashif. My guest, for reasons of his own, wishes to remain anonymous. We have come for a cloud casting, having heard that you are the finest and most discreet wizard of that art in Liavek."

Jen stared. Erlin said, "My art is honored, Your Grace," and bowed so low that Jen feared for the neckline ribbon. "But of course Your Grace understands that fine magic must of necessity command a fine fee . . ."

"Of course," Count Dashif said. "As it should be. We are prepared to offer you ten levars."

Just in time Jen kept herself from gasping.

"For a single question," the count added smoothly. "Where do we—"

"On the roof," Erlin said. "This way, Your Grace. My children, talented apprentices, shall of course accompany us."

A narrow stairwell curved from the corner by the hearth to the roof; the top steps were thick with cobwebs. Erlin swept through them, lifting her skirts higher than strictly necessary. The count stood back to allow the nervous merchant to precede him. Jen and Cav came last, and Jen pretended to tie her sandal so she could whisper to Cav. "Something's wrong. You don't address a count as 'Your Grace,' that should have alerted him that Mother isn't . . . that she doesn't . . ." But Cav, she saw, was not listening.

Liavek spread out below them in a sun-splashed mosaic of twisting streets. To the east lay the flowered glory of the Levar's Park, crossed by the sparkle of the Cat River; to the south, the green copper roof of the palace. Above, masses of white clouds floated in turquoise. A brisk wind whipped Erlin's gown against her knees and Jen's unbound hair into her mouth. It was a perfect day for cloud casting.

Count Dashif twisted his bracelet slowly around his wrist.

"Now if I knew what question you wished cast . . ."

"Ah, that is where the superior nature of your wizardry must come into play, mistress. My guest has a question, but being unused to consulting cloud casters, he does not wish to influence the answer by even phrasing it. And of course I do not wish to influence the answer, either." He stroked the jeweled bracelet with his left hand, and met Erlin's eyes.

Jen felt herself flush with indignation. Erlin might not be . . . well, she might not be what she thought she was. But she was a wizard, a cloud caster, and for the count to suggest . . .

Erlin herself gave no sign of anything. From her bodice (the merchant looked hastily at the distant river), she drew out the square of fine linen that was her luck object. Easily concealed, not likely to be stolen, sturdy enough to wash, the color of the sky. It was embroidered with silk clouds faded now to the color of cream.

Please, Jen begged silently, *please let her have the power this time, at least this one time again—*

And Erlin did. Jen saw the moment her mother's face changed. The spurious haughtiness and tawdry theatrics fell away, and in the planes and taut curves was the cloud caster Erlin might have been.

She held her luck loosely in both hands, palms closed only enough to keep the soft linen from blowing away, and raised it to the sky. From the blue cloth a thin line of vapor rose in wisps. It spiraled slowly upward, misty in the sun, until Jen could no longer follow where it blended with the clouds above.

The clouds began to change shape.

First there were masses of uncarded wool, fluffy and white. Then the wool directly overhead began to thin, to stretch, to spin into long filaments against turquoise sky.

The merchant gripped both hands tightly together.

Erlin began to rock back and forth. Her lips parted, her eyes closed, and a light sweat filmed her forehead. Above her, the filaments of cloud began to sway. At first they moved all in the same direction, as if blown by a light wind. Slowly some of them changed direction, coalesced, came apart, and formed a definite pattern—but not a pattern Jen had ever before seen in a cloud casting. It looked like a ladder, with two long filaments crossed by short ties. Yet somehow Jen knew that it was not a ladder.

"The railroad," Count Dashif said quietly.

Beside the first casting, a second began to form. Huge clouds folded in on themselves, becoming compact, dense, and blocky.

Roofs began to form. Doors, windows, and a peculiarly shaped gate, decorated with the head of a spitting camel.

"I know that place!" Jen said aloud, before she could stop herself. It was Camel Alley, a dilapidated street running southeast from just inside Merchant's Gate, and notable only because its dilapidation and teeming tenements were more typical of Old Town than of the area around Merchant's Gate. Jen had trawled for clients there—but never alone.

The merchant moaned. Jen found herself gripping Cav's fingers; they felt dry and still. Erlin's swaying became wilder, and as the other four craned their necks toward the sky, the cloud railroad began to blow toward the cloud alley. It was a snaky sort of blowing, as if the railroad writhed in indecision. Below, on the street, a small crowd had gathered, mostly jeering youths whose baggy pants blew in the opposite direction to the clouds, extravagant banners of chartreuse and scarlet and vermilion and lemon.

All at once Jen felt Erlin's luck tingle over her mind.

It had happened before, during an intense cloud casting. She was Erlin's daughter, she had had lessons in investiture for three years now, and she knew that her own talent was strong. She would not be able to influence Erlin's spell, but she was able to catch the spillage of magic, tingling and teasing her mind. She liked it.

Cav pulled his hand out of hers as if it were on fire.

As Jen turned toward him, the writhing railroad reached the alley in the clouds—and froze. Slowly, slowly, the tracks reared, like nothing so much as a ghostly cobra preparing to strike, until it loomed over the dilapidated buildings. There, it swayed, moving now to strike the alley, now to miss it. The sky darkened, and the jeering crowd fell abruptly silent. The merchant fell to his knees. His eyes never left the sky.

Dazzled, Jen looked from the clouds to her mother—she had not known Erlin could do all that—and so saw the moment it happened.

"I think you will have your decision soon," the count said in his musical voice. He addressed the merchant, but his gaze was on Erlin, and his right hand caressed the jewels in the bracelet on his left wrist.

Erlin's dark eyes were huge, vulnerable, and strained with the moment of magic. Jen thought numbly what it must be costing her to hold that power back for even a moment. Why was she doing it? Why was she hesitating?

Almost imperceptibly, the count shook his head.

Erlin shuddered. The tingling in Jen's mind wrenched itself hard, and then turned itself wrong. She clapped both hands to her temples. Wrong, *wrong:* water burning, wood melting, magic forced into a shape it did not want to go . . .

But Erlin forced it. The cloud railroad struck at Camel Alley —and missed. The tracks curved around the alley, not through, and all the buildings stood.

The merchant cursed suddenly, clearly, with disappointment.

The tracks stood clear for only a moment longer. Then the illusion began to melt back into clouds. Erlin gasped and collapsed against the balustrade. The fiery wrongness left Jen's mind, and she blinked in the sudden brightness of the paling sky.

"My guest and I wish to thank you," Count Dashif said smoothly to Erlin. "You have been most helpful."

The cloud caster looked at him with dangerous eyes.

"How could she do it?" Jen demanded of Cav, who said nothing. "How *could* she?"

The two sat on the roof, in the navy blue hour just before night. There was still enough light to see each other's faces: Jen's preternaturally sharp, anger limning the bones; Cav's a dun pudding.

"She knew what answer the count wanted, and she gave it to him. That poor merchant thinks the land is worthless now, or at least not worth the gold it would be if the railroad wanted it. And she did it with her luck. She sold her *luck!*"

Cav said nothing.

"It would be one thing to steal the bracelet—*I* thought of that. But the best cloud casting she's ever done, real power and magic —how could she?" Jen fell silent a moment. Then she cried with all the drama of Erlin herself, "If that's what being a cloud caster is, then I don't want to be one! I won't be like her!"

"You will damn well be what I say you will be!" Erlin's voice cried. Her hand thrust over the top of the stairwell, followed by the rest of her. "How dare you!"

Jen jumped up and clenched her hands. "How dare I what?"

"How dare you judge me!"

Jen thrust herself forward. Erlin stepped to meet her, and mother and daughter stood inches apart, glaring. Erlin raised her chin in the haughtiness of a great lady correcting a servant; Jen lowered hers like a market fighter.

"I said you will not presume to judge me!"

"I will judge anyone who betrays her greatest gift!"

Erlin's chin creased with the weary skepticism of someone who has learned from life; Jen raised hers.

"When you are older, you'll understand things hidden from you now."

"I will never be old enough to sell my one talent!"

Erlin let her chin go soft and maternal; Jen tightened hers in incipient hysteria.

"You have many talents, Jen dear. When you are a cloud caster—"

"I won't be a cloud caster! I won't be anything! Do you think after what I've seen today, after what you did—"

Erlin slapped her, lightly. Jen cried out as if she had been pushed over the balustrade. Erlin reached for her, quick tears filling her eyes. Jen pushed away her mother's arms, then flung herself into them, sobbing wildly. The two women clung and wailed. After two minutes of that, Jen bounded away, flinging her arms wide toward the sky.

"How could you betray . . . that? It's like betraying life!"

Erlin's tears disappeared and she smiled with superior patience. "Don't be so dramatic, dear. It's a bad habit."

Cav made a sudden movement, but did not look up from studying his clasped hands.

"*Me!*" Jen shrieked. "It's you, you're a . . . you did—"

"What I did, I did for you! I've never done anything except for you and your brother! Just because I wanted to afford valuable luck pieces for you two, just because I didn't want you to have to invest your luck in a ragged piece of cloth as I was forced to, just because I wanted the very very best for my children"—she started to sob, pathetic sobs of maternal hurt—"wanted *lovely* luck pieces, so Cav will be tempted to go through with his investiture and be able to earn a respectable living and not die poor and starved and alone like I've been since your father left—that's all I wanted, to tempt Cav, to please Cav; this is all *your* fault, Cav—"

Cav neither moved nor blinked.

"Yes, it is!" Erlin cried. She put a handkerchief, scarlet and lace, to her eyes. "All I've ever wanted is to make something of my children, everything I've done has been for that, if you had only met me halfway, Cav, I wouldn't have done what Jen hates me for now—I wouldn't! Cav, my son, if you had only helped me know what to do, if you had only shown some spirit, if you had only wanted something—"

Cav looked up. His broad pasty face caught the last of the

daylight. Erlin stopped ranting and stared in astonishment. Jen stopped flinging her arms about and stared in astonishment.

Cav said, "I want to invest my luck in the railroad."

He would not explain. The women begged and cried and raged and pleaded and fell on their knees and threw things and hugged him and hit him. Feminine ranting filled the shabby little house: feminine shrieking, feminine tears. Cav would not be worn down. He wanted to invest his luck in the railroad.

Finally, Cav gave Jen some words that she supposed were an explanation. They were, at any rate, the most words he would string together on the subject of the railroad.

"It's solid. It's hard. It goes somewhere."

Jen, red-eyed, tried to consider this. "Solid"—unlike clouds. "Hard"—unlike a square of embroidered linen. "Going somewhere"—unlike Erlin's endless overwrought schemes, circling back on themselves to collapse in tangled hysteria.

"But you'll die!" Jen wailed. "No one has ever invested luck in a railroad. We've never even *seen* a railroad!"

They went to look at it. The three of them trooped out to the Merchant's Gate one hot day just before sunset, a procession solemn as a funeral. The women's faces were extravagant with swollen protest, Cav's as impassive as clay. Erlin wore black.

There was not much to see. Although railroads had existed in Tichen for thirty years, construction on Liavek's first line had only begun six months ago. Track was being laid in Hrothvek, Saltigos, and Trader's Town, none of which would reach Liavek until the next year. Within the city, work had begun on the Central Station, although so far this edifice was represented by a low wall, some wooden framing, and a great deal of mud. The track of the spur line, which would eventually run inside the New Wall (including through what was now Camel Alley), was not yet begun.

Outside the Merchant's Gate, surrounding what would become the Central Station, lay the land that would become the train yard. It stretched between the Golden Road and the Cat River, a maze of half-laid rails gleaming red in the bloody light. Some of the track, which was wood capped with a thick strip of steel, disappeared into long, low sheds; some of it circled back on itself; some of it just stopped, metal ends raw against the soft mud. Much of it still stood in great heavy piles around which the ruts of carts bit in deep ditches.

"Impossible," Erlin said. "My dear son—you must see—a

place like *this* . . ." She stubbed her toe on a half-buried rail and
uttered a small scream.

Cav's face shone.

"Cav," Jen said in a small voice, "what would you invest your
luck *in?* The tracks are laid in pieces—see, they fit together at
these lines—they're not a unity. Not at all. And this idea of a
'train'—there isn't any train. Not yet. There won't be a train
until the Levar's fifteenth birthday. And this station—oh, Cav,
you know how bad it is to invest luck in a building! What if it
burns down, or is destroyed like the houses in Camel Alley will
be, or—there's nothing here to invest your luck *in!*"

Cav said, "I want to invest my luck in the railroad."

"But *Cav*—"

"I forbid it," Erlin said. "There is no argument. I absolutely
forbid it." She stood very straight, her black shawl billowing
around her like a sail.

Cav did not answer. Jen said, in the same small voice, "Investiture is so difficult anyway. . ."

Erlin turned on her. "Now don't you start! You've had the
finest in training, it's cost me a fortune, and except for that I
might have lived on Wizard's Row myself . . . saving every
minute . . . clothes on my back . . . time I cast for a margrave . . .
best I know how. . ." They were no longer listening. Jen, appre-
hensive and wan, gazed at Cav. Cav gazed out across the muddy
farmlands and darkening road, out toward Trader's Town, out
beyond that to the unknown and empty and silent Great Waste,
out where the railroad would go.

The twins had been born a little after dawn, Jenneret first and
Caveril just a few minutes later, after a labor that had cost Erlin
only five hours of discomfort. Nothing she could do had made
labor longer, or harder. The birth had been notable only in that
Cav, even when slapped on his broad little ass, had refused to
cry.

For this investiture birthday, Erlin had spent every copper she
had, buying great quantities of sweetmeats and marzipan, good
wine, masses of blue and white silk to shroud the windows, and
two luck objects. Both Cav and Jen had walked through the last
few weeks subdued and obedient, with little to say, but the sight
of their luck objects should cure *that,* Erlin thought. Matching
turquoise amulets bought at one of Liavek's better shops, the
Tiger's Eye, from a tall black-haired woman who—though not

even a wizard!—had stared with insolent amazement at Erlin's gown.

Well, in a few more hours no one would ever stare insolently at her and hers again. The twins were destined for great things. She, Erlin, could feel it. They would be cloud casters of such fame that nobles would come even from Tichen and Ka Zhir to consult them, and they would be celebrated in song and story. And Erlin, too, of course, as their mother, honored and revered for this triumphant outcome to her tragic struggle to survive after desertion by a spindly-souled lover.

She wondered how one set about having the Desert Mouse company do a play about one's life.

The evening before the investiture, all was in readiness. Jen and Cav and she had scoured, had baked, had purchased sweet-smelling Farlander candles, had hung the voluminous blue and white silk over all the windows. The twin luck pieces, turquoise amulets carved with such intricate scrollwork that the mind could make of it anything it would, including clouds, lay on twin silk pillows before the hearth. Just before midnight, Erlin disappeared into her room to bathe and perfume herself, and to dress in the brocade gown. Nothing else would do for this, the crowning night of her life. In a few years, of course, she would have clothes and jewels far greater than this, greater than the bracelet from Count Dashif (so unfortunate that it had had to be sold). She would need them to receive guests at Cav and Jen's home on Wizard's Row. But for tonight, the brocade was the best she had, and nothing less would do.

She smiled at herself in the old mirror, by the midnight light of the expensive candles.

"Mother," Jen said, "Cav is gone."

Erlin turned slowly toward her daughter. "What?"

"Cav. He's gone."

"No. He can't be. You're mistaken. Look again, you impossible child!"

"I think," Jen said, "that he's gone to . . ." and then could not say it. Into Erlin's face rushed a look so terrible that Jen took a step backward. Thunderheads mounted there, heat lightning flashed; in the ominous rumble small animals dashed for cover. Between stiff lips Erlin got out, "Get me a footcab from the inn. Or a bodyguard. Whichever you find first."

"But—"

"Whichever is faster."

"It's almost ti—"

"*Go!*"

Jen went. Running down the dark street to the inn, two thoughts crashed in her mind: *My investiture*, and *Oh, Cav—*

Bursting back inside with the incurious but greedy guard, she was amazed to see that Erlin still wore the brocade gown, that the amulets were gone from the hearth, and that Erlin thrust at her a thick bundle of blue and white silk.

"Erlin . . . *not at the—*"

"Run!" Erlin cried, with a furious glance at the bodyguard. "Come! Run!"

"*Run*, mistress?"

"You heard me! Run!"

"I do not run, mistress. I—"

"Double your fee!"

Jen gaped; Erlin never paid double anything. The man's eyes narrowed and he nodded. Erlin picked up her preposterous skirts with one hand, and Jen saw the moment the storm actually broke.

Running through the moonlit streets of Liavek, Jen felt a stitch in her side. Erlin, panting and gasping, would not let them stop for an instant. People still strolled the warm and sweet-smelling summer streets; in Old Town youths jeered at them, in the Levar's Park soldiers and flower sellers and lovers watched bemused as the weird trio tore past, Erlin's gown flapping like brocaded fins. Jen could not catch her breath.

"Mistress . . . if we stop . . . a m-moment . . ."

"Run!" Erlin shrieked. "Hurry!"

Through the deserted residential section north of the park, where shuttered walls hid private gardens and stately homes. Through poorer streets again, less deserted. An inn, a well, a square, the smell of pot-boil. Dogs barked at them, cats stared with glittery eyes. Erlin's face, under sweat in the moonlight, looked crazed. The armpits of her gown darkened, smelling of camphor.

They were in Camel Alley, within sight of the Merchant's Gate, when Jen knew the stitch in her side was not a stitch in her side.

"Erlin—"

"Run!"

The birth luck tingled, beginning somewhere under her left arm, near her heart. It spread upward to her shoulders, down along her arms to her quivering fingers. Jen had studied hard; the luck felt much stronger than in previous years, and the disciplining of it for investiture, the fruit of all those long and expensive lessons, took over her mind. She slowed to a walk, stopped. All of a sudden her stomach lurched.

"M-mother..."

And then Erlin was beside her, peering and gasping into her face, and Erlin's hand was holding Jen together by the firm grip on her shoulder.

"You, guard—stay here by the gate. Keep a sharp eye on my daughter. And triple your fee if you don't watch what she does!"

"I—" the bewildered man began, looked at her face, and said no more.

Erlin led Jen, dazed and sick, over the maze of half-finished tracks to the shadows of a long shed. Swiftly she spread the blue silk over the ground, up to a nail on the rough wall, over a scraggly bush, and pushed Jen to sit in the nest of cloud-strewn sky. Above, stars shone in cloudless glory. Erlin put both turquoise amulets in Jen's hands.

"You can do it. You know how to do it, my daughter."

"But we...practiced for a twin investiture. I only learned how to do it *together*—"

"You can do it. No one in my family has failed at investiture in one hundred thirty years!"

"Cav—"

"You can do it, Jen!"

Erlin smiled at Jen, a smile so terrible that Jen closed her eyes. Birth luck coursed through her. Erlin straightened, walked to the other side of the shed, and bellowed in a voice of such power and fury that the bodyguard, lounging against the Merchant's Gate, jumped to terrified attention.

"Caveril Elanoren Demarion! You are decayed fish heads if I don't see you in three minutes flat!"

Three minutes passed, three hours. More. Jen could not do it. She *knew* how to invest luck, she *felt* it—but the luck would not flow in one direction, would not mount and crest, like a dark smooth wave, into the turquoise amulet. It...balked. There was no other word for it. Did luck have a life of its own, was it alive? What was she going to do?

Where was Cav?

Erlin could not find him. The unfinished railroad yard was vast, and it blended into the farmland and scrub brush from which it was only half-born. There were a thousand places for a boy to hide. If there had been clouds, she might have cast for him—but there were no clouds.

"Caaaavvvvv!"

At the note in her mother's voice, Jen shuddered.

"Mistress," a far different voice said, so close to Jen that she jumped in her blue silk nest and raised to the speaker a frightened, sweaty face. With a shock, she saw that it was past dawn. A man, dressed as if he had stopped at the railroad yard after a formal party in the city, loomed above her, his face backlit by the sun. There were flintlock pistols thrust through his sash.

The calm musical voice said, "But surely you aren't here, doing this, alone."

"What are you doing here?" Erlin tottered up to them, stumbling through a muddy pothole. Her brocade skirts hung in tatters, her hair whipped around her muddy face, her eyes burned like acid fires in the Great Waste. Count Dashif regarded her fastidiously.

"Mistress Erlin the Cloud Caster. What a very strange place to encounter you again."

"Get away! Go away! My bodyguard—"

"Has been dismissed. This is my land, you know."

"Your—"

"Recently acquired, most of it, and in the process of being reacquired by the Levar's Council, for the railroad." He smiled. "A profitable transaction for all concerned. But one that does *not* lend itself as a site for petty investiture."

Before Erlin could react to that, Jen moaned. She did it loudly, and only half deliberately. Erlin dropped to her knees and flung her arms around her daughter; the count frowned. "How much time has she left?"

Jen looked up at him over a faceful of muddy brocade. Erlin cried hysterically, "Moments! Less than an hour! My daughter!"

Jen said, with difficulty, "Cav is here somewhere. My brother. On your land. It's a twin investiture—you have to find him!"

Count Dashif smiled. "I don't *have* to do anything, young mistress. And given that, why should I?"

"Because it might be bad luck for your land if an investiture failed and I died here. Two investitures—Cav's, too. Two deaths!"

The count considered this. He studied the position of the sun, holding a finger to the horizon. He considered Jen once more, and sighed.

"I see no reason to assume that. But . . ." Dashif drew his pistols. Almost carelessly, he fired a shot in what looked to Jen's dazed gaze like a random direction. It hit a pile of rails and ricocheted, producing two sharp cracks followed by a single yell.

Erlin screamed.

"You've killed Cav!"

"Certainly not. The yell came from that direction over there —there isn't a boy alive free enough of self-importance to think a pistol shot isn't fired at him, and yell in response. Not even your lumpish son, mistress. Bring the young mistress, if they need to invest together."

Jen could barely walk. The birth luck, hot and thick, foamed around her in all directions like a boiling river, so that she could not see. She staggered against Erlin, knocking them both down more than once. After a time she felt the count return to support her other side, and heard his low noise of fastidious impatience.

But her vision cleared when they reached Cav.

He lay in a shallow indentation covered with scrub, just to the right of the outcropping of rock. He must have dug the indentation himself, for the scrub was freshly cut and the ditch lay between two of the laid rails, ducking underneath one of them. To this rail Cav clung, full length, arms and legs wrapped around the wood and gleaming metal, and cheek pressed to it as to a lover.

As soon as the count glimpsed this, he dropped Jen. He hurled himself into the ditch beside Cav, reaching to pry the boy loose from the length of track. Cav clung like pitch, and the count drew his second pistol.

When he dropped her, Jen had sagged against Erlin, and they both had gone down. But when she saw the drawn pistol, lightning shot through her. Cav was in danger, Cav would be hurt! Jen rolled into the ditch and threw herself onto the count, knocking the pistol from his hand.

At that moment Jen, finally in contact with Cav, felt her birth luck mount and crest, and the dark wave of it flowed strong and powerful in one unified direction. Count Dashif screamed as if he had been burned and snatched at his legs where they rested against Jen's body. He scrambled out of the ditch, howling in pain.

"The amulet!" Erlin cried. "Jen—the amulet!"

Both amulets had been left in the blue-sky nest by the shed.

Jen closed her eyes and squeezed Cav. The luck flowed out of her into Cav, and a great peace descended, a timeless emptiness. But only for a moment. Into that emptiness came another thing, hard and unchanging and reliable as the bedrock underlying all the treacherous clouds in all the airs that ever existed.

Then that thing, too, vanished from her, and suddenly it was Cav's body that smoked and burned. Jen screamed, the same scream Count Dashif had given at the moment of her investiture, and climbed off Cav to huddle, dazed and weak, by the huge rock.

The length of rail Cav was holding began to glow, shining with an inner illumination no metal ever had. The glow was silvery, faintly undershot with red, and it made the track look even harder and more solid than it was.

All over the railyard lengths of track began to glow.

Piled in squared-off stacks, slicing across the muddy ground, welded to each other or not, the metal strips and wooden rails glowed brighter and brighter, until Jen shoved her shaking hands against her eyes. Dimly she was aware of her mother groaning, and of the count cursing with a roughness she never would have associated with that melodious voice.

Then it was over. Jen lowered her hands. Cav crawled out of his ditch and stood upright before the three of them, and he was smiling with satisfied wanting.

"But what . . . what will he be able to *do?*" Erlin asked piteously. She slumped in her chair in the Inn of the Dancing Spider. The inn stood just within the Merchant's Gate, a discreet travelers' lodging with a great many discreet parlors, one of which Count Dashif had, with tight-lipped rage, commanded from the instantly cowed innkeeper. The four of them sat staring at each other. The count drummed his knuckles on the wooden table. Jen tried to take a sip of tea, but it would not go down. She stared at Cav, who was somehow Cav no longer. He was, for one thing, her luck piece. But only for one.

"Mistress," the count said brusquely, "I don't *know* what he will learn to do. He should not have been able to do what he has already done. Not only because His Scarlet Eminence will not like it at all, but also because the investiture itself was impossible. Railroad tracks are not a unity."

Jen found herself saying, "They are to Cav."

"Oh, what do you know about it!" Erlin snapped. "You've ruined your own chances—investing your luck in a living being! What if he died?"

The count's knuckles grew still, his eyes thoughtful.

He turned to Cav. "What can you do, boy? What can you do with the Levar's railroad?"

"I don't know."

"What do you *want* to do?"

Cav smiled, and said nothing.

The count studied him a moment longer, smiled in his turn, and rose from his chair. His hand lay on the butt of one pistol. Jen felt fear slide through her like icy and brackish water. She stood and faced him.

"You can't ever have Cav killed."

Count Dashif gazed at her with such impassivity that she was incongruously reminded of Cav himself—the old Cav. She thought, too, of Dashif saying *I don't have to do anything.*

"He *is* the railroad," Jen said.

The count did not change expression.

"I saw it. At the moment my birth luck invested in Cav. I saw his luck flowing out. Only it didn't go into just the rail he was holding, or the rails in that place. It's all the rails everywhere, even the ones not anywhere yet. It's the *railroad*. Cav is the whole thing."

Dashif raised an eyebrow. "Not possible."

"For Cav it is." Despite the brackish fear, Jen sighed. When had any of them understood Cav? His silent stubbornness was the bedrock under their emotional weather, as buried and as dark. She blundered on.

"I *saw* it. Cav believes—no, he knows—the tracks are one whole thing, forever and ever, solid and permanent and . . . and connected. If you change the tracks, hook up more to these or take some away, it's still all the same one thing to Cav. It's still his tracks. It's the same as if . . . as if you change the bedrock under Liavek. The bedrock is always there, no matter how much you dig or drill or blast, because the earth needs it there, to hold Liavek together. Cav *needs* the railroad, to hold himself together. So it's his luck piece, all the tracks, even the ones still coming."

"Ridiculous!" the count said in a strangled voice.

"Well, *I* think so," Jen said. She was so tired.

"Do you mean," Dashif asked, "that Cav could do this because he believed he could? That he was ignorant enough or talented enough to believe he could?"

"Yes," Jen said. Was it the truth? She didn't know. She said it anyway; the count's hand lay, still, on his pistol.

"Ah. And does this curious investiture include the tracks in, say, Tichen?"

"I don't know. Maybe when they're hooked up with our tracks."

"Ah," said the count again, and his hand suddenly shook. Jen, astonished, raised her eyes to his face, but whatever had been there was already gone. He said, "Then possibly Cav's luck will someday extend even to Tichen, if he reinvests it in the tracks each year."

"I guess so. But . . . doesn't Tichen already have the best magicians in the world?"

"They do indeed," Dashif said, and his hand moved off his flintlock. He sipped his tea. "So far."

There was a little silence. Jen let out breath she did not know she had been holding.

"But of course," Dashif continued, "we have no proof of any of this. We shall all have to wait and see."

"Yes," Jen said. "The only proof we have is what you just said—that what Cav already did was impossible, so he must have a very powerful talent. He might be a very powerful wizard. Possibly."

It was the first time any of them had used the word "wizard."

"Possibly," Dashif agreed. He watched Cav.

Suddenly Erlin sat up straight in her chair. Her ravaged face gleamed. "Powerful. With a luck piece that will stretch *everywhere.*"

The count's eyes slid slowly toward the woman in the ridiculous gown.

"Of course," Erlin went on, as if to herself, "he would have to be within three paces of *some* tracks. No house on Wizard's Row. But still, a special one of these little cars that will run all over the tracks—velvet seats, ivory trim—people coming to him, control over all these strange trains—and you said even trains in Tichen, to be hooked up someday? You might find it profitable, Your Grace. We might *all* find it profitable."

The count looked at Cav, then at his mother. Erlin fingered the expensive twin amulets in her lap and smiled.

"I warn you, Your Grace, that I drive a very hard bargain."

"I don't doubt that for a moment, mistress," the count said. His voice sounded curiously strangled. "May I add that there may be certain . . . constraints on any plans you may have for your son? Her Magnificence the Levar has honored *me* with responsibility for overseeing the railroad for her Council."

The two measured each other; their polite smiles and hard eyes were twins. Suddenly Cav laughed. Startled, Jen looked at him; she did not ever remember having heard Cav laugh out loud before. He held out his hand and pulled her toward the door. The doughy feel was gone from his fingers, and to her dazed eyes he suddenly looked taller, thinner, harder. Not like himself. Like . . . a rail? Cav?

Erlin said, "My son, the Wizard of the Railroad."

Cav laughed again, a laugh that could have meant anything, and pulled Jen with him out the door and toward the railroad yard beyond the Merchant's Gate.

Appendix One: A Liavekan Songbook

"City of Luck": The Liavekan National Anthem

"City of Luck," the Liavekan national anthem, was first penned by the Levar Andrazzi the Lucky who said that the words came to her in one of her famous Shift Dreams. The music, however, is based on an old Tichenese herding song, which Andrazzi claimed she listened to endlessly as a child. Her nurse during the *90 and 1*, the traditional three-month period in which young nobles are suckled successively by members of the court to "spread the luck around" (a custom no longer honored literally), was the daughter of a Tichenese herdsman.

The song's powerful chorus is a later intrusion, often attributed to an anonymous member of the Dashif family, but denied by the current count. That chorus is often heard in the dirty sinkholes of Ka Zhir, with the first line inverted, so that numerous and—alas—scurrilous rhymes may be made upon the word "luck." We will not rehearse any of those rhymes here.

City of Luck

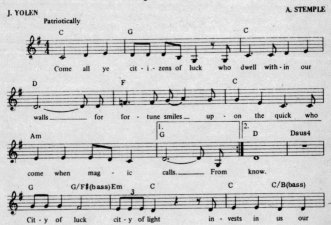

J. YOLEN   A. STEMPLE

mag - ic might that all our en - e - mies will fear____
____ the luck that reigns from year to year.

City of Luck

Come all ye citizens of luck
Who dwell within our walls,
For fortune smiles upon the quick
Who come when magic calls.

From shining strands and tragic shoals,
From Docks to Wizard's Row,
The summoned magic works its weal
As Liavekans know.

    (chorus) City of luck, city of light,
               Invest in us our magic might
               That all our enemies will fear
               The luck that reigns from year to year.

Oh, Liavek, thy towers gleam
Unworldly in the sun;
Uncorporeally made
To decompose when day is done.

For day by day and night by night
Thy magicians labor long,
Their mothers' labors echoing
To make the magic strong.

    (chorus) City of luck, city of light,
               Invest in us our magic might,
               That all our enemies will fear
               The luck that reigns from year to year.

The Ballad of the Quick Levars

J. YOLEN   A. STEMPLE

The Ballad of the Quick Levars

Translator's Note: This scurrilous Zhir ballad is usually sung by a
drunken song-rhymer accompanying himself on the seven-stringed peg-boxed
gittern and the ample bosom of a local slattern. The bitter wines of Ka Zhir,
mixed with the resins of the barrels in which the drink ferments, serve to
coarsen vocal chords, which is why it is a tradition in the taverns of Ka Zhir
to *sing-shout.* This is one of the more popular tunes, with the usual anti-
Liavekan sentiment.

'Twas the season of Buds, when the Cat overran
All her banks with a horrible miaou,
That the infamous year of Quick Levars began—
Though to this day no one knows how.

Number one was Azozo the Ancient-of-Days
Who became a Levar as a crone,

And she died the first moment that her antique bum
Touched that cold and implacable throne.

Next Bukko the Baby, still toothless and small,
Whose drools were considered so wise
That even before he had learned how to crawl,
He'd conspired in his own demise.

Then Cruski the Crabby whom nobody liked,
Her unfortunate death no one mourned.
And Denzzi the Deadhead who nonetheless hiked
To a wood against which he'd been warned.

And just a day after, Emmazi the Eager
Was caught in a bedroom that caved
In, and Froz-Factual died of a meager
Supply of the trivia he craved.

Gondo the Ghastly was popped in an oast
As the joke of a baker who drank,
And Hazli Half-hearted choked on the toast
When she tried the same baker to thank.

Oh, the rota is endless; it took a whole year
Of quick deaths and destruction and doom,
Till nary a niche remained empty, I hear,
In the fabulous Levar's Great Tomb.

The bright line of succession by now was quite gray
So the nobles who ruled such affairs
Passed a law that no Levars of less than a day
Could pass on the Great Throne to their heirs.

Eel Island Shoals

by John M. Ford

Translator's Note: It is doubtful that the Eel Island Shoals deserve the terrifying reputation this song gives them. However, ships are still wrecked there, despite harbor charts and warning lights; and there is something dramatic and poignant in a ship being lost within sight of safe harbor. And "Eel Island Shoals," while its lyrics are hardly inspired, can be made by a talented singer into a compelling performance piece.

The Fin Castle light is a thrice-blessed sight
To the sailor come finally home,
But keep a sharp eye with Eel Island hard by
For the breakers hide teeth 'neath the foam.
Now Liavek's lee of the terrible sea
Safe harbor, fair landing, home port—
But the Sea of Luck rolls past the Eel Island Shoals
And shatters the ships there for sport.

Keep a hand to the oar where the sea eagles soar,
And steer wide of Eel Island Head,
For the waves and the stones don't spare timbers or bones
And the sea does not give up its dead.
Hold fast to your lines till the Baymouth's behind
And Eel Island lies in your wake,
For the Sea of Luck rolls past the Eel Island Shoals
And reaches for bodies to break.

Watch tiller and tide, for the shallows are wide
And the ships and their sailors are small,
And the spray-shrouded rocks where the sea vultures flock
Know nothing of mercy at all.
So bear toward Fin Castle as you are bound past,
Mind the sails, keep the glass to your eye
Where the Sea of Luck rolls past the Eel Island Shoals—
And sometimes the lucky sail by.

Pot-boil Blues

by John M. Ford

Translator's Note: While the pot-boil is often considered to be the highest achievement of Liavekan cuisine, it is useful to remember that it is also the lowest common denominator, as, er, celebrated in this song.

"Pot-boil Blues" has numerous variations and extra choruses. Often performed as a "show-stopper" in the best places in the City, it is popular at all levels of Liavekan society.

They got a lot of fancy places on the Merchant's Row
That you can visit when it's time to dine
And if your pocket's full of silver, you're a man to know
Then all the people there will treat you fine
But if your ship's not in the harbor and your good suit's sold
And it's a while until your birthday's due
You better step up to the stockpot with your spoon and bowl
And join the potluck on the pot-boil blues.

> *We got a couple of potatoes with the evil eye*
> *We got an onion that would make a granite statue cry*
> *We got a fish a starvin' alleycat would pass right by*
> *We toss 'em all into the pot-boil blues.*

They got a bunch of fancy overeaters called gourmets
Who say the Liavekan pot's an art
They talk about how you can season it five hundred ways
But on this side of town we ain't so smart
Now if you're newly on the bum and you're not used to fare
Like stringy carcasses and worn-out shoes
You know it really ain't polite to ask just what's in there
When takin' potluck on the pot-boil blues.

> *We got a little hump of camel, not the choicest cut*
> *We got a strip of bacon stolen from a sleeping mutt*
> *We got a marrowbone from something, but I don't know what*
> *They'll be delicious in the pot-boil blues.*

You've got to boil it till whatever's in there disappears
And keep it stirrin' so the grease don't set
Up in the mountains they've been boilin' one two thousand years

And rumor has it that it ain't done yet!
It's true the taste is pretty grisly and the portion's small
But though this surely ain't the life we'd choose
If it's a choice between the pot-boil and no pot at all
Give us the potluck on the pot-boil blues.

   We got an artichoke looks like it's had a heart attack
   We got some cheese that wouldn't make a mouse a decent snack
   We got a couple bites of somethin' that I think bites back
   It all goes right into the pot-boil
   Every night's a pot-boil
   When you're taking potluck on the pot-boil blues.

Appendix Two: A Handbook for the Apprentice Magician

1. Tricks of investiture

Living things can be invested with birth luck (though this is always to be considered rash) and, in very rare cases, pieces that form a greater whole can be invested with birth luck (though this is always to be considered mad). The folly of investing luck in a living thing should be obvious: The person or pet might flee, or somehow reveal that it is a magician's invested object, or die.

The danger of investing in a divided whole, such as a wooden puzzle or a deck of cards, is compounded by its difficulty, for the process is far more complex than that of common investiture. It requires meticulous preparation of the thing that is to be invested (for example, a deck of cards must be cut from a single sheet and be prepared during an elaborate ritual as a preliminary to the act of investiture). Even if the ritual of investiture is successful, the invested object may only be used when the magician and all of the pieces of the object are within the customary three paces of each other. If one of the pieces is missing, the luck cannot be used, and if one of the pieces is destroyed, the luck will be freed.

Since such investitures are done, and done successfully, investiture may be no more than a test of the magician's ability to perceive and sustain belief in a "unity." This theory is supported by the latest Liavekan understanding of physics, which suggests that all objects are constantly changing on the molecular level. And yet, though many magicians accept this theory, not one has been able to invest luck in a poem, a theorem, a god, or a joke. The student magician is advised to invest luck in simple, durable, physical items.

2. A magician's birthday

Since Liavek's solar year is 365¼ days long, the actual hours of one's birth period will occur at different times each year with respect to the calendar. A magician is always aware of the discrepancy between the calendar year and the solar year. That discrepancy is reconciled only by the extra calendar day given every four years during the Grand Festival.

Since all Liavekans publicly celebrate their birthdays during Festival Week (excepting, of course, the Levar, whose birthday is at midyear), many young magicians are fooled into thinking that their own birthdays are secret. So long as one has family, friends, or neighbors, this is not so. Someone almost always remembers the time of year that a magician's mother secluded herself for a few days or weeks or months, and from the tiniest clues, a rival can deduce a magician's birth hours. A rash magician might try to eliminate family, friends, and neighbors in the hope of being safe from enemies—a course that is likely to create more enemies. The wise magician will always behave an ethical manner, from a sense of self-preservation if not of morality.

3. A brief history of magic

In primitive times, inhabitants of the world lived in awe and fear of the effects of birth luck. The practices of early magicians may never be known, but it is certain that their skill was less than that of the youngest student of magic today, for until the secret of investiture was learned, magicians only had power during the hours of their births. The name of the magician who discovered that luck can be invested in a vessel and used throughout the year is not remembered, though the oldest college of magic was established in Tichen in 2533, and Tichenese records show that the principles of investiture were the first things taught to the would-be magician. It is possible that investiture was known several centuries before that time and kept as a secret handed from magician to apprentice.

4. Of magic and medicine

The student magician is strongly advised to avoid the practice of medicine without completing an extensive course of study in medicine. The casting of a simple spell of healing can be easy; its consequences can be deadly.

(a) If the spell deals only with effects and not with causes, a patient may walk about in apparently perfect health for days or weeks, and then collapse without warning.

(b) Since an ignorant magician's spell is dependent purely on magic, it will fail on the magician's birthday, when all the magician's spells fail. Should the magician's luck be freed or destroyed by an enemy or an accident, or should the magician die, the spell will fail. When this happens, if the original illness or impairment is not the sort cured by the passage of time, it will return, at least as strongly as it was at the time of the spell or, in the case of a degenerative ailment, more strongly.

The magician who knows nothing of medicine is advised to send ailing clients to a doctor of medicine or to an unlettered healer of good repute, regardless of whether that doctor or healer is a magician.

Any student magician will do well to consider acquiring a degree in medicine. Doctor-magicians are rare and very well paid. However, those magicians who wish to keep their birthdays secret should consider other occupations. A doctor who is a magician is honor-bound to reveal when reinvestiture draws near so patients who are dependent on magical treatment may seek another doctor. Some doctor-magicians will form joint practices so that they may offer overlapping treatment to each other's patients.

COLLECTIONS OF SCIENCE FICTION AND FANTASY

Fantasy from Ace
fanciful and fantastic!